SMUGGLERS NOTCH

JOSEPH KOENIG

SMUGGLERS NOTCH

VIKING

VIKING
Published by the Penguin Group
Viking Penguin Inc., 40 West 23rd Street,
New York, New York 10010, U.S.A.
Penguin Books Ltd, 27 Wrights Lane,
London W8 5TZ, England
Penguin Books Australia Ltd, Ringwood,
Victoria, Australia
Penguin Books Canada Ltd, 2801 John Street,
Markham, Ontario, Canada L3R 1B4
Penguin Books (N.Z.) Ltd, 182–190 Wairau Road,
Auckland 10, New Zealand

Penguin Books Ltd, Registered Offices:
Harmondsworth, Middlesex, England

First published in 1989 by Viking Penguin Inc.
Published simultaneously in Canada

1 3 5 7 9 10 8 6 4 2

Copyright © Joseph Koenig, 1989
All rights reserved

LIBRARY OF CONGRESS CATALOGING IN PUBLICATON DATA
Koenig, Joseph.
Smugglers notch.
I. Title.
PS3561.03345   1989   813'.54   88-40307
ISBN 0-670-82341-4

Printed in the United States of America
Set in Times Roman

For Howard Smith

SMUGGLERS NOTCH

1

The second time around the block the girl was still there. He sped by as though he didn't see her and then tromped down on the brakes, fishtailing into the curb lane, making a show of it. In the mirror he watched her studying the van, unable to make up her mind. He saw nibbled lips not too shy to assert themselves, dark eyes that were deep set and vulnerable, the prettiest thing about her. Hurting eyes. He wondered how they looked with tears in them.

She came off the curb slowly and walked to the passenger's door. With one foot already inside she hesitated, sizing him up, recoiling slightly when she saw the bed done in blue velveteen in back. She was a short girl in a pea coat a couple of sizes too large, with the collar raised against the first real snow of the season. The way she looked at him, she was the one doing the favor.

He turned up the radio, flooding the space between them with digital sound. "Shitty day to be out," he said. "Been waiting long?"

"A half hour, maybe." She cupped small red hands together and blew against her fingers. "Is there any chance you're going all the way to Montpelier?"

He showed her his best smile. "How'd you know?"

She folded down her collar. Shaking the snow from straight black hair, she made herself comfortable on the seat, and he leaned across her lap and pulled the door closed, sensing her body tense until he retreated to his side of the engine hump. Without checking the mirror he left rubber all the way to the corner, nearly clipping a blue Toyota that hadn't cleared the intersection.

"Next time," he told her, "just so you'll know, don't thumb so close to town. Most drivers won't bother to stop when they can smell home."

They crossed over the Passumpsic River into St. Johnsbury. Listening to heavy chains torture the broken pavement, they trailed a salt spreader through a shopping area shrouded in Halloween's black and orange. Up a slippery-steep hill and around the library, the countryside took over, and a two-lane highway brought them between frozen fields where dairy cows breathed billows of gray.

He wound down his window and reached outside to swat away wet snow that the wipers had packed into a corner of the windshield. "You can expect six to eight inches," he said. For no reason the girl could see, he laughed. "You live in Montpelier?"

The vulnerable eyes bounced off his. Up close they were dark brown, as dark and delicious as chocolate chips. "Uh-huh."

So she wasn't a talker. One of the rules he lived by, one of a few, was that hitchhikers didn't owe you a thing—not gas money, or a smile, not even a word. It was all right by him if she found her tongue, but then again it didn't matter. "Name's Paul," he said.

The girl smiled faintly, as if she were hardly there. In her mind she wasn't. Back at her boyfriend's, she was replaying a squabble that had ended with a declaration that she would never see Ben again. And this time she meant it! . . . Well, maybe *one* more time, but only to return the pea coat she had grabbed in her hurry to get away, and to pick up her own ski parka, which she had left hanging on the door.

"I said my name is Paul." Snapping his fingers in front of her face.

"Mine's Becky."

"You don't look like a Becky," he said without taking his eyes off the road. "More like Rebecca."

She smiled absently. "Okay, have it your way. Rebecca."

" 'And they called Rebecca' "—he was looking right at her now—" 'and said unto her, Wilt thou go with this man? And she said, I will go.' "

"I don't get it."

"Genesis," he said. "Chapter twenty-four, verse fifty-eight. Very apropos, don't you think?"

"You're weird."

"Not really." He flashed the good smile again, but this time he took something off it, like a junk ball pitcher mixing his speeds.

"No one's called me Rebecca since I was a little kid."

"Rebecca's a beautiful name," he said. "And you're a beautiful girl. How old are you, Rebecca?"

"I'll be eighteen tomorrow."

A crash fence bisected the road and then it divided into four lanes. Holding the van at an even seventy, he took a hand off the wheel and put it around one of hers and shook it. "Let me be the first to wish you a happy birthday," he said solemnly.

"You're not the first. But thanks anyway." She pulled back her hand and fumbled inside her pockets. "Mind if I smoke?"

Becky opened her window a crack and removed a thin cloth sack from her coat. She emptied the bag into a square of gummed paper which she twirled into a loose cylinder. Then she depressed the lighter on the dash. While she waited for the element to heat up, she tuned the radio to a C & W station and began whistling.

The boy dialed back to heavy metal. "Girls can't whistle," he said.

Was that a law or just his dumb opinion? But before she could say anything the lighter was ready and she took a long, soothing drag and exhaled languorously through her nose.

The boy had his hand in front of her face again. "I'd like a hit of that."

Becky placed the cigarette between his first two fingers and immediately he began to cough. "This is tobacco, for Chris' sake."

"What'd you think it was?"

"Oh, boy," he said. "Have you got a lot to learn."

"About what? About dope? I don't think there's a whole lot you can teach me about dope."

The highway narrowed for the block-long Main Street of Joes Pond and he came off the gas and returned both hands to the wheel. "About life," he said.

The girl looked up sharply. He saw her glance at the window, open her mouth as if she were about to say, You can let me out here.

"I could teach you plenty." He tried the smile again, but this time was unable to make it fit. ". . . But only if you asked nice."

Becky squirmed against the door and sat catercorner with the back of her head resting on the glass. For the second time she took a good hard look at him. He was about twenty, twenty-two at the most, wearing the autumn uniform of a Green Mountain yankee—checked wool jacket, iridescent hunter's cap with the earmuffs down, twill pants and oiled boots—a type she regarded as canny but trustworthy, though this one seemed like a real creep. He was a slender boy and, from what she could see, lightly muscled, the biggest thing about him the Adam's apple it looked like he cut the two times a week that he had to shave. Hardly a threat—especially after everything Ben had taught her about kneeing a man where it hurt most. Whatever

idea she was entertaining about jumping from the truck evap-
orated when a green-and-gold Vermont state police car turned
after them at the only red light in the settlement and dropped
back four car lengths.

"Think you know about life?" she said. "To me it looks like
this is maybe your second time ever out of the Northeast
Kingdom."

"You'd be surprised."

"I'll bet I would. Tell me, from your vast experience—" She
held back till he turned toward her and could see her laughing.
"Tell me about life."

If she was getting to him, he didn't show it. "There are certain
things I've learned," he said in his stolid country twang, "things
you only wished you knew."

"Oh . . . ? Like what?"

"For one," he said, "I know better than to get into a van
with a stranger."

She tried to laugh again, but felt her throat constrict. "Are
you trying to frighten me?"

She looked at him closely once more, but his face told her
nothing new. Then he pushed back his cap and she saw perspiration trickling out of the close-cropped hair over his temple,
out of the two-dollar haircut, and suddenly the van was much
too warm. But, then, why had she begun to shiver? She searched
the mirror for the trooper's car still glued to their bumper. "You
don't, you know," she said, more for her own benefit than for
his. "You don't scare me one bit."

"Why would I want to do that?"

The question was why he was doing such a good job of it.
"Let's change the subject. Are you from around St. Jay?"

"Malletts Bay." When he caught her looking at him as though
she didn't know what the hell he was talking about, he said,
"It's not in the Northeast Kingdom. It's on Lake Champlain,
above Burlington."

She was trying not to listen. She'd had her fill of this know-it-all hick tooling around in his fancy van. Still, she didn't have to be told, they were a nice few miles from Montpelier, and it might not be such a bad idea to rein in her resentment, or at least to keep it from spilling over. Again she framed the police cruiser in the glass. What's it like there? she wanted to ask. But what came out was, "I wondered where you got so smart. I'm sure Malletts Bay is a real swinging place."

"It's not so bad."

He said nothing more, and they rode in silence for another twenty minutes as the dairy spreads gave way to neat farms where Morgan horses grazed in wooded pastures losing definition in the snow, gentleman's farms. Then the highway funneled into a village street lined with pillared mansions, one in three topped with glass-walled widow's walks like those where whalers' wives once had strained for a glimpse of home-bound sails—a hopeless affectation in northern Vermont, a hundred miles from the ocean. Without signaling, the boy turned onto US 89, the interstate skirting the capital.

"Where do you think you're going?" Becky asked, the annoyance starting to show again. "I get off here."

"Jeez." He smiled sheepishly. "I'm so used to taking 89 that my brain forgot to tell my hands what to do."

"The next exit's Waterbury, and that's another eleven miles from here." She glanced out at the old road bending away behind them and felt her stomach knot as the police car followed it into the city. "Why don't you just pull over and I'll walk back down the ramp?"

"I can't let you do that."

"Why?" Cracks were showing in the upper register of her girlish soprano. "Why not?"

"It's too dangerous. And besides, it's against the law and I could get a ticket. What we'll do, I'll drive to Waterbury and then I'll get off and turn around and bring you back."

"You don't have to. I'll just—"

"It's no big deal," he said, gunning the engine to make further debate meaningless. "Anyway, missing Montpelier was my mistake. It's the least I can do."

"Thanks. I . . . I appreciate your going so far out of your way."

West of Montpelier the interstate took dead aim at Burlington's snubbed skyline and beyond the lakeshore the high peaks of the Adirondacks. He steered into the slow lane and kept the van on course with his little finger. "It's funny how sometimes the left hand doesn't know what the right's doing. What I mean," he said, "is I was planning on bringing you right to your door, and instead I went on by the city like it wasn't there. Can you give me a clue why I did that?"

The girl started to say something, but he cut her off. "Me neither. But it certainly doesn't make me look very bright, does it? So why don't we just blame it on Malletts Bay, if that's okay by you."

She didn't respond to that. She was thinking of Ben again, and only in part of where he had taught her to kick a man. What had they been fighting about in the first place? She remembered a silly disagreement that was mostly—no, entirely—her fault, and how she had used it to hurt him. As soon as she was home she would call and apologize for everything, let him know how much he meant to her.

A tinny metronome distracted her, and she became aware of a flashing green arrow on the dashboard. In a wedge of clear glass carved out of the snow she saw the Waterbury exit. As the truck began to slow, her hands buried themselves in her pockets again, but the tobacco pouch was empty. She slouched in her seat. "Are we almost there?" she asked.

"That's right."

He came off the interstate cautiously, feeling his way along the ramp. Small flakes gusted around the van in dry swirls, overwhelming the windshield wipers. He touched a knob on the dash and the rubber blades beat to a faster tune, but still the girl scarcely could see ahead of her. By her watch it was nearly five o'clock, and if they didn't step on it Ben would be leaving for work before she made her call.

Where the ramp emptied into a four-lane highway he hit the brakes hard, and she was thrown forward so suddenly that it took all her strength to brace herself against the dash. "What was that about?" she asked.

"Some retard cut us off," he said. "You okay?"

"I think so." And another thing about Ben, he was a careful driver.

They turned and then they turned twice more and crawled along at thirty-five. She rubbed the heel of her hand against the fogged glass and was rewarded with a better view of eddying snow. Through the side window she saw the occasional light of a sullen farm defying the storm. Then a tractor-trailer swung around their right, raising a curtain of brown slush across the windshield, and as the boy used his washer she realized they were on a mountain road above a town she didn't recognize.

"I thought you were taking me back to Montpelier," she said.

"I am."

"But this isn't I-89. It isn't even going the same way."

"Well, no," he said. "Didn't you see the sign back there? The eastbound lane's closed on account of the storm. We have to take secondary roads."

"I didn't see anything." Her eyes followed twinned beams inside a white tunnel that seemed to close behind them. "There's no need for you to drive all the way to Montpelier. I'll get out and then you can find the interstate and be home in no time."

"Way out here in the woods? What'll *you* do?"

"Me? What about me?" The soprano fractured into a shrill falsetto. "You don't have to worry about me."

As though he had thought it out a long time before, he shook his head. "That doesn't sound like such a hot idea."

"I can take care of myself, thank you," she snapped. "You can drop . . . No, I'll walk to town and wait out the storm there. Now I'm telling you to stop. I want to get out."

As the van skidded to a halt, she buttoned her coat, trying to store the warmth that she would need outside. What *am* I going to do all the way out here? she asked herself. But even a night in the blizzard was preferable to another moment with this weirdo. She looked out at a dark woodlot where sugar maples melted into the spruce forest of the high country, and tugged her collar around her throat.

"Good-bye, and thanks again." She felt for the door handle. Unable to find it, she flattened her palm against the panel and swept widening circles. Inches from the window crank her hand closed on a jagged stub of metal. "What is this?"

"Let me explain."

"You damn well better."

"Behold," he said, and cleared his throat theatrically. "Rebecca is before thee, take her and go, and let her be thy master's son's wife, as the Lord hath spoken."

Turning her back, she wound down the glass. Behind her she heard him asking, "You see what it means? Don't you see that?"

She was groping for the outside handle when he grabbed her by the shoulders and jerked her against him. "No," she lied, "I don't know. What does it—"

"What it means," he said in that earnest voice of his, "is I'm gonna fuck your brains loose now."

Slender arms wrapped themselves around her and bundled her easily over the top of the seat. She landed on her hip, the fall cushioned by a scrap of Oriental carpeting that covered the ribbed floor of the truck. An adjustable wrench lay beside a toolbox just out of reach. But before she could crawl toward it the boy vaulted the backrest and wrestled her onto the bed. A soft bed, and so comfortable, the blue velveteen cool against her flaming cheek. If only he'd let her alone, it would be so easy to shut her eyes and sleep. . . .

He was all over her then, pressing his mouth against hers, chewing on the nibbled lips, the touch of his skin enough to make her gag. She remembered hearing someplace that the best way to turn off a man was to puke in his face, but despite her revulsion she couldn't do it. She hugged herself tightly and brought her knees up to her chest, curling herself into a ball. Maybe, just maybe, he'd give up and—

"Take off your clothes, Rebecca." When she didn't respond, except to move her eyes away from his, he added, "I mean it."

"My father . . ." she said. "My father is a lawyer in the attorney general's office. That's why I live in Montpelier. You don't want to get in the kind of trouble he can make for you. If you let me go, let me go now, I won't tell anyone."

"Is that right?"

The girl nodded, and for an instant he might have been going for it. But then he shrugged his narrow shoulders and said, "You can tell," and pried her arms away from her body and began unbuttoning Ben's coat.

She flailed at him with tiny fists. She aimed short kicks at his crotch the way Ben had taught her, feeling herself go numb as they bounced unnoticed off his thighs. He had the coat off by then, and she thought she was going to vomit in spite of herself as he slipped his hand under her red cashmere sweater and moved it over her belly, digging under her bra with icy fingertips.

"That's a pretty sweater," he said. "I'd hate to see it torn up. So why don't you do us both a favor and take it off yourself?"

The girl shook her head.

"Okay, have it your way." He ripped the sweater open, the

shell buttons popping like scattershot against the wall of the truck. Then he wrenched her into a sitting position and pulled the ruined cloth from her shoulders.

"Leave me alone." She brushed her wrist under her nose. "I haven't done anything to you."

"Not yet," the earnest voice said, and gave way to a brittle laugh.

He shoved her down, and she crossed both arms over her chest, holding onto her bra straps as if they were lifelines. As he unbuckled her belt, she saw him backlighted in a halogen glow. He flattened himself against her until the grinding of a heavy car receded down the hill, then knelt between her ankles, tugged her jeans below her hips, and bunched them against the top of her boots.

"Now your underwear." When the girl began swinging her head from side to side, he said, "And this time I want you to do it yourself, Rebecca."

Her head moved faster, and he cradled it in his hands and put his mouth close to her ear. "Would it make a difference if I said, 'Please?' " he whispered. "Pretty please?"

"What if I ask like this?" He showed her his fist, but only for the time that it took to drive it into her stomach.

The air rushed out of her in a sob and she doubled onto her side. Her hands clenched involuntarily into fists of her own, and he took both of them in one of his and with the other punched her over the heart.

"Now, Rebecca?" he asked. "Now will you do that one little thing for me?"

So faintly that he almost missed it, the girl nodded. She reached behind with trembling hands and fumbled with her bra.

"Can I help?" he said softly, and brushed her hands away. He unhooked the bra and dropped it on the rug and then stepped back to study small breasts cloaked in a fabric of goose-flesh. "Now your underpants, Rebecca."

Again the girl shook her head. She was whimpering, try-ing without success to choke back the tears that seemed to excite him.

"Please, Rebecca," he said, and made another fist.

The girl raised her legs and kicked feebly at him, as if to say I *tried* to resist, and then she pressed her thumbs under the elastic and pulled her panties down around her ankles.

"Good, Rebecca. That's very good."

He backed away again, and it occurred to her that maybe now he'd take out a camera and snap a few pictures and throw her naked into the snow, maybe that was all. She'd settle for that, be grateful for anything but to have him at her again. But then he began taking off his own clothes, folding them neatly over the seat until he had on only his underwear and she was wondering where all the muscles came from.

"Always save the best for last," he smiled as he stepped out of his shorts.

His knees were between hers, spreading apart, opening her. His mouth clamped onto hers, his tongue maneuvering inside until she remembered what Ben had said to do in such a situ-ation, and she gritted her teeth and then she ground them. She heard the boy grunt. But when she opened her eyes, the smile was still there. He said, "You shouldn't have done that, Re-becca. Really, you shouldn't."

He brought both fists down on her stomach, and when she covered up with her arms, the fists found her face and then her stomach again, and after a very long time that was really less than a minute she began to lose consciousness. But before she did she saw him reach for her belt and felt the webbing scrape against her throat, and then she felt another kind of pain, more intense than anything she'd ever experienced, and deeper, as if she were being torn apart. . . .

When she opened her eyes, he was lying at her side with one leg wrapped in hers, snoring lightly. Her entire body burned, the pressure of her fingers on her breasts enough to make her wince. There was the taste of salt in her mouth, and as she moved her tongue over her lips she licked away flecks of blood. The belt was still looped around her neck, the other end between the boy's fingers, so that when she pushed herself up on her elbows he stirred. She lay back again, glimpsing more blood between her thighs.

If only she could get her hands on the wrench . . . Her eyes fastened to the gray iron, as if a magnetism of her own making could draw it into her grasp, but there was no way to move past the boy without waking him. Softly, so as not to frighten herself more, she began to cry. Not even Ben could help her now. About all that was left was to pray. But what came to mind from eight years of Sunday school were only a few scraps from the Bible. *Behold, Rebecca* . . . Under her breath she cursed God instead.

Never looking away from the sleeping boy, she began to undo the belt. She worked the loop around her chin and had it nearly over her forehead when he tugged her down and pinned her arms under his.

"Where do you think you're going?"

"You're choking me."

"I wouldn't blame you for wanting to take off," he said matter-of-factly, and gave her some slack. "Only I can't let you go yet, you understand?"

The girl didn't nod or say anything.

"There's something I've been meaning to ask you, Rebecca the attorney general's helper's daughter. I never did get your last name." Waiting for an answer, he tugged at the belt again, but not so hard.

"Beausoleil," she gasped.

"Your family originally Canucks?" He seemed impressed. "Pretty people, the frogs," he said, and kissed her.

Her hands rushed up against the side of his jaw. But then

the belt closed around her windpipe and she lay still and shut her eyes and counted slowly to 50 as he climbed on her, counted to 100 and then 150, trying not to let him see her tears, 200, 250, until the numbers ran out. And finally he was beside her again and she thought he was going to sleep, but then he said, "I like you, Rebecca Beausoleil, I like you a lot. It'd be nice if we could get together sometime and do this again."

He laughed and scratched his chest, which was as smooth and hairless as hers. "Well, not exactly like this. Now that we're an item," he said, and laughed some more, "we could take in a movie and then go to my place and really have ourselves a high old time. What do you say to that, Rebecca Beausoleil?"

He put his face close to hers, and she thought that he was going to kiss her again. If he did, she'd try to do the one thing Ben had never told her about, which was to smile and pretend she was enjoying herself and wrap her arms around him as if she couldn't get enough of him and moan to him and whisper in his ear, and maybe then he'd have enough of her. And as she made up her mind, she began to hate Ben for being too jealous to tell her how easy it was. And, more than that, to hate herself, too. But just then the boy's mouth tightened and he looped the belt another time around his fist.

"Except we sure as hell can't if you blab about what happened," he said. "I could get in a shitload of trouble if you did that."

"I won't tell anybody."

"Well, then, I guess there's not going to be a problem after all, is there, Rebecca?"

The girl opened her mouth, but made no sound. She mouthed the word "No."

"Let me hear you say it."

She shook her head.

"Say it, Rebecca."

"No . . . no problem," she gasped.

"I'll sleep better tonight knowing that." He let go of the belt and was loosening the loop around her throat when suddenly he said, "Only how can I be sure you're not lying to me?"

"I wouldn't—" Her head, her whole body shaking.

"You could just be saying that."

"I don't want to make trouble."

"It's not like I don't want to believe you." He pressed his cheek against hers and she lay still again and tried not to squirm away. "But what if it slips out what happened and somebody puts a bug in your ear about going to the police, and the next thing I know they're looking for me?"

"I . . . I couldn't do that even if I wanted to."

"Why not?"

"I don't know your name," she said, "or your address. I didn't get a look at your license plates. I wouldn't know how to find you again."

"No?" He looked hurt. "That'd be a shame. Worse than the other. So in case you *do* want to call, my name is Paul Arthur Conklin, and I live on Sturgeon Cove Road in Malletts Bay, and my phone—"

"Stop," she screamed. "I don't want to know."

"I thought you said you'd see me."

"*You* have to call."

He kissed her neck and her face, and then he was on top of her again. She shut her eyes and wallowed in the thin mattress, tunneling away from him. "Now you're getting into it," she heard him say. But then his hips stopped moving and he hiked himself up on his arms. "Only you do know my name, Rebecca, and there isn't a damn thing I can do about it."

The belt shortened around her throat, pressure building inside her head as if all the blood in her body were being squeezed into the space behind her eyes. "Do you get off on this, Rebecca? I hear some girls do."

She tried to answer him, but the words were trapped deep

in her throat. She needed air, but the trapped words blocked her windpipe and she felt herself growing light-headed. She said, "Fuck it," but only to herself, and dug her nails into his back and sliced his shoulders, then jabbed them at his neck and dragged them to his cheeks, feeling the slippery warmth in her fingers, clawing at his eyes while he twisted away to cinch the belt against the fragile bones in her voice box. She heard his heart pound, drowning hers out, hers barely making any sound as he said, "Do you like it, Rebecca? Do you like it? Do you? Do . . . Do . . ."

Ben, she thought, why didn't you tell me about . . .

Her heart beating faintly.

Then not beating at all.

He pressed a cheek against her breast, listening, and when he heard nothing pulled away to stare at her. Other than a lopsided grimace frozen on her lips, she wasn't much different from before. Tears had formed in the corners of her eyes. As he slipped the belt over her head, they began to roll down her face, and he flicked his tongue at them and swallowed them.

"Such beautiful eyes. Such beautiful, beautiful . . ." He nestled against her and tilted her hips toward him. Again his knees burrowed between hers, muscling unresisting legs out of the way, forcing himself into the still body. "Rebecca," he whispered, and kissed the bluish lids.

He slept. In forty minutes the cold woke him and he pulled the velveteen spread around his shoulders and snuggled against the girl. Already her skin was cool and clammy, but he warmed himself spilling kisses on the back of her neck until he dozed.

When he got up a second time, he hurried into his clothes. He placed the girl on the carpet and scavenged beneath a mound of oily rags for a dented kettle which he emptied of corroded battery clamps and scraps of cable and then carried outside. The storm was at its peak, crystalline spear points cutting through his flannel shirt as he dug the pot into a snowbank at the edge of the road, tamping the flakes beneath bare hands till he had all he could use.

He found clean rags in the glove compartment. He dipped one into the snow and washed the girl's body, glazing the grayish skin. A trace of red had dribbled from her mouth, and he blotted it away with the mascara that caked her cheeks like sorrow's residue.

"So beautiful . . ." He discarded the soiled rag and used a fresh one to pat the body dry, then swaddled it in the velveteen spread. "So *clean.*"

The light from a passing car paralyzed him like a jacked deer, and he listened for other vehicles before shouldering the body into the woods. In a clearing ringed with bare trees he stumbled, and the girl slipped from his arms. He let her down between the roots of a large oak and then leaned against the trunk, taking great gulps of frosted air. Papery bark fluttered from the limbs of twisted birches like silver flags.

"And they blessed Rebecca," he whispered, "and said unto her, Thou art our sister, be thou the mother of thousands of millions, and let thy seed possess the gate of those which hate them."

He peeled away the cloth to kiss the dark eyes one last time as the blizzard began to hide her. Then he walked back through the pines between piles of blown snow.

2

Before dawn, on four hours of sleep, Lawrence St. Germain loaded his skis into the back of a Cabot County sheriff's car and bulldozed a path from his cabin to the gravel township road. He drove fifteen miles to I-89 and exited at Waterbury, riding the cleared lane north past the Trapp family lodge turnoff to Stowe and into the mountains. Where Route 108 was closed to traffic through Smugglers Notch, he entered the Mount Mansfield ski area and parked at the foot of the gondola.

Careful not to scuff the unmarked finish, he slid his new K-2's out of the back seat. He kicked off spit-shined black oxfords and hurried into racing boots and nylon gaiters that protected the legs of his tan uniform trousers. As he stepped clumsily away from the Ford, he was hatless, his .38 Chief's Special heavy against his thigh. Through the streaked windows of the gondola house he could see the woven cable on which red cars were strung like battered beads. Safety inspectors were due by that afternoon, and in two weeks the lift would open to the public. But for the next several hours he had the mountain to himself.

The early light was alive with pogonips, particles of frost that glinted in the frigid air. He carried the skis around the empty lodge and fit his boots over the blunt track of a snowshoe rabbit that followed the shadow of the cable up the mountain. A clump of whittled alder showed where deer had come to browse at the edge of the trail, and higher up he saw the stringy droppings of a lone coyote. He kept climbing—not quite 7,000 feet to go, 2,000 of them vertical.

Beside a gash in the trees where the Rimrock trail met Gondolier, he hesitated. The Front Four, the mountain's steepest terrain, hung over Rimrock like plummeting fairways. But the challenge of frozen mogul fields would have to wait for January's deep snows. Keeping to Gondolier, he trudged toward a waterfall that was hardening into rippled slabs against the slope. There he paused to swing his skis to the other shoulder before continuing toward the top.

Alongside the Toll Road off the Lookout double chair was the tiny fieldstone chapel where he had been married. Hard to believe now that the mountain had been such an important part of his life that he had insisted on a slopeside ceremony with everyone schussing down afterward to the reception at the base lodge. Following the honeymoon—two weeks at Aspen—he'd gone years without putting on his skis, preoccupied more with the new lieutenant's bars on his uniform collar than with the bride he made so little time for that eventually she had left him, saying something about marriage being the doom of romance— theirs. He'd started skiing again after the divorce, and missing Annie so badly that he burned up the phone lines to her parents' place in Key West, keeping on her case till she moved back in with him and they fashioned the cautious arrangement that kept them mildly engaged and out of each other's hair and that surely was the death rattle of both marriage and romance.

The sun was inching above the Octagon warming hut when he reached the Cliff House. He stood by the ruled stick that measured two feet of accumulated snow, sighting north along purple mountains dissolving against the Canadian border. To the east heavy clouds pressed down on Mount Washington's uncertain summit. Almost reluctantly, he dropped the skis and stepped into the bindings and poled toward the Perry Merrill.

The new K-2's turned effortlessly in the virgin powder, and he glanced back with satisfaction at the precision of his curved track. Around a corner of the mountain where the wind had blown off most of the cover, he tightroped down a narrow strip of white bordered by granite outcroppings. With his poles on his hips he crouched into a racer's tuck, savoring the burst of speed it produced. Then the Perry Merrill—the merry peril, he'd called it as a kid—veered back to Gondolier, and he skied the fall line down its rocky heart toward the waterfall between the gondola towers.

Over the years he guessed he'd seen seven broken legs there, expert skiers sitting back defensively as the mountain fell away beneath them, surrendering to the urge to panic. Though he could spot its symptoms at a distance, fear was mystery to him, something he took pride in never having had to conquer in himself. Relaxing, maintaining his tuck, he raced to the lip of the waterfall, holding back until his ski tips were over the edge before throwing himself forward to soar toward a patch of soft snow and land awkwardly on one foot, then regaining his balance and gliding easily down the slope.

He stayed on Gondolier, building speed as he let his skis run free, and then moderating his descent with gentle traverses. After a while he entered lower Chin Clip, which dropped gradually through hardwoods toward the base lodge. His skis were on his shoulder again when the crackling of his radio through a window left open two inches sent him hurrying into the lot. A voice he recognized as a sheriff's dispatcher was asking where he was.

He pulled off a pigskin glove, unlocked the Ford, and reached for the microphone with fingers stinging from old frostbite. "St. Germain here," he said.

"Thought you went missing, Lieutenant. We've been looking for you all morning."

"Couldn't have." He slid onto the seat, clawing at the snaps on his boots. "It's not eight o'clock yet."

"That ain't the point. Marlow wants you now, wants you an hour ago."

"What about?"

"Somebody *has* gone missing," said the voice on the radio. "Marlow wants you to find 'em."

"Hold on." St. Germain took off one boot and then the other, then stuffed his scarcely feeling feet inside his shoes. "Now who did you say—"

"Name's Rebecca Rachel Beausoleil. W F 18, 323 Ethan Allen Street, Montpelier. Brown hair, brown eyes . . . you getting this?"

"*How* old?"

"Eighteen today," the dispatcher said.

"Ed, you caught me at a bad time. I'm over to Stowe just now. There's two feet of powder on the mountain and the only tracks in it are mine. I'm not in the mood to go hunting for a snot-nose girl probably gone less than two days, who's—"

"Less than one, Lieutenant."

"Less than one, then . . . who's no doubt shacked up with her boyfriend, or her boyfriend's best friend, or the two of them, for all I know or care."

"This one you do," the dispatcher said.

"The hell I . . . Why do you say that?"

"Because her father's Raymond Beausoleil, the new state's attorney for Cabot County, and 'cause if you don't, Marlow's gonna bust you down to—"

But the rest went unheard as St. Germain twisted the key in the ignition and the radio was drained of power as the cruiser surged to life and roared out of the upper lot. The big car skidded onto the highway, a christie turn on two wheels, and found traction, and St. Germain retraced his route past eight miles of shuttered restaurants and motels. On the outskirts of Stowe he went southwest toward Tremont Center, homing in on the radio mast over a clapboard building with grilled windows.

He came inside the rear entrance, turning to allow his shoulders through the doorways. The colonial-style structure, on the register of National Historic Landmarks, had been erected in 1787 by R. L. Cabot, the timber merchant who had lent his name to the county, and it was St. Germain's complaint that eighteenth-century Vermonters must all have been under five feet tall. St. Germain, since he was a high school senior, had stood six feet four inches, and in the dozen years since that time had filled out to 220 pounds, most of them rock-hard. He squeezed through the empty corridors toward a door leaking light through a window with SHERIFF painted between ruled lines on the pebbled glass.

St. Germain opened the door and then knocked and then bent down to strip the gaiters from his trousers. Behind an undersized desk John P. Marlow faced a man wearing a camel's hair topcoat and with a gray fedora in his lap. The fifty-nine-year-old sheriff, in his ninth two-year term, was in the same uniform as his lieutenant, but without two rows of ribbons over the breast pocket. "Larry," he said, trying not to glare, "you know Ray Beausoleil."

St. Germain snapped to his full height with his right hand extended. The man in the topcoat leaned the least bit to latch onto it and then let go. "Lieutenant," he said.

"What can we do for—"

"Ray's daughter, Becky, didn't come home last night," Marlow interrupted, "and he has reason to believe she might be in some trouble."

The little cockteaser with the big round eyes and the rounder heels is gone half a day and we're supposed to jump like trained dogs? he wanted to say. We could try the hot-sheet motels on the Barre–Montpelier Road, except she probably knows by now to check in under an assumed name.

But what he said was, "Is that right?"

Beausoleil leaned back, raking manicured fingers through styled hair going silver at the temples. At his feet St. Germain noticed a monogrammed attaché case done up in soft black leather. "About six weeks ago she took up with a St. Johnsbury man. His name is Benjamin Lederer and he's thirty-three years old," Beausoleil said with evident distaste. "By profession he's a grease monkey, by avocation, I believe, a dope dealer. Since he sunk his hooks into her, Becky's been acting totally out of character. But she's never gone so far as to do anything like this before, stayed out all night, I mean."

"And you want us to bring her back, do you, Mr. Beausoleil?"

"Yes."

"If she spent the night with him of her own free will, there's not much we can—"

Marlow inched closer to his desk. "Hear the man out, will you, Larry, before you jump to conclusions? Just this one time."

"She's only eighteen," Beausoleil said, redness starting to creep under his blue jowels. "And impressionable. A pushover for someone like this Lederer."

St. Germain walked to a folding chair against the wall and lowered his bulk onto it carefully.

"I don't expect you to make an arrest," Beausoleil said. "I just want my daughter home. And I want her to know what a disgrace she has become to her family."

In a hollow voice St. Germain said, "I still don't see where that's a job for us."

"Lieutenant, I've spent six years in the attorney general's office all over this state, and I know better than to consider any sheriff's department a candy store with free goodies on the shelves. I understand full well the nature of your responsibilities. I also know that days, if not weeks, go by in a rural county of this size without anything more demanding than traffic patrol to take up your time, and so I don't think it's asking too much for you to drive up to Lederer's home with your dome lights blazing and your siren screaming and scare the living shit out of my daughter on her eighteenth birthday."

"Have you tried talking to her?"

"I phoned late last night," Beausoleil said. "And again this morning. And got nowhere both times. Lederer insists Becky left his place yesterday afternoon and that he hasn't heard from her since."

"I mean did you ever sit down and talk to—"

"Larry," Marlow said angrily.

St. Germain shifted his weight uncomfortably, so that he was facing the man in the topcoat. "What I'm trying to say is that Lederer could be telling the truth, you know."

"He's a liar and a fraud," Beausoleil said unhappily. "Else what would my daughter be doing with him?"

When Raymond Beausoleil had gone, St. Germain opened a window to let out the faint scent of gingery cologne lingering in the room. "I can't figure out why you didn't give him the gate," he said to his boss. "Everybody knows the kind of girl Becky is."

"I didn't," Marlow said, "because in less than two years I'm finally taking off this badge and I believe it might not be a bad idea for the state's attorney for this county to have a working relationship with the man I hope to succeed me. Does that answer the question?"

"But you know—hell, he knows, too—that all we can do is go through the motions. Even if I find her, Becky's old enough to do whatever it is she wants to do and with whoever she wants to do it. I can't run her in for sleeping with her boyfriend and staying out all night. I can't even give her a good spanking, which is something I might at least enjoy."

Marlow twirled a toothpick in the small space between his front teeth. "Larry, there's times I think you're thick as shit.

The man's not trying to change his daughter. He's scared witless that he's lost what little control he ever had over her, so he feels he has to throw his weight around here, the other choice being to do nothing and let it eat him up inside. Of course he thinks this office is his candy store. And as far as he's concerned, you're the clerk. He's not asking, he's ordering you to ride out to St. Johnsbury quick to report that his daughter's all right even if she is having the time of her life letting this Lederer screw her every which way. And when you tell him that, what he'll do, he'll look extremely pained that you didn't bring her back with you and murder Lederer in the bargain."

St. Germain fit his hat squarely on his head and walked to the door. Marlow, watching him, said, "I never told you that being a cowboy was all there was to the job, did I?"

"No, John, you didn't."

"It's being a diplomat, and something of a suckass, that's most of it. So now that we both understand that, how's about taking Jeffcoat for company to St. Jay and then coming back and telling Ray Beausoleil what he wants to hear."

"Yes, *sir*," St. Germain said.

"And, Larry, if it's not too much trouble . . ."

St. Germain paused with one foot already out the door.

"Take off the other goddam gaiter before you make an ass out of the whole goddam department."

At the end of the corridor St. Germain ducked inside a double-doored room, half of which was given over to three cells fitted out with bunk beds and new clamshell-white American Standard force flush toilets so immaculate that the deputies preferred them to their own single-stall john in the basement. Beyond the bars were four wood desks, bruised and wobbly, and slatted chairs to match. At one of these, filling out a vehicular accident report, sat a man with a boy's face in the baggy tans of a Cabot County sheriff's officer.

Walter Jeffcoat was in his third year with the department,

although only his first in uniform after eighteen months as a probationary officer assigned to clerical duties. On the seat beside him was an eight-pointed policeman's cap with badge number 138 reflected in the shiny bill. From time to time he looked down at the shield incredulously, as though affirming his membership in an otherwise exclusive club, then touched the point of his pen to his tongue as he searched for his place on the page.

When he heard St. Germain's heavy step and his, "Morning, Wally," inside the bullpen, Jeffcoat got up out of his chair and stood stifly beside it. Stretched ramrod straight he was five feet five and three-eighths inches tall, nearly three inches below the minimum height requirement for the department, and, at 135 pounds, more than 20 pounds underweight. Contact lenses disguised the 20-80 vision that was also in violation of standards. Because he was the first young officer to have been appointed to the force in five years, and was believed to be the only person in the county who would risk his neck for the starting salary of $10,776, he was considered by his superiors to be among the most valuable men in uniform, if a little bit naïve.

"What's doing?" St. Germain asked.

"Couldn't be busier, Lieutenant." Jeffcoat nodded proudly toward the pile of completed accident reports, forgetting for the moment the disdain with which other officers regarded paperwork. "After I'm done," he added quickly, "it's my day to bring traffic charges in District Court."

"Insurance companies'll have to wait," St. Germain said. He grabbed for a Styrofoam cup beside the papers on the desk, and Jeffcoat saw his protuberant Adam's apple bob twice before he put it down. "So will the speeders. We're going for a ride."

"Where to?"

"For starters, to Shep's diner. I've been over to Stowe just now, working up a monumental appetite."

Jeffcoat stood more at ease. "You been ski—" The familiarity in his tone brought him up short. Social invitations were rarities from other officers, most of them hardened former military men who treated him as a gofer at best, more often as a kid brother who was always underfoot. Invitations from the big blond lieutenant who was Marlow's crown prince were the rarest of all. "And then?" he asked warily.

"To St. Jay. Montpelier after that. There's a fellow, I think it'd be a good idea if you were around when I talk to him, so I don't end up committing felonious assault after he hears what I have to say."

Jeffcoat squinted longingly at his accident reports. "Armed fellow?"

"Nope. Come on, Wally, put a move on."

Jeffcoat didn't budge. "Why would you want to do something like that," he asked, "assault the man?"

St. Germain picked up the cap with badge 138 above the bill and whisked some lint off the tan cloth. Then he slapped it down low over the baby-faced officer's eyes. "Tell me, where am I going to find somebody to do it for me?"

The farmhouse was an architectural collage, its various parts arranged in no particular order, a Cape Cod cottage between a geodesic dome and a greenhouse radiating purplish growth light attached to a redwood garage. The man who met them out in front seemed to have fallen into the same style. He was tall, as tall as St. Germain, but broader, with a full beard and coarse black hair parted down the middle and gathered into a pony tail that whisked against the small of his back. He was wearing a blue reindeer sweater over faded, dirt-caked overalls, red ostrich-skin cowboy boots, thick eyeglasses with black frames, and a gold Romulus watch. In his hand was a long shovel, which he scraped at the yard as the cruiser pulled into his drive and the two officers came outside.

"Mr. Lederer," St. Germain said. "This is Deputy Jeffcoat. I'm Lieutenant—"

The broad man stared at the outstretched hand, but made no move toward it. "You're looking for Becky, ain't you?"

"Miss Beausoleil didn't come home last night. We have reason to believe you were the last person to see her."

"Like I told her father two times over the phone, she ain't here."

"He says he's not sure he believes you."

"That's his problem."

"Uh-uh," St. Germain said evenly. "Becky's his problem. What you're handing out about her, that's yours."

"In that case, let me explain a little better," Lederer said. "She still ain't here."

"Where—?"

"Don't know." Lederer dragged the shovel over the snow as though he had seeds to cover in the white furrow. "Don't care either."

"But she *was* here," Jeffcoat put in, filling a short silence as if he were expected to say something.

"Yeah," Lederer conceded, "but that was yesterday, and Becky's a pretty fast mover, if you know what I mean."

"What time was it that you saw her last?" St. Germain asked.

"Don't remember. We had a dumb spat and she—"

"What kind of spat?" Jeffcoat interrupted. He looked to St. Germain for approval, and the senior officer poised a phantom kick at his shins.

"The same one we've been having since I met her."

"About what?" St. Germain tried. "If you don't mind our asking."

"What I mind," Lederer said, "is your being here in the first place." He scraped another hole in the snow and then clamped his hands over the top of the shovel and rested his chin on his knuckles.

St. Germain put an edge to his voice. "Tell us anyway."

Lederer blew his nose in the snow, thinking it over. "Why not?" he said. "You can tell her old man it was over how many guys she was screwing while she was moving her stuff in with me."

Jeffcoat opened his mouth again. A dirty look from St. Germain shut it. "How'd it end?"

"The way they always do," Lederer said, "with her screaming and throwing shit and running out threatening she won't ever see me again. She left her jacket on the door where she could've grabbed it if she wanted, so I don't expect it'll be long before she's back."

St. Germain was looking at the greenhouse and the slender stalks pressed against the glass. "It didn't bother you when her father said she hadn't come home?"

"You knew Becky, you wouldn't be worried she was spending the night out in the cold."

Jeffcoat asked, "Do you have her jacket here?" And this time St. Germain wanted to pat him on the back.

"In the greenhouse. With the rest of her crap."

"There might be something in the pockets that we can use," St. Germain said. "Mind if we come in and have a look?" He was moving toward the glass building when Lederer's, "I do," caught him by surprise.

"Then why don't you bring it out for us, and make everybody happy?"

"It don't make me happy. Let me see your warrant."

"Lederer, I'm asking you nicely, get me the girl's—"

"Not without a warrant."

"You think I don't know what you're growing in there? I couldn't give a shit if you hung a sign and sold it by the bale. All we're here for is to find out what happened to Becky Beausoleil. She means anything to you, you'll—"

Lederer let the shovel fall and took two quick steps forward. "The warrant. I want to see a fucking warrant."

St. Germain stood his ground, his hands clenched into fists, then suddenly backed off toward his cruiser. "Okay, have it your way."

Jeffcoat caught up with him at the passenger's side. "He's right. We don't have any business going in—"

"Get in the car, Wally."

The rear wheels kicked up angry braids of slush as St. Germain buried the accelerator and the cruiser leaped ahead of an oily pall. Lederer jumped back as the car bore down on him, the Ford gathering speed as it veered off the drive, swerved around a shallow fish pond, and crashed through the greenhouse doors, bringing down the wall and two large plates of waxed glass from the roof. Jeffcoat was still trying to fasten his safety belt as St. Germain tore open his door and ran into the ruined structure.

Lederer picked the shovel up out of the snow, holding it across his chest as he sprinted after St. Germain. "You're a dead man, cocksucker," he hollered.

St. Germain stopped and turned around, his fingers drumming against the stiff leather of his holster. "Say something?"

Lederer lowered the shovel and they stood so close that St. Germain could smell the morning coffee on the other man's breath. "You're going to be sorry you ever—"

"I doubt that." Toeing bits of glass out of the way, St. Germain went into the greenhouse. Under a long shelf lined with clay pots, each one containing four neatly spaced seedlings and a fertilizer spike in rich humus, he saw a blue parka sticking out of an open carton. On the opposite shelf five-foot vines pushed sprays of pointed leaves out of larger pots, and he lifted one of these over his head and let it crash against the floor. Then he snatched up the jacket by a sleeve and unzipped the pockets. There was a knot of crumpled tissues in one and in another a tin of throat lozenges. When he pried off the lid he found three fat joints and some loose marijuana, which he poured onto the broken glass and ground beneath his heel. He patted down the inside, coming up with a ballpoint pen and a slip of paper on which was written, "Muenster cheese, milk, cornflakes, grape jelly." He offered it back to Lederer, and when the bearded man kept his hands at his sides, let it flutter between his feet. Then he put the jacket on top of the carton and carried everything to the cruiser.

He pulled on his gloves and whisked away the debris on the hood. A headlight was shattered and some chrome was missing from the grille, but he saw no real damage to the car. When he looked back inside the ruined greenhouse, Lederer was bunching the potted rows beneath plastic drop cloths, as somber as any citrus farmer at the first warning of frost.

"*You'll* pay for this."

"Don't count on it," St. Germain said. Then he loaded the carton into the trunk and backed away.

"Jes*us*, Lieutenant," Jeffcoat said, still trying to fasten the belt. "I don't believe you did that."

"Tell you something." St. Germain looked both ways before turning the Ford onto a desolate country road.

"What's that?"

"Neither do I."

Marlow was out of the office when they returned to headquarters. St. Germain found him downstairs in the communications room, tinkering with the antique radio that held the county together while the dispatcher looked on over his shoulder.

"I can't understand why you won't junk that thing and replace it with something modern," St. Germain said, "say, since the time of Marconi."

"And how's the county supposed to meet your salary while we try and pay it off?" Marlow pulled his head out of the radio. "Hand me that tube over there, will you? And, Ed, what about putting up a pot of coffee?"

The dispatcher went out and St. Germain poked through a

collection of silvered tubes and handed one to his boss. "This what you're looking for?"

"Uh-huh. Did Ray Beausoleil bite your head off when you told him what his daughter's been up to?"

"Didn't get the chance," St. Germain said to Marlow's back, which stiffened at the words.

"Why's that?"

"We still don't know where Becky went. She's not at her boyfriend's. She was there yesterday, all right, but he insists she left. He's a queer duck, growing sensimilla in a big greenhouse right in the open. . . . Was, anyway."

"What do you mean *was*?"

"It's not important, John. What is, though, is that he's every bit the class act Beausoleil said he was. I wouldn't want to be any girl who stepped on his toes. And Lederer admits he and Becky were fighting all the time."

"So what does that prove?"

St. Germain let the excitement out of his voice. "Nothing, I guess," he said, chagrined. "It's just something to keep in mind. What do we do about Ray Beausoleil now?"

"Don't you think you've got your priorities out of order? Shouldn't it be Becky we're worrying about?"

"The girl's a tramp, everybody knows it. Lederer says she's probably shacked up with someone else."

"I don't know it," Marlow said, a steely edge undercutting the fatherly tone he reserved for St. Germain. "And until you can tell me where she is and what's happened to her, neither do you. Why not give her the benefit of the doubt and try running her down?"

"You're the boss."

"I am," Marlow said. "But only for the next thirteen months, or till it finally sinks into that handsome blond head that you can't take anything for granted, not when an eighteen-year-old girl's well-being is at stake. Then, with any kind of luck, the sheriff's office becomes your headache. So how about *you* figuring out what we do."

St. Germain buried his hands in his pockets. "I'll call the *Free Press* and the *Herald* and the *Times-Argus*. TV and radio, too."

Marlow laughed humorlessly, the sound rattling in the guts of the old radio.

"What's funny?"

"You are," the sheriff said. "You're what . . . thirty years younger than me . . . and it's like we're light years apart. The way *I'd* go about it, first I'd send her description to Chittenden and Lamoille and Caledonia counties and the state police, then notify the hospitals and morgue. And I'd be thinking of rounding up some of her friends, girls if she's got any like that, and asking if they have a notion where she could have gone."

"I was getting to it."

"In the meantime, you're concerned more about making a name for yourself than you are about the girl."

"Becky's made her reputation." St. Germain moved into the corridor, nearly bumping into the dispatcher, who was juggling three containers of coffee. "I'm still working on mine."

"Come back here."

"I'm going upstairs," St. Germain said. "I have calls to make."

"Larry—"

When St. Germain brought his bulk inside the doorway, Marlow was standing with his back to the radio. "A reputation's not worth shit if it isn't backed up by something substantial."

St. Germain dropped two sugars in black coffee and inhaled the steam. "I don't see the harm in having my picture in the news before election year."

"You worry so much about your image, pretty soon that's all there'll be."

"Come on, John, who's being cheated if I like playing the hero every now and then? Are you saying the taxpayers aren't getting full value out of me?"

"You are," Marlow said, and went back to the radio.

Plows had come by while he was away, walling the long drive with boulders of packed snow. He left the cruiser at the side of the road and mounted the barricade, high-stepping toward a cabin of burnished logs.

The woman in the garden was tall and thin, with sloping cheekbones providing an angular framework for pale skin livid with the cold. She was wearing waffle-soled boots and a maroon skirt, a man's overcoat with a knit scarf under the collar. With a chewed-up broom she was batting clumps of snow from barren hedges bent nearly double against themselves. For long minutes St. Germain stood beside a sugar maple riddled with tapholes, watching her plump the bushes lovingly with bare hands. In the four years he had known her, he never tired of just looking at Annie. Now that he had her to himself again, he knew he'd better get his fill.

When she went inside, he followed. The smell of supper on the stove relaxed him in the same way that a few beers with the boys had served the same purpose during the months when they were living apart. He hung his gun belt on a coat tree and put his cap over it. The fleece-lined parka that was supposed to look like part of his uniform he wore into the bedroom, where he found her darning his socks.

Without looking up from her sewing, she said, "You're home early."

"You could pretend you were happy about it."

"Must we start right away? You haven't even taken off your coat yet."

"I was ragging you, Annie."

She put down the sock and leaned across the bed to kiss him, letting him cup her breast in his hand as he always did no matter how polite her call for affection. "So was I." Lingering on his lips. "How was skiing?"

"Huh?"

"You remember, Mr. Lieutenant. When you left this nice warm bed, it wasn't six o'clock in the morning. Because, you said, you had to try out your new skis."

"It was okay, I guess."

"You *guess*?"

"Tell you the truth, I'd about forgotten I'd been to Stowe today. We had some trouble, and it's still on my mind."

"You didn't do anything to make John mad . . ."

"No, not like that. A girl went missing last night. I'm trying to find her."

She rethreaded the needle and jabbed it into frayed Argyle. "It seems like you're always trying to find a girl."

"For crying out loud—"

"Ease off, Larry. It was a joke."

"I'm not in the mood for comedy," he said. "We looked in every bed you'd expect her to turn up in. Nothing. Her dad's the new state's attorney, and if we don't bring her to him soon, there'll be all kinds of hell to pay."

"Only if you grab the check."

"You don't understand. This is a real son of a bitch on our back. It'd be his pleasure to make life miserable for the department."

"That's my point," she said. "You have no business in the sheriff's office." The tall woman bent lower as she propelled the needle with a thimble that was a silver blur on her finger. "Instead of camping out in the woods, wasting your life with the Keystone Kops, you could be making something of yourself."

"I thought you like the country."

"I do," she said. "But one day I hope to have a child—yours, if you can get up the courage—and I'd hate for him to become the next log cabin President."

In spite of himself, St. Germain began to smile, then thought better of it. "If it was good enough for Abe Lincoln—"

"It's not good enough for *my* child."

"Maybe it won't have to be. John's making some more noises about me taking over when he retires."

"So we trade the cabin for a shack in town and you can grow old early like he did playing cops and robbers? Take off the white hat, cowboy." She made two quick stitches, knotted the thread and snipped the end between her teeth. "You promised me things would be different this time around."

St. Germain dropped beside her and put an arm over her shoulder. "You should have known better than to believe me. I'd have said anything to have you back."

"Damn you." She squirmed away and twisted around to face him. "You're only twenty-nine, not too old to finish your degree. In a couple of years you could be working regular hours, bringing home decent money—"

"Doing what?" He shuddered. "Teaching?"

"What's wrong with that? You're good with kids."

"There's a kid who needs me now."

"Oh, shit," Annie said.

"What if I've been wrong about her? What if she's lying by the side of a road somewhere, hurt bad?"

"*I* need you," Annie said. "You don't have to teach. Stowe's starting to hire again, and they're paying management trainees thirty thousand to start. You could be outdoors as much as you like."

"For all I know, the girl's been snatched." St. Germain went on as if she hadn't said anything. "Annie, this could be the one I've been waiting for, the case to hang a career on."

"You're impossible."

"If Becky *has* been kidnapped . . ." He got up from the bed and began tracing a circle in the floor around a yellow scatter rug. "And the more I think about it, the less unlikely it sounds . . . there could be a ransom demand coming."

"Now you're fantasizing."

"I'm going to ask Beausoleil if we can put a tap on his phone. I'll also contact the state police about getting a tracking dog over to Lederer's place."

"Whose?"

"Becky's fellow . . . And see if he can pick up a spoor."

"The whole thing stinks, if you ask me."

"If I can get that poor kid back from whoever grabbed her, the election'll be just a formality."

"I thought you said the poor kid is a slut."

"It's not my job to judge 'em, Annie. Only to find 'em."

"What about our weekend? We were going to Montreal . . ."

St. Germain stopped pacing. "And if there's no call for ransom, I'll get a helicopter in the air, and if that doesn't work, I'll ask for volunteers to check every vacant building in the county, have the governor's office authorize a reward."

"I said, "What about . . . ?"

"Sorry, Ann." He leaned over to kiss her, and his hand slid automatically to her breast. "Maybe if we get lucky quick . . ."

Annie didn't answer. She reached inside a small cloth bag and pulled out another sock.

3

Hunters found the body.

They were down to three by then, two men and a boy, die-hards from a party of six that had spent most of the night in the tavern of a Hogback Mountain lodge, losing two of their number to hangovers before the day got started and another on the forced march through two feet of fresh snow to a bivouac in the woods. Now, in the early dusk, they trekked back, lugging a trussed 170-pound buck—a fine trophy, the boy had been told, although he wondered if his wisecracking uncles would mount the eight-point rack or the white-tailed hindquarters, like he'd seen over the men's room at the lodge. The boy, who was twelve and small for his age, urged his frozen feet not to quit. Two hours before, excited by the kill, he had worn himself out in the struggle with the carcass. Exhausted now and shivering in the chill downpour that had taken them by surprise, he lagged behind, scarcely able to shoulder his unfired Winchester.

In an opening in the trees the boy dropped back farther to rest on a stump. Staring blankly through clouds of his breath, his interest was drawn to a swatch of blue in the field of white. With the first strength that he could spare he pushed himself across the drag marks to investigate. The blueness seemed to be expanding at his feet as the rain washed the forest floor. He kicked away some of the snow and then peeled off his mittens and scraped more with his hands, uncovering cloth that was stiff and unyielding, anchored to the ground by a cumbersome form around which it was loosely molded. He tugged at a corner and looked inside, and, feeling colder than he could ever remember, he fell to his knees to dig like a dog for a trophy of his own.

The lips were the bluest, as blue as the bedspread shrouding the rest of her. When he had cleared away the snow, he pushed back the cloth and filled his eyes with her body. She was the first woman he had seen without clothes, but the first dead person as well, and he didn't know whether to smirk or to scream. The choice was made by a voice sounding a little like his own, pleading with his uncles to forget about the deer and come back for him, no matter how far they had gotten.

Trying without success to avoid peeking at her again, he knelt beside the woman and pulled the cloth over her. The wind blew it away and he went in search of a heavy rock to weigh it down. Another voice was calling to him then, floating above the storm. "Hello, Tim, you all right?"

The boy hesitated, trying to quell the tremor in his throat. "No," he hollered. "I need you fast."

When they found him, double-timing it into the clearing, flushed and breathless with their rifles in their hands, he was squatting with his back to the dark patch in the snow.

"What you bagged there, boy?" One of the men grinned. "We didn't hear no shot."

The child didn't answer. Clinging to his Winchester, he stood up and moved away and the men gazed down at the pale form in the bedspread.

"Holy shit," one said. "Tim, did you shoot her?"

"Don't be a fool, Ralph," the other man said. "This girl's been dead awhile. And even an idiot could see where she ain't been shot."

"Well, what's her body doing out here in the weather?"

"Ain't our business. Far as we're concerned, we didn't see nothing. Let's get going."

The men shouldered their rifles, retreating toward the path through the clearing. "Sure was a looker, though," Ralph said.

"Ain't you coming, Timmy?" his other uncle called back to the boy. "There's lots more girls where this one come from."

Tim shook his head. "We can't just leave her here like this."

"Why not? It's the way we found her, ain't it?"

The boy went back to the body and stood over it with the Winchester across his chest, groping for something to say, something they couldn't twist around to make him sound like a dumb little kid. "It ain't right," he tried finally. "That's why."

"Listen, son," Ralph said. "You know our tickets've been filled since opening day. Last thing we need's two carcasses out of season. We call the authorities on this, they're going to arrest us for the deer, if not the other. You might consider that."

The boy dropped down on his haunches. "But it ain't right."

"Tell you what we'll do, Tim," his other uncle said. "Soon's we get the buck out of the woods we'll go looking for a phone and you can let the sheriff know what you found, and where, so long as you don't leave any names. It a deal?"

Before the boy could answer, he was being prodded out of the clearing, the three of them jogging through the rain, glancing over their shoulders. They went an eighth of a mile before they found the deer where Tim's uncles had left it under a mossy underhang, and the boy, not so cold anymore, led the way to the truck.

When the dispatcher reached him with word about the body in the woods, St. Germain was less than a block from the sheriff's office. He continued into the lot, made a U-turn around the building, and raced out of Tremont Center headed back the other way. At Waterbury he turned toward Stowe, sighting through flailing wipers along a highway cleared of snow. Outside the village of Moscow he crossed the Little River on a road that went to dirt pitted with icy puddles as it climbed alongside Miller Brook toward Lake Mansfield.

He counted three Cabot County cars parked on the brushy shoulder with their right wheels in the ditch, four if you included the meat wagon from the coroner's office. He left his cruiser behind the others and used his five-cell flashlight to pick a way into the trees. Up ahead he made out the shape of a man in a hooded parka moving slowly through the snow, and doubling his pace he caught up easily with Wally Jeffcoat. The young deputy broke stride and spun around when St. Germain laid a heavy hand on his shoulder.

"Mind if I lead?"

"Who the . . . oh, it's you, Lieutenant." Jeffcoat grinned with embarrassment. "You scared me out of two years' growth."

"I hope not," St. Germain said. "I've been counting on you fitting into your uniform one day."

Jeffcoat grinned some more and then looked guilty about it. "They're saying it's the Beausoleil girl they found."

St. Germain moved ahead, following the probing beam of his flashlight. Two feet of snow had softened into a carpet of slush that oozed inside his shoes. The rain was starting to mix with large flakes that found the back of his neck, transmitting a chill down into his shoulders.

At the edge of the clearing he doused his flash. Lit by portable arc lights, four men cast exaggerated shadows against the silver trees. St. Germain recognized Marlow and Deputies Dick Vann and Artemis Gray, along with the Cabot County coroner, Dr. Sajit Singh. "G'evening, Loot," one of the deputies said, and then both walked away with their eyes on the patchy snow.

Quietly, as though trying not to disturb the dead, St. Germain arranged his massive silhouette among the others. "What've we got here?"

"The Beausoleil girl, most likely," Marlow said. The stark light brought out new lines in his crinkly forehead. "None of us have seen her since she was little. If this is her, she didn't look a thing like her old man."

The body lay on a sodden cloth secured around the hips by two flat stones. Other than a curious half-smile the features were as composed as if she had shut her eyes expecting a wake-up call that never was to be delivered. St. Germain knelt beside her to brush away some slush that had accumulated between the parted lips. "She kill herself?" he asked.

"What makes you say that?"

"I can't see any indication of foul play." When Marlow offered no opinion except to shrug his shoulders, which had become a code between them to keep talking, St. Germain said, "Her boyfriend told us they'd had an argument, a real humdinger. Becky wouldn't be the first gal to make a man sorry for what he said by taking a walk in the woods on a snowy night."

"A long walk," Marlow said. "We didn't find a car."

The coroner, who wore a white turban and a bristly black beard, stepped into the light. In his hand was a leather bag like those physicians carried, but Sajit Singh was one medical man who viewed the living with disdain, holding it against them that they were unqualified to receive his skills. St. Germain turned his back. That he despised the dark-skinned man, making himself something of a bigot in his own eyes, troubled him as greatly as did the coroner's contempt for healthy people. More than once Marlow had tried to tell him that his real problem with Singh was that the Indian had not lived in Vermont for five generations, like everyone else St. Germain respected. But whatever the reason, St. Germain couldn't stand the sight of him, and made no more apologies for it.

"It is to your misfortune, not to mention my own, that in a good year this state is lucky to see a dozen homicides," Singh said in a high singsong. "Neither of us has nearly enough experience with violent death."

St. Germain came near tilting his head as though he hadn't heard right. If Marlow had not been standing there, he would have decked the Sikh ghoul. He calmed himself by studying the blunt tips of his shoes in the snow. In a way, he had to admit, Singh was right; in seven years with the department this was only his second murder—if that's what it was—the other being a knifing that had been less a case for sheriff's investigators than for a porter with a damp mop and strong stomach.

"Do you see the marks in the girl's neck?" Singh asked as if he were conducting a high school biology class and Becky Beausoleil was of no greater significance than a dissected frog.

St. Germain turned to the body. "No, I don't."

"They are there," the Indian said confidently, and moved one of the arc lights so that it shone into the bloodless face—indecently, St. Germain thought. "Look again."

St. Germain shielded the corner of his eyes with his palm. Close up, Becky was prettier than any girlfriend of Benjamin Lederer's had a right to be. More innocent-looking, too, without a speck of makeup, and as Marlow had said, with none of the cramped features of her sourpuss father. What was hardest to take, she seemed younger than eighteen years, much too young to end up a frozen corpse on her birthday.

"There," Singh was saying, "just below the left side of the jaw, you should be able to see them now."

On a line with her ear St. Germain noticed a thin red stripe across the throat. More redness was visible below the point of her cleft chin where the skin appeared to have been abraded. "Yes, I see."

Singh made no effort to hide his glee. "That," he said, "is irrefutable evidence of strangulation by ligature. The girl was murdered."

St. Germain's eyes shifted to the blue cloth fluttering over well-formed breasts that seemed to have lost none of their sensuality in death. He shuddered then and zipped his parka. "Was she raped?"

"That will have to wait for the laboratory tests. And those cannot begin before I have completed my postmortem. Until that time, you see how she is dressed . . . draw your conclusions from that."

St. Germain took the blue cloth between his fingers. "It's some kind of blanket," he said to Marlow.

"Bedspread. Makes a hell of a snowsuit."

"She deserved better than this," St. Germain said. "Anyone would."

He stood under a yellow pine searching for his cigarettes and the Zippo lighter that his father had carried onto the beaches of Normandy and that later made up the bulk of his estate. In the woods behind him he heard the splat of leather soles against the soupy snow. "Who're we waiting for?" he asked Marlow. "State police?"

A man emerged from the trees, wearing a camel's hair top-coat that was soaked through across the shoulders. Without a word to anyone he went into the circle of blinding light and looked down at the body in the bedspread. St. Germain watched for tears but didn't see any. Ray Beausoleil stood silently over the girl for five full minutes, his concession to emotion the unconscious working of his jaw. Then he backed into the darkness. "You'll arrest him *now,*" he told St. Germain.

"Beg your pardon, sir."

"Lederer, you ass. The man who did this to my daughter."

"There's nothing I'd like more," St. Germain said. "But we have no evidence against him. He says she left his place in the afternoon, and there isn't anything to contradict—"

"Let me worry about the evidence. When we need it, it will be there. You worry about bringing him in."

St. Germain's head snapped back, as if he had caught a whiff of a bad odor, and Marlow moved quickly between them. A long time ago, he had found that stepping between his lieutenant and the people his lieutenant did not like was becoming an increasingly larger part of his job. Because he shared St. Germain's prejudices, he would just as soon have minded his own business as a rule and let nature take its course. He was looking forward to nothing about his retirement with greater anticipation than to the missed opportunities to intercede.

"I'll run out myself, Ray," he said. "If there's any reason at all, we'll have him behind bars by—"

Beausoleil walked away from the uniformed men to stand closer to his daughter. "I want him locked up tonight."

St. Germain took a drag on his cigarette and then stubbed it out against the wet pine bark, listening to the faint hissing sound. "John, it would be a waste of your time going to the Lederer place."

"The least I can do for Beausoleil is to talk to the man."

St. Germain shook his head. "Lederer had nothing to do with this. Take it from me."

"You said yourself that he was a dope dealer, a bully. How in Heaven's name can you be so sure he didn't hurt Becky?"

"Because that son of a bitch in the camel's hair coat says he did."

The high ground, the loading dock near the back entrance, went as it always did to the cameramen, Minicams from the Burlington and Plattsburgh stations jockeying for position with still photographers from the newspapers. The radio crews and print journalists were waiting inside. When Marlow saw the cars with the call letters splashed along the sides, he cursed under his breath and braked his Ford. "I hate to have to do this to you," he said to the man beside him on the seat. "But those piranhas'll eat me up alive if they see you like this. Put your arms behind your back. I'm going to cuff you till we get in, for their benefit only, I want you to know."

Benjamin Lederer dug his fingers into his scalp and rubbed vigorously, making up in advance for lost opportunity. Then he held his wrists together at the base of his spine. and twisted toward the window. "You've treated me square. I can't complain."

"It's the least I can do," Marlow said as he snapped on the bracelets and sped the rest of the way into the lot, "after that cowboy took down half your place with one of my cruisers."

Marlow came out first, ducking away from the cameras. He opened the passenger's door and brought Lederer into head-quarters, jostling him once or twice for effect, but ignoring the pleas for, "Look this way, Sheriff," and, "Just one of you and him together."

In the quiet of the bullpen he found St. Germain at Jeffcoat's usual place, behind an ashtray heaped with two-inch butts. "You don't look well, John," St. Germain said. "Where'd you pick up that rash?"

For the only time since he had taken him into custody two hours earlier, Marlow saw Lederer tense. His feet dragged against the linoleum as if he were digging in his heels. "Easy, you're almost there now," the sheriff whispered, glaring at St. Germain behind his prisoner's back. "Don't louse things up for both of us." Then he unlocked the handcuffs and Lederer went inside the cell and tested the thin bunk mattress. "Anything you want, just ask."

"How about a blonde?" Lederer said. "The lieutenant have a sister?"

"What was that, you bastard?" St. Germain yelled, knocking over his chair in his hurry to get out of it.

Marlow intercepted him near the barred door and bulled him away. "Get out of here," he said. "He's just trying to get your goat, same as you're doing to him."

"I'll give him my goat. I'll give it to him up his—"

"I want to talk to you." When St. Germain pressed closer, Marlow said, "That's an order, damn it."

St. Germain lingered in front of the cell, staring the broad man down. Lederer stood over the toilet and unzipped his fly without averting his eyes, and St. Germain moved off toward a neutral corner.

"That welcome party," Marlow asked, "did you arrange it?"

St. Germain, distracted for the moment, relaxed. "Just because I'm some kind of egomaniac doesn't mean you should be deprived of good ink for a job well done. Hell, you wrapped up a major murder investigation in—what?—less than twenty-four hours."

"Sometimes I don't know why I even keep you on," Marlow said disgustedly. "You've just made a clown out of me in front of the whole northern half of the state. Lederer no more could have killed that girl than you or I. When I told him how she'd been found, he bawled so bad it was all I could do to keep from joining in."

"He did *what?* Those were crocodile tears."

"It may be hard for you to believe someone like him's got feelings, but he was in love with her. No way he harmed her either. Ask me how I know, and—"

"Yes, John, I'm asking."

"Don't be impertinent . . . how I know, and thirty years as a cop tells me you don't jump to conclusions about a man because of the way he looks. Those tears were real."

"I still think you're wrong. But I'll take your word for it," St. Germain said. "I have to. Ray Beausoleil doesn't. Which means Lederer's already good as tried, convicted, sentenced, and appeal denied. If he didn't kill Becky, that's too bad . . . and, then again, maybe not. He's hardly a solid citizen; seems to me there's the matter of some time he should be paying the state for drug charges never brought."

"Drug time's not the same thing as murder time. And Ray Beausoleil can go and screw himself."

"Yeah, but once Ray sets the hook, he doesn't let go." St. Germain glanced toward the cells and added, "Unfortunately," as though it were expected of him. "It's out of our hands."

Marlow circled around, pinning him in the corner. "Not until the legislature says it's okay to strap a man in the hot seat and dim the lights. Till then," he said, jabbing a hard finger at St. Germain's chest, "your job's convincing Ray that Lederer couldn't've killed his daughter."

St. Germain showed his palms at arm's length, like a traffic cop bringing a heavy truck to a stop. "I'm not beating my head against that wall. I've got two weeks' vacation that've got to be used up by New Year's, and Annie'll have my scalp if we don't spend 'em with her people in Key West."

Marlow cuffed the hands out of the way. "Or you can build the man a new greenhouse. Your choice, but you owe him."

A big voice from the cells said, "Listen to him, St. Germain," and then laughed till the flushing toilet drowned it out.

Lederer's arrest had come too late to make the morning papers, and next day the worst November blizzard in Vermont history relegated the story to the second section. Nearly three feet of wet snow blanketed the Champlain Valley and Green Mountains from southern Quebec to the Berkshire Hills. Large sections of Burlington and Montpelier had been blacked out when power lines toppled, and forty thousand rural and farm residents were still without electricity as the storm was entering its second day. St. Germain, snowed in at headquarters, huddled in a tattered county blanket dreaming of sunstroke in the Florida Keys, waking to the realization that if getting the chill out of his bones depended upon springing Benjamin Lederer rather than finding new grounds to keep him locked away, it was time to stock up on thermal underwear. At the arraignment a District Court judge had set cash bond of $250,000 on a count of first-degree murder and ordered Lederer to submit to sixty days of psychiatric evaluation at Waterbury State Hospital, which would determine if he was capable of understanding the charges against him and assisting in the preparation of his defense. The preliminary hearing was slated for the second week of December. If probable cause was found, and St. Germain couldn't remember the last time that it was not in a major case, the evidence would go before the Cabot County grand jury by the end of the year.

From time to time St. Germain interrupted his idyll in the Keys to rack his brain for a fresh avenue of investigation. Because he was up against a circumstantial case backed up by Ray Beausoleil's legal muscle, he could develop no point of attack. Witnesses would be required to prove Lederer's innocence— for despite Constitutional guarantees suspects in all felony prosecutions were presumed guilty until proven otherwise. St. Germain had no idea where to begin. Any juror with two eyes would vote to convict without the benefit of testimony. About the best he could do was to advise Lederer to get a haircut and a shave.

St. Germain was splashing cold water against his face when Wally Jeffcoat, looking like his ball had gone through the lieutenant's window, came into the bullpen to tell him that he was wanted on the phone.

"Annie?"

"Not unless she's started whistling through her teeth when she talks," the deputy said in a rare attempt at humor that he wished at once he had kept to himself. "It's someone from out around Hunger Mountain, says there's something you don't know about Ben Lederer."

"All I need," St. Germain said. "He's probably got what Beausoleil wants to soup up old sparky."

"I don't think so. He's hard to understand, but it seems like he's saying he can clear him."

St. Germain hustled the deputy into Marlow's office, where the phone was off the hook. As he pressed it to his ear, Jeffcoat lingered at the doorway, casually eavesdropping.

"Hello . . . Hello?"

No answer.

"Shit, I think he hung up. What's his name?"

"Martin," Jeffcoat said.

"Mr. Martin, are you there?"

"Who?" The voice sounded used up, barely awake, as if its owner had been dozing. "Who's that you want?"

"Mr. Martin?"

"My name's Martin," the voice said, more alert this time. "But it ain't mister. It's Martin Tucker. This Marlow?"

"The sheriff's not in. I'm Lieutenant St. Germain."

"I'd like to talk to him."

"I said he isn't— What is this in reference to?"

"Hello, Marlow?"

St. Germain's lips tightened and he slapped his hand over the mouthpiece. "If this guy doesn't start making sense quick," he said to Jeffcoat, "I'm going up to Hunger Mountain and wring his neck for him." He moved his hand away. "The sheriff is out," he said slowly and distinctly, as if there were a problem with Tucker's hearing. "Can I help?"

"Yeah. These Nip cars, they stink."

"What's this?"

"Ain't I speaking loud enough?"

"Yes, sir," St. Germain said, debating whether to drive out and throttle him right away, or to listen some more and do it later.

"Every last one of 'em's no good. Get in an accident, you can kiss your ass good-bye. They reach sixty thousand on the speedometer, the darn things fall apart like the one-horse shay. There's two inches of snow on the ground, they're worse'n useless."

"Sir." St. Germain forced himself to say the word. "I don't see what this has to do with—"

"Goddamn Toyota kept me locked up in my own house two days. Like solitary confinement—no heat, no electric, no hot water, no food except Friskies and what little I had in the fridge and that got spoiled. No TV or radio neither. Bad enough I near froze to death and starved, I was climbing the walls doing it. That's how come you didn't hear from me before."

"Sir," St. Germain tried again. "Is there some information you have—"

Tucker brushed the interruption aside. "Wasn't till a couple hours ago the power come back on and I could take off my sweaters, and then the plows come by and dug me out and I had to get in 'em again to run down to the store for something to eat and a *Free Press,* and that's when I saw it."

"Saw what?" St. Germain asked.

"You sure Marlow ain't there?"

"Saw—"

"The picture of that fella they got for murdering the girl in the woods by Lake Mansfield."

St. Germain held his breath, waiting for more.

"You still there?" Martin Tucker said.

"What about the picture?"

"*What about it?* You got the wrong fella, that's what about it."

"Why do you say that, sir?"

" 'Cause I was in St. Jay when that little gal got picked up thumbing, and that fella with all the hair wasn't who took her."

"Are you sure?" St. Germain asked.

"Sure I'm sure," Tucker said, and laughed indignantly. "The fella that give her a lift, he was driving a van is what he had. Big one, with the fancy wheels with the writing on the sidewalls. And he looked younger than the hairy fella."

"You're positive about this?"

"Didn't I just say so? He near squashed my Toyota like a Jap beetle with that van of his, didn't he?"

"I wouldn't—"

"Wished he had, too, the piece of shit."

"Is there anything else you remember about the van?" St. Germain asked.

"It was blue," Martin Tucker said.

"You're—" St. Germain caught himself. "What shade of blue?" he asked patiently.

". . . Or black."

"Try to remember. This could be important."

"Yeah," Tucker said. "Blue or black. I'm sure now."

St. Germain took another tack. "What about the man behind the wheel?"

"He was white."

St. Germain extended his index finger and twirled it in a circle beside his ear, but he did not hang up on Martin Tucker. "I'd like you to come by the sheriff's office," he said, "so we can talk at length about what you saw in St. Johnsbury. It shouldn't take much of your time, and it might mean an innocent man being let out of jail and a guilty one put in his place."

"Well, I don't know . . ." Tucker said. "Can it wait till I finish polishing my car?"

Jeffcoat was stacking large, leather-bound volumes on the floor when two men clad identically in red plaid jackets, baggy wool pants, knit caps and mittens entered the area where St. Germain had pushed the best of his sorry collection of chairs close to his desk. They were tall and raw-boned, with narrow eyes and parchment cheeks showing gray streaks of chronic frostbite. Hilljacks, St. Germain said to himself, hard-drinking, inbred, no doubt half-crazy hilljacks—brothers, or, more likely, half brothers, the older one's thin features curling into a pleated caricature of his companion. St. Germain put out his hand to the wrinkled man.

The younger one, who was not young at all—about forty-five, St. Germain estimated—peeled off a mitten and reached for the hand. "Pa," his tired voice said, "you take the truck back to your place and I'll call when I want a lift." To the lieutenant he said, "I'm Martin Tucker."

"I thought you'd be the—" St. Germain waved his hand in front of his face, wiping the slate clean. "Never mind," he said. "Please, sit down."

Tucker dropped onto the slatted chair and quickly put his feet out to steady himself. "Well," he said, and opened his jacket. "Fire away."

St. Germain kept an eye on Tucker's father until Jeffcoat had him by the elbow and was showing him to the street. Then he placed one of the leather books on the desk. "This is what we call our Rogues Gallery," he explained. "This particular album shows everyone arrested for a sex offense in Vermont over the past fifteen years. There's a strong chance the man who killed Miss Beausoleil has a previous criminal record. If he does, his picture will be here. We're hoping you'll recognize him."

St. Germain opened the book to a color Polaroid of a man with his back to a V-shaped mirror allowing right and left profiles beside a full-face portrait. On his chest was a plaque with movable letters spelling out his name, the date of his arrest, and the county in which it was made. The following pages contained similar photos of other men, most with the fish-eyed stare of the witness looking back at them. Although, to the casual observer, there was a flinty sameness about them, to Martin Tucker they were as easily distinguishable as would be a large and errant brood of children to their own father. St. Germain crumpled the cellophane from a box of Camels as Tucker inspected the pictures with the quiet thrill of a librarian sitting down to a review copy of the next best seller.

"Any questions," St. Germain said, "just ask."

Tucker nodded. He flipped the page and then four more before he looked up and said, "I know this boy."

St. Germain stood up so quickly that he knocked his lighter off the desk.

"This Sam Baker," Tucker said, jabbing his finger at a snapshot. "He married my cousin Fay in Beebe Plain and brung her and her little girl, Connie, to his place in Island Pond. Wasn't but two months when Fay learned he was doing things, vile things, to Connie. It's a comfort to see they got his picture in here."

St. Germain bent for the lighter. He inspected it for dents and found none he didn't recognize. "Then that's not the man you saw—"

"I see Sam Baker again," Tucker said, "you can make room for my picture in your book here, what I'll do to him." He turned the page.

When Tucker had leafed through the volume, St. Germain started him on a second one. There were sixteen in all, Vermont's roster of convicted felons dating back to the early 1970s. Over the next four hours Martin Tucker got up out of his broken chair on only two occasions, once to use the deputies' toilet downstairs, and later to phone his father with word that he would be spending more time in Tremont Center than he had planned on, and that the nice lieutenant would drive him home. It was nearly five o'clock when he slammed the last book shut, massaging his red eyes with his thumbs. "Tell you one thing," he said confidently. "That boy's never been locked up for nothing before."

"It's too soon to say." St. Germain stubbed out his last cigarette against his heel and let it fall to the floor. "If he has a juvenile record, but hasn't been charged as an adult, we wouldn't get to see a mug shot. Juvenile records are sealed by the courts."

"Well, what are you gonna do about it? We can't let him get away with what he done."

St. Germain pushed the books aside and rested his elbows on the desk. "You come back tomorrow," he said, "and we'll have a police artist here to work up a composite of the man you saw. If it's any good, we'll put it on a flyer that'll go out all over New England."

"Sounds reasonable." Tucker pushed up from his chair.

St. Germain nudged him down again. "In the meantime, maybe there's some more we can get done today."

Tucker reached inside his jacket for a watch attached to a torn leather strap and tapped it against his palm. "It's getting toward evening," he said. "My pa . . ."

"About the van," St. Germain said over him.

Tucker shook his head. "Like I told you, I was too busy trying to scat out of the way to get a fix on it. I still ain't real sure about the color."

"What about the license plate?"

"Now you mention it," Tucker said, "it was green. Shiny new Vermont tag—like a quarter million other folks around here have, that helps any."

"It could. If the truck was carrying Vermont plates and the boy driving it knew enough to find the road to Lake Mansfield in a blizzard, he's no flatlander." St. Germain rummaged through an ashtray for a two-inch butt and brought out his lighter again. "I just wish I knew which damn hill he's hiding behind."

Toward midnight, when Marlow returned from a conference with state police homicide detectives, he found St. Germain nodding in the swivel chair in his office. "Trying that on for size?" he said.

St. Germain opened his eyes one at a time, and then jumped to his feet.

"Sit down, Larry. What's so important it can't wait till morning?"

"The witness, Tucker, the one I didn't think anything was going to come of him . . ." St. Germain moved away from the chair, kneading the bunched muscles at the base of his neck. "Turned out he could make sense when he wanted to. We ran the mug books by him. He didn't come up with the ID, but he says he'd recognize the boy if he saw him again. He's trying for us, only there's not much he can do if we don't have the right picture to show him."

Marlow took over the vacant seat and leaned back all the way, sighing. The lines in his face had deepened perceptibly, and what shape his insides were in was something that his lieutenant didn't want to speculate about. The rare major investigation, even more than natural calamities, made the sheriff's job the killer that everyone said it was. St. Germain wondered if he, too, would grow old before his time.

Marlow used his hands to pull a leg up onto his desk. "What does he say about the van?"

"He didn't get much of a look. I'm thinking about taking him to Burlington and driving him around the auto showrooms till he spots something familiar, and then asking the Department of Motor Vehicles for a printout on all registered owners."

"I like that."

"Don't know that it'll accomplish anything, though. And if things don't pan out, we're up against a stone wall."

"I'm acquainted with that wall," Marlow said. "About all you can do when you feel it creeping up on you is sit tight and pray the son of a bitch doesn't drag another girl inside his van." He hoisted the other leg. "Murder investigations are drab affairs, most of them, tedious and full of waiting for the other side to gab too much or screw up in some other way. Except in the movies, they don't lend themselves to the manufacture of heroes."

"I can't sit," St. Germain said, and began pacing the room as though he had to prove it.

Marlow hid an exasperated look behind a yawn. "You get a good likeness put together and a picture of the van, bring them to Fort Abenaki. Plenty of GIs living off base drive trucks. Maybe one of them's your choker."

"I doubt it," St. Germain said. "Everything points to a local boy."

"Try UVM, then, and St. Mike's and Lyndon College. Should be enough instate students mixed in with the rest of them to give you a run for your money."

"Guess I'll have to," St. Germain said with little enthusiasm. He paused and then snapped his fingers. "Cancel that, John. If he was in school not long ago, I know a better place to look."

When Martin Tucker returned to sheriff's headquarters the next day, St. Germain and Jeffcoat were waiting in the bullpen behind a mound of Danish and three containers of tepid coffee. "G'morning," St. Germain said as if it had been wrung out of him. "You're forty minutes late, you know."

"Don't I know it," Tucker said. "The goddam Toyota give out again. Had to call my pa for a lift."

St. Germain moved an apple turnover across the desk and then reached toward a stack of oversize books on the floor.

"Got some more of them rogues, I see," Tucker said, and threw his jacket over the back of a chair.

"Uh-uh. These are high school yearbooks."

"What for? The boy we want, he was voted most likely to succeed?"

Tucker turned toward St. Germain to see what effect his little joke was having and was pleased when the lieutenant smiled. "Could be," St. Germain said. "You're going to tell us."

"I am?"

"If he's from around here, this is where he went to school. Deputy Jeffcoat and I've been trying to put our hands on the yearbooks from every high school in this part of the state. It's a good bet his picture is in one of them. You shouldn't have any trouble recognizing him when you see it, now should you?"

Tucker looked again at the pile on the floor, which seemed considerably higher than it had at first glance. "How many of those books did you say?"

"The last five years from each school."

"But how many is that all told?"

"It's not important," St. Germain said, and interposed himself between Tucker and the stack of volumes. "Far as you're concerned, his last name could be Aaron and his'll be the first face you see in the first book. Now get to work."

The first face in the first yearbook that Tucker cracked that morning was, indeed, that of an Aaron—Charles F. Aaron—but he was not the boy with the van. Neither were any of the other youngsters smiling uncomfortably from the glossy albums of Montpelier Central, Mount Mansfield Union, Chittenden County Regional, or any of the fifteen schools Tucker went through without so much as a second look. Around noon, when the pile of books dipped below five, St. Germain drove away from headquarters, leaving Jeffcoat in charge of the witness. He returned four hours later with simulated cowhide volumes from two dozen more high schools and religious academies. As he carried them wedged under his chin into the bullpen, Tucker stood up rubbing tired eyes. "No," he said. "No more, please. I look at another pimple I'm gonna break out myself."

St. Germain dismissed him with a terse, "You've got to," and opened one of the new books in front of him.

Tucker peered inside as if he were about to be sick. "I ain't interested in no more senior trips to the Statue of Liberty, or the junior proms, or volleyball teams. I don't give a crap about the French clubs, or the rock climbers, or the cafeteria squad, or the future homemakers, not even the Catamount Choraleers. How long I gotta do this?"

"Till you find him," St. Germain said. He turned the pages for Tucker, making certain his witness went through the pictures carefully, getting a good look at each face before moving on to the next. "You know how important it is."

They leafed through four more books before Tucker slid his chair away from the desk past St. Germain's restraining arm, fanning at his eyes with the flat of his hand. St. Germain walked him around the parking lot and then drove him to Shep's diner for a sandwich and all the coffee he could hold. It was eight o'clock when they came back to the bullpen to start on the six remaining volumes.

St. Germain was preparing to concede that maybe the witness had been looking at too many pictures when Tucker's finger glued itself to the page and his bloodshot eyes opened wide. "That's him there," he shouted hoarsely. "That's the one."

St. Germain stood up quickly and leaned over Tucker's shoulder. "You're sure?"

"Positive."

"How can you be—"

"I *know*," Tucker insisted. "Ain't that good enough for you?"

St. Germain tilted the page toward the light. Under the small square photo of a teenager with a smooth face and shy smile was the inscription:

PAUL ARTHUR CONKLIN
Keep on truckin'

"Take a break for now," St. Germain said, slipping into his parka. "I'm going to find out what the rest of the world has to say about this kid."

The shirt was his favorite, off-white with thin blue pin-striping and the extra long tail that made it the only one he owned that stayed inside his pants—and he groaned when he saw it on her. She had bundled herself against the midnight cold, hands hidden in the forty-inch sleeves, the lightly starched collar turned up and crumpled against the pillow. With a pickpocket's touch he began undoing the buttons, but then she rolled onto her back and the moonlight found the dark patch where the cloth fell away from her hips and he was forced to admit that the shirt did more for her than it ever would for him. Without taking off his shoes he crawled into bed beside her and felt for the warm curve of her breast.

"Wha . . ."

"Montreal," he whispered in her ear. "We'll start off there, say, a weekend getting used to each other again, then fly direct to Islamorada and never come in out of the sun."

"Larry, 's that you?"

"Some other guy," he said, and gently closed his hand. "What do you say, anyway? How's it sound?"

She used her fingertips to massage her temples. "You caught him?"

"Not yet. But we know who he is. Tucker ID-ed him, and then I went to his town and asked around, and it's him. Got to be."

"Slow down. I'm only half awake."

"No," he said, "I'll bust if I can't let it all out now. His name's Paul Conklin and everybody I talked to, the ones who'd say anything, told me about the kind of kid you'd think of first when you learned what happened to Becky."

Annie reached down around her knees and tugged a patchwork quilt over her. "I'm glad for you, Larry."

St. Germain raised the other side and slid under. He placed his hands on her hips and turned her toward him and kissed her. She fit herself snugly under his massive body and wrapped her arms around his back and dug her feet under his ankles, straining against him until he broke away to get out of his clothes. "Don't bother opening your eyes, Ann," he said. "This is just a dream, the best you'll ever have."

"Too late. I'm up." She lifted a corner of the quilt, lowered it over his shoulders as the bed dipped beneath his weight.

He pushed himself against her, warming himself, and then drew away. "Tomorrow I'll run out and grill him, and unless I miss my guess I'll be reading him his rights by suppertime. We can start packing now, if you like." He kissed her again, but she didn't respond, and when he tilted her head into the pale light, the groggy smile was gone from her mouth.

"Not real romantic, am I?" he said. "Sorry, but I'm slightly obsessed." He came close to nuzzle the special spot behind her ear, and when even that failed to move her, he whispered, "Ann?"

"Look in the corner, Larry." She squeezed herself against him, but her face mocked the urgency in her body. "Do you see that valise? I'm all packed, no matter how you and Becky Beausoleil's killer are planning to spend the week."

4

Frost heaves had broken the old road's spine, so that its distance should have been measured in vertical feet. St. Germain slowed to forty as he followed it away from the highway onto a jagged peninsula that jutted into the lake like a beckoning finger. Six miles of ruined pavement gave way to a crushed rock lane that snaked between tall pines shading a summer colony boarded up for the season. Where the limestone thinned to dirt topped with gritty slush, black paint, dripped onto a wood slab, announced STURGEON COVE ROAD.

He rode his brakes as he scanned vacation homes disguised as rustic cabins with screened porches and two-car garages and the inevitable satellite dish aimed over the bay, bungalows and glass A-frames, each with a floating dock hauled onto the beach in anticipation of January's crushing ice. Although the main body of the lake stirred with the wind, a dull glaze had settled over the cove, and a flock of Canada geese on that. St. Germain held the car at fifteen, searching for signs of post-Labor Day life. As he shouldered the cruiser between two stalwart tamaracks, relics of a forest that once had swept down to the shore, he saw that he was not alone.

A Jeep Wagoneer with a plow blade mounted on a winch blocked the drive of a bungalow painted a runny redwood color.

Parked head to head was a blue van with wide tires boasting *Michelin* in raised lettering on the sidewalls. A grimy smudge hung over the redwood's roof and another, paler, seeped from under the van. St. Germain prodded the cruiser to twenty and followed the snowy track around the cove.

He emptied his ashtray in the slush and began filling it again without taking his eyes off the house. In time, a teenager wearing a checked jacket came out and poured a quart of oil under the hood, while a youth a few years older dragged a heavy sack out of the rear and left it with some others in the yard. The boy in the jacket sniffed the air like an animal sensing a predator on the wind, looked through the trees toward the far shore of the cove. But if he noticed the Cabot County car, it made no impression on him. His companion backed the Jeep out of the way and together they drove off in the van.

St. Germain waited for the crunch of tires on wet pebbles before he put the cruiser in gear. Keeping two hundred feet behind, he stalked the boys back to the highway. As he turned south toward Burlington, he pulled down the visor and maneuvered it over the side window, blotting the low sun. When he could see without squinting again, the van was disappearing on I-89. He nudged the needle to eighty and began to reel it in.

An eighteen-wheeler with ST. JOHNSBURY in serifed capitals along the side kept pace as he came off the ramp, and he had to fight the urge to curb it. He swerved around the cab and settled into traffic as the interstate skirted Burlington across new suburbs feeding on the dairyland to the east. The highway broadened to three lanes climbing the shallow valley of the Winooski River. St. Germain held steady at seventy, biding his time, never far from the van. Beyond the Central Vermont Railway trestle the interstate insinuated itself between old Route 2 and the water, the roads running so close together that St. Germain caught smiles from weathered men cruising the pitted asphalt on plodding farm implements. The state road went to concrete at the Cabot County line, and he watched his speedometer till he clocked the van less than three miles under the speed limit, then moved up on it beneath flashing domes.

When the driver failed to pull over, St. Germain touched his siren. Brake lights fluttered and then glowed as the van sliced across traffic and beached itself on the shoulder. St. Germain rolled to a halt fifty feet behind. He stepped out cautiously, alert for truckers unable to pass up the easy chance to dust a county cop, studying the van as though hieroglyphs told a story in the white grit dulling the buffed finish.

"What'd we do?" the driver called out to him. "Why'd you flag us?"

St. Germain scowled. He walked toward the front and looked in. Up close the driver was younger than Tucker had described him, younger even than in the two-year-old photo in the yearbook. In the passenger's seat the older boy had knitted his companion's irritation into a hard mask. To whichever one cared to answer, St. Germain said, "You in some kind of hurry?"

The driver met his gaze and held it. "We weren't speeding. I had one eye on the dash the whole time you were behind us."

St. Germain poked his head inside the van, showing off his scowl. "Have your speedometer calibrated," he growled. "And try keeping both eyes on the road." He glanced behind the youngsters, but a heavy cloth suspended from the ceiling blocked his view of the rear. "Let me have your license and registration."

"I don't see why you're stopping us when I didn't—"

"Let him have it, Paulie," his passenger said. "Maybe then we can get the hell on our way."

"No," the driver said. "It's a matter of principle. I wasn't speeding."

"Fuck principle. We want to be moving."

"What was that?" St. Germain snapped, as if the profanity

had been meant for him. He was addressing the boy in the passenger's seat, but looking at the driver, at the scabs like crusted seams on the back of his hands and his cheeks.

"No offense, Officer. I was telling my brother to use his head for once in his life and give you his license. If you've already made up your mind, there's nothing he can do about it by being a hardass, is there?"

"Shut up, Mel," the driver said. "I never went over fifty. If he wants to write a ticket, he can run me in first. I'm not gonna stand for this."

Too fast for St. Germain to follow the motion, Mel backhanded his brother. Then he plucked a tattered billfold from Paul's back pocket and offered it to the lieutenant.

"Take out the license and registration and hand them to me," St. Germain said.

Paul snatched the wallet away and slid some papers from the plastic sleeves. St. Germain carried them back to the cruiser. He raised headquarters on the radio and asked if Marlow was in his office.

"I'll see," the dispatcher said, and nearly three minutes went by before St. Germain heard his boss's gruff, "Yeah?" crackling out of the speaker.

"John," he bellowed, not trying to contain his excitement. "Wait'll you hear who—"

"Where are you, damn it? There's an active murder investigation you're supposed to be heading, in case you've forgotten."

"I haven't forgotten." Subdued, but letting Marlow know he hadn't spoiled his good time. "What would you say if I told you I've got Paul Conklin on ice ten miles from Tremont Center?"

"Probably I'd ask you to turn in your gun so we could work up a case against you. How many bullets did you put in him?"

"Very funny," St. Germain said. "I just pulled him over in

that van of his on I-89. Anything special you'd like me to ask him?"

"There's something I want to ask you. I want to hear how you got him away from Malletts Bay. What did you do, kidnap him over the line?"

St. Germain swallowed back a wisecrack. "It doesn't matter. What does is that he's here."

"It matters plenty," Marlow said. "We don't have a warrant for his arrest. Christ, we haven't even applied for one yet. If you blow this case for procedure, I'll have you proofreading Jeffcoat's accident reports till you go blind."

"Relax, John, everything's on the up and up." As though it were his final argument to sway a holdout juror, he paused for effect and then added, "I swear."

"I'll take your word for it," Marlow said reluctantly. "I have to."

"What do we want out of him?"

"You have no cause for interrogation, so be careful. Bust his chops, put him in a thoughtful frame of mind, and let him go. What've you got him for, traffic violation?"

"Uh-huh."

"Don't cite him. We don't need a written record of this. And, Larry, in the future, don't be so damn eager."

When he went back to the van, moving slowly and deliberately to let the boys know they were not going anywhere for a while, St. Germain found Paul Conklin glaring at his brother. Mel had his thumb pressed against his upper lip, bunching it under his nose. "Get out, you two," St. Germain ordered. "I'm taking a look inside."

"What for?" Paul said.

Mel pulled his hand away from his mouth and St. Germain saw a puffed lip, dark flecks of blood. "Where do you come off searching us? We didn't do nothing."

"We'll see," St. Germain opened the door. "Out."

"You better be ready to drag us," Paul said.

"My pleasure," St. Germain said, calling his own bluff. As he leaned inside, he noticed white powder on the patterned floor mats like sand in a toddler's beach toy. "I've got reason to believe you two are transporting drugs."

Paul Conklin forced a hollow laugh. "You're the one that's blowing smoke."

"We don't even *do* dope," Mel said. "Right, Paulie? You've got no business accusing us of moving it."

"What's that on the floor?"

"Huh?" The boys gaped at the mats and then Mel looked up and said, "It's gypsum. My brother and me, we renovate old houses. We're doing a job in Shady Rill. That's where we're going. We must've spilled some. It happens all the time."

"I'll bet it does," St. Germain said. "Now get out."

Paul shook his head and both boys stayed where they were. St. Germain stared without blinking until Mel averted his eyes, kneading his swollen mouth. St. Germain walked to the passenger's side and Mel pushed open his door and dropped onto the shoulder. His brother sat motionless as the bravado went out of him, and then he swung his legs over and stood beside the van.

"Turn around," St. Germain ordered. "I want you with your backs to traffic while I search your vehicle."

He climbed in through the driver's door and poked at the mats with his toe. For all he knew the white powder *was* dope, but how was he supposed to tell when he had never made an arrest for anything stronger than marijuana. Funny thing, but he wouldn't recognize hard drugs if he was caught in an avalanche of them. He rolled the powder in his fingers. Feeling gypsum's coarseness, he scooped some into a glassine bag anyway and slid over to the passenger's seat.

A collection of road maps accordioned like a jack-in-the-box as he opened the glove compartment. He swept out some rags and a screwdriver and two flat tablets that said TUMS in raised letters. The breeze from a passing truck whisked the heavy cloth against the back of his head and he swiped it aside and saw an unmade bed and, stacked in a corner, four large paper sacks like the one Mel Conklin had lugged out of the van at Malletts Bay. Around a caricature of New Hampshire's Old Man of the Mountain was the inscription, GRANITE STATE GYPSUM.

Speakers were mounted in the walls and exposed wires ran up front and under the dash. On an Oriental rug a rocking chair with an amputated runner lay on its side. St. Germain squeezed between the seats. He kicked the crippled chair and a toolbox out of the way and got down on his hands and knees and reached for a dark tangle of cloth wedged under the bed. He unraveled an extra-large pea coat knotted in dungarees with a twenty-three-inch waist that were too new to have been washed, a torn sweater, bra and panties.

He balled the garments together and brought them into the front. "Come here, you two," he called outside. When neither boy was in a hurry to move, he dropped his voice and said, "Now," and the Conklins came sullenly to his door.

"What's this stuff?" St. Germain asked.

"What does it look like?" Paul Conklin said.

"You tell me."

Mel affected an exaggerated simper. "Those are mi-ine," he lisped.

Paul elbowed his brother away from the van. "They belong to my girlfriend."

"Don't believe him, Officer. Where'd he ever get a girl?" Mel licked the tip of his pinkie and smoothed a bushy eyebrow. "He just loves playing with my undies."

"You don't want to be breathing through your mouth permanently, you'll shut up," Paul said.

Mel shut up.

Paul snorted, as if to show the advantage in staying on his

good side. "What's this got to do with dope?" he asked St. Germain.

St. Germain had no answer for that. He pinched some more of the powder, licked his fingers as he'd seen television detectives do, and spit. He glared at the brothers as though the taste had confirmed his suspicions, and when he could think of nothing else said, "I don't want to see you in my county again."

Paul took back his license and registration. "Considering as how you didn't find any drugs," he said, "you might have to."

St. Germain walked to his cruiser and followed the van off the shoulder. He tailed the brothers to the next exit, clocking them at seventy-seven miles an hour when he turned off for Tremont Center. Back at headquarters he found Marlow at his desk, looking over Jeffcoat's paperwork with a pained expression. When Marlow saw him, the pain seemed to become unbearable.

"How'd you make out?"

"I gave 'em a hard time and sent 'em packing," St. Germain said. "Like you wanted."

"That all?"

St. Germain nodded. "Why? You sound surprised."

"Any time you don't make more trouble than the situation calls for, it surprises me." Marlow focused bloodshot eyes over tortoiseshell half-glasses. "You never did tell me how you happened to spot him in the county."

"I guess not." St. Germain hesitated and, when Marlow didn't press him, said, "Conklin's clawed pretty bad. I don't think it's a cat that did it either. I had a look inside the van and there was a pile of girl's clothes something tells me fit Becky Beausoleil fine. I'm ready to make the arrest."

"No, you're not. We can't use that information to get a judge to sign a warrant, not the way you obtained it. As far as the law's concerned, we haven't questioned Conklin. Far as you're concerned, he isn't even a suspect."

"How do we make him one?"

"That's the problem," Marlow said. "Intuition doesn't stand up in court anymore. Any novice two weeks out of law school knows to deflect the issue away from the evidence to how we came to get it. We're the ones on trial. We've got to show that Tucker was on the money all along when he said Conklin was the boy he saw in St. Jay."

"I doubt he'd impress a jury. He couldn't convince you the world's flat if he fell off of it."

Marlow gazed through his lenses at an accident report and scribbled something in the margin. "It won't hurt his credibility if he can pick Conklin out of a show-up. How about letting him try?"

"I'll go to Shady Rill right now."

"Where?"

"The brothers are fixing up an old home there."

"Why don't you let them put in an honest day's work, then?" Marlow said. "Conklin must have figured out you have more than a passing interest in him, so I wouldn't count on his being agreeable next time he sees you. Better wait till tonight, when you can be reasonably sure he's back at Malletts Bay, and then run out with Vann and Gray and a Chittenden County officer or two so no one's feelings get ruffled, and when everybody's in place and knows what he has to do, when the potential for trouble's been minimized, then ask nicely if it would be inconveniencing him to accompany you to headquarters, and you can haul him in by his ears if you like."

"All that for a punk kid?"

"The punk kid choked the life out of Becky Beausoleil, looks like. It wouldn't put him out giving you a hard time."

St. Germain leaned so close that Marlow had to tilt his head to see him clearly. "He goes a hundred and fifty pounds soaking wet, and his pleasure's hurting people with his hands. I can take him with one of mine tied behind my back. Why bother anyone else on this?"

Marlow was waiting for St. Germain to be reasonable, knowing he was wasting his time. "If it makes you feel better, Larry,
I'll tell the photographers to come in tight when you bring
him in."

"You know that's not what I mean," St. Germain said, wondering if, in fact, it wasn't. "I just don't like playing to the
notion he's some sort of celebrity. He'd think it was worth
twenty-five years out of his life if I showed up like General
MacArthur dictating the terms of surrender to the Japs. Why
give him the satisfaction?"

"Give me some satisfaction. Take Vann and Gray."

St. Germain shook his head stubbornly. "I still can't see
where it's necessary."

". . . And the Chittenden officers. It's procedure."

"Okay, but keep your detectives. I'll take Wally. A little
excitement, and I do mean *little*, ought to do him good."

Marlow started to nix the idea when he glanced at the accident
report again. "If you think he can handle it . . ." He took off
his glasses and folded them in a pocket. "I don't suppose it
could hurt his handwriting."

Papers were spread around the bullpen, but Jeffcoat was
not at his usual place. St. Germain heard one of the new
toilets sucking hard enough to pull a man in and looked inside the cells. Jeffcoat grinned back self-consciously, then
turned his back as he adjusted his zipper. With his personal
bar of soap he washed his hands in cold water and patted
them dry in the fluffy towel that he brought from home each
day and kept with his civilian clothes in his locker in the
basement.

"Got something you'll want to hear," St. Germain said.

Jeffcoat's eyes lit up. "Sheriff Marlow's decided to order portable breathalyzers after all? I've been lobbying for them since
I saw them in the catalogue. They're a swell idea, a real im-
provement over the—"

St. Germain tried not to groan out loud. "Better than that.

I'm going after a suspect in the Beausoleil case and I want . . . I need you to help me."

Jeffcoat's smile froze and then cracked, and his hand slid gingerly to his gun and nudged the barrel as if it had been pointed at a vital organ. "You're pulling my leg, aren't you?"

"Nope."

"Why me?" Jeffcoat asked cautiously. "No one else seems to think I'm equipped to deal with anything riskier than sorting out bodies after a head-on."

"I do," St. Germain said, trying to sound as if he meant it.

Jeffcoat drew himself erect. To St. Germain it appeared that he had made himself larger, like a blowfish.

"I won't let you down, Lieutenant."

"It never crossed my mind. I'm . . . the department's counting on you."

"What do you want me to do?"

"You can begin by treating yourself to a big lunch. Late afternoon we're running out to Malletts Bay. I don't know that we'll be back for supper."

"Where's Malletts Bay?"

"On Lake Champlain. Chittenden deputies'll meet us, and then we'll drive to the cove where this boy lives. Name's Paul Conklin. He's only about nineteen—and while I don't expect he'll make trouble, like John says, you never know. I'll go in with one of the local officers while you lay back in case something comes up we didn't plan on. Is that exciting enough for you?"

Jeffcoat's hand clung to the holster that lay like a vestigial appendage against his thigh. "We'll find out soon enough," he answered with too much swagger.

"Wally, just say yes or no."

"Yeah," Jeffcoat chirped. "You bet. I've been waiting forever on this."

* * *

The bullpen was still deep in accident reports when St. Germain returned a few minutes before four-thirty. Jeffcoat was nowhere around. St. Germain checked the cells, but saw only Silas Cumming, one of Tremont Center's habitual drunks, charged with malicious mischief for tossing a bottle through the window of the Smart Tavern after a bartender refused him service and eighty-sixed him for life. A container of steaming coffee beside a cigarette burning down to the filter on one of the desks hinted at a calamity so sudden that St. Germain was reminded of pictures of Pompeii in his eighth-grade history text. The newer calamity he blamed on his deputy's cold feet. He was trying to remember Dick Vann's home number when Jeffcoat came in, cradling a silver thermos bottle.

"Thought you'd found something else at the last minute," St. Germain said, relief disguised as mild amusement. "Where were you hiding?"

"Shep's Diner. Missing dinner's no big deal, but if I can't tank up on coffee when I want it, you'd be surprised how cross it makes me."

"Guess I would." St. Germain dusted off the billed cap with badge 138 stuck in the tan fabric and spun it around his finger. "Got everything you need?"

"Let's see." Jeffcoat patted down his pockets, automatically caressing his holster. "I think so."

St. Germain pressed his hands against the smaller man's shoulders and eased him toward the corridor. "Then say good-bye to Silas and let's get going."

He stayed behind the deputy all the way to the parking lot, cutting off every opportunity for retreat. Outside, Jeffcoat hesitated and wedged the thermos under an arm.

"Why you stopping here?" St. Germain asked.

"You didn't say if we're taking your car or Joe Louis."

"We'll need both of 'em. If you want to talk on the way, flash your lights and I'll pull over."

"What about the Chittenden deputies?"

"I've decided not to—" St. Germain began. "There's been a change in plan. They're tied up with a major investigation of their own and can't spare the men. We're going to have to tackle this by our lonesomes."

"Whatever you think's best," Jeffcoat said, and remained where he was.

"Move, Wally. What's the matter?"

"Nothing, Lieutenant. I just wanted to thank you for going out on a limb for me, using me in a big case. This really is something, putting a murderer under arrest and all."

"Isn't it, though?" St. Germain filled his lungs with cold air. "God, I love being a cop."

They walked between the rows of cars to the Brown Bomber, the hand-me-down cruiser that had been Jeffcoat's own since he joined the department. The deputy tossed his thermos on the seat as St. Germain unlocked the new turbocharger Marlow had ordered especially for him and that had caused a near rebellion in the squad room when it was still just a rumor. When he twisted the key, the engine roared as if it were being let out of a cage. Jeffcoat was on his bumper as he led the way to the interstate.

The sun was flaming out behind the Adirondacks, backlighting the high peaks in an orange glow that boiled out of hidden valleys. St. Germain groped for the visor and shifted it over the tinted glass. In the mirror a Chevy with sandblasted paint was nosing ahead of the Brown Bomber. St. Germain touched his brakes, rode them lightly until the intruder was squeezed out from between the police cars and Jeffcoat's boyish features became distinct again.

He cut his speed some more at the Burlington bypass and halved it for the ruined road to Malletts Bay. Behind him the Brown Bomber dropped back again, headlights blinking furiously. St. Germain ignored the signal until they reached the summer colony and he had circled out of sight of the Conklin place to a cove where Canada geese hunkered down for the night. At the water's edge a shantytown of ice fishing shacks waited for winter's hard freeze. A shack of his own stood beside Long Lake in the mountains. First thing back from Florida, he would move in with his Coleman stove and his Watchman, hardly see Annie for two months except when she came by to tell him to grow up and come in out of the cold.

He parked behind twin cedar trees, wondering why police cars weren't equipped with camouflage netting. The Brown Bomber crept alongside and Jeffcoat stepped out, adjusting his holster on his hip.

"I've been flashing you ever since we came off the highway," the deputy said, crankiness masquerading as professional concern. "You didn't see?"

"We were too close to Conklin's place to risk stopping. What's on your mind?"

"Nothing now. You were driving so fast I was bottoming out trying to keep up. You know what Joe Louis's suspension is like. I was afraid I'd scrape off my muffler and they'd hear us all over the lake."

"It never occurred to me."

"I hope that's all that—" The tone of his own voice brought Jeffcoat up short. "Well, no harm done," he said. "Which house is his?"

"The bungalow in the pines, the red one. See it?"

Jeffcoat shielded his eyes against reflected light that seemed to sizzle in the snow. "The one with the van in front?"

"Uh-huh. I'll drive down and say he's wanted at headquarters for something or other concerning his truck. We can tell him later we think he killed a girl in it."

"What's *my* job?"

"Conklin's got an older brother who could make a pain of himself without too much encouragement. I don't see his Jeep around, but that doesn't mean it's okay for you to daydream. If he jumps on my back, I'd appreciate it if you'd come down and pull him off. If I need you for anything else, I'll wave my arms over my head."

"That's it?" Jeffcoat asked. "That's all I have to do?"

St. Germain appraised the deputy and then reached out and straightened his collar. "Better comb your hair, Wally."

"What's that got to—"

"And learn to smile." He pinched Jeffcoat's cheek. "You want to look your best for the cameras when we bring him in."

With Jeffcoat stashed where he wouldn't trip over his feet, St. Germain backed into a U-turn. He killed his lights, picking out the way with the dregs of the sun. In Chimney Corner, across the bay, the big waterfront homes glowed like beacons in the growing darkness—Burlington's new money getting an early start on a weekend in the country. Skating on frozen slush, the cruiser cut across the summer colony to Sturgeon Cove Road and followed it onto the Conklin property. Woodsmoke swirled over the redwood's roof in yellow light rising like warm air. St. Germain swung around the van, demolishing a powdery hill beside the remains of a paper sack.

He came out in a hurry, slamming the car door, using up what little surprise he had left. The air was flavored with greasy meat frying, a barbecue he was glad to have missed. It made him hungry just the same. Though he had warned Jeffcoat to have a big lunch, he could remember eating only four doughnuts since a breakfast of apple pie.

A track in the slush ended at three stairs and a porch. A brown mat thinned by lug soles extended a conditional welcome in faded letters as he hunted for a doorbell. Not finding one, he pounded the redwood with the side of his hand and checked to see if the color had come off.

He waited half a minute and banged again, harder, then peered through a window. Smiling back was the chubby weather gal from the Plattsburgh TV station framed by the lower forty-eight on a twelve-inch screen. He knocked one more time and tried the knob, surprised when the splintered wood didn't rattle. Angry, but not sure why, or at whom, he went around to the back.

The path was littered with old engine blocks and washing machines, rusted refrigerator motors, three '57 Chevies cannibalized for parts—Appalachian megalomania spilling into the tony Champlain Valley. He walked through the junk into a yard doing double duty as a stunted baseball diamond. The rear of the bungalow was unpainted, the redwood stuff an affectation for salesmen and passersby. The windows were insulated with heavy sheets of plastic that were secured around the frames with duct tape. St. Germain tried to see inside, but it was like looking for goldfish in a bowl that needed a change of water. There was a dark green door that seemed wedged into the jamb like a cork hammered in a bottle. With his knuckles he played it like a drum.

He heard footsteps, thought he did, light ones like stocking feet on a carpeted floor. But no one came to let him in and the sound went away. He moved along the cluttered porch to the side of the house and peeled the tape from a double window, allowing a clear view of a box spring upright against the glass. He pressed the plastic into place again and retreated into the snow.

The moon was rising out of the mountains, a brass button among pinheads in a velvet sky. St. Germain looked for the cove where Jeffcoat was supposed to be keeping an eye on things and felt queasiness come over him when he easily spotted the Brown Bomber between the cedar trees. He went to one of the old Chevies and glanced in. Other than torn cushions leaking brown batting, the interior was picked clean; even the knobs had been plucked from the dashboard. As he was straightening up, he backed into something hard, something that hadn't been there a moment ago and that began inching along his spine. Cold metal made his flesh creep as it traced a circle in the back of his head. A confident voice he had heard not many hours before warned, "Use it or lose it."

A shudder ran through his body, but he made no other motion. He was trying to concentrate, to remember what the training manual said about being caught in a spot like this. But what came to mind was that old radio comedian, Jack Benny he thought it was, and the mugger with the voice like Bugs Bunny who was always saying, "Your money or your life," and Jack not answering right away, then getting the big yucks when he'd finally say, "I'm thinking, I'm thinking."

St. Germain already had thought it out. As soon as he had the upper hand, he was going to break someone's head.

"What was the choice?" he asked, as Jack would have, but holding himself rigid, making it plain that he knew he had no choice.

"I've got a twelve-gauge shotgun aimed where it'll break you in half," Paul Conklin said. "Cuts a real tight pattern. The choice is, you do what I say or we'll see exactly what you're made out of, Mr. Muscles."

St. Germain raised his hands above his shoulders.

"Did I tell you to do anything?" Conklin asked.

Cautiously, St. Germain lowered his arms.

"Put your hands up," Conklin said. "And keep them there till I tell you not to."

St. Germain complied. It was going to be a long night, and he hoped to be around when it was over.

He felt the boy's fingers at his holster. A part of his body seemed gone as they came away with his revolver. Then the fingers found his pockets and removed his wallet and car keys.

"Take off your gun belt," Conklin said. "Let it drop on the ground."

St. Germain tugged at the strap and the holster fell into the slush. His head didn't move. He was trying not to look any-where, especially not in the direction of the Brown Bomber. He was wondering if Jeffcoat had seen the boy set his trap and how he would respond. Then Conklin ordered him away from the car, and as he moved into the shadow of the house he realized the scene was screened from the deputy's view.

"Now your other belt," Conklin was saying.

"My pants'll fall down."

"Your problem. Take it off."

St. Germain opened the fancy brass buckle with the Cabot County seal that he had made up special for everyone in the department on a trip to Boston the year he was promoted to lieutenant. The stiff leather was comforting in his hand. If the boy came near enough, he would use it to whip out his eye.

"Drop that," Conklin said.

St. Germain pulled the strap through the loops, felt his pants slide down to his hips. He let go of the buckle and grabbed for the waistband.

"Stay like that," Conklin said. "It'll give your hands some-thing to do. Now let me see your face."

Tamping a circle in the snow, St. Germain turned around. Paul Conklin was in his checked jacket and twill pants, his hair in spiky tufts as if he had just rolled out of bed. Binoculars hanging from his neck and the pistol in his fist reminded St. Germain of a bird-watcher out for blood. At his feet was a thin metal rod. He laughed as he ground it into the slush.

"Yeah," he said, "look at it, look at it good. Bang bang bang. There's my shotgun."

St. Germain felt the skin on his face tighten.

"I could shoot you just like that." Conklin snapped his fin-gers, the popping sound like handmade gunfire. "Say I thought you were a prowler."

"You could," St. Germain said. "But you wouldn't get any-body to believe you."

"Let me worry about that part. Why're you snooping around my house?"

St. Germain pinched his waistband against his midsection. He brushed his knuckles against his forehead and brought them away, clammy.

"I asked you—"

"You know what I'm doing here, Paul."

Conklin's hand began waving as though he had forgotten there was a gun in it. St. Germain couldn't forget. "Your truck," he said quickly, ceding the first round to the boy.

"What about it?"

"Day before yesterday, a van like yours was in a hit-and-run accident on Main Street in Tremont Center. Somebody owes five thousand dollars to the owner of a green Ford."

The construction of a sloppy smile seemed to exhaust Conklin's anger, and the gun stopped waving. St. Germain smiled, too. If he could keep the bullshit flowing, the boy probably would invite him in for a beer.

"That's all?" Conklin said and lowered the weapon. "Just a car wreck?"

"It's why I pulled you over this morning. If you can prove you weren't near Tremont Center, I'll have to let you go."

"Let *me* go?" Conklin jabbed his hand for emphasis, then stared at it as if he were surprised to find the revolver there. "You're gonna let me go? That's a laugh."

"Well, Paul?"

"Well, what?"

"Were you in Tremont Center with your truck?"

Conklin's eyebrows came together and he shook his head.

"Then why don't you give back my gun and we can forget this ever hap—"

"I know I wasn't," Conklin said, "'cause I've been keeping prett' much to home since I killed that girl last week. Rebecca something or other, wasn't it?"

The sweat turned to ice on St. Germain's forehead. "What are you talking about?"

Conklin pushed the gun out in front again. "You think you're talking to some kind of simpleton or something? You think I didn't know what you were up to when you flagged my truck? One more day and you wouldn't have found me here. I was heading . . ." He stopped, picking a destination. "It doesn't matter. The thing is, I would have been gone. And now look what you're making me do."

"I'm not making you do anything, Paul," St. Germain said in the firm but nonthreatening voice the training manual advised.

"Another thing, you're not my pal, so stop Pauling me. From now on, it's Mr. Conklin to you, got that?"

St. Germain nodded.

"What's *your* name?"

"Lawrence St. Germain. Lieutenant, Cabot County sheriff's office." Expressionless, like a prisoner of war.

"I'll call you Larr, if that's all right with you."

Sure, St. Germain wanted to say, but it'll cost you, on top of everything else. But what he said was, "You're the one with the .38."

Conklin tilted the gunsight at his head and scratched the side of his nose with it. "You don't have to remind me, Larr."

"What are you planning to do with it?"

"Bang bang bang," Conklin said again.

St. Germain felt the stripped Chevy press against his hips, although he didn't remember backing into it. He came forward slowly, inching over the iron bar, hoping the boy wouldn't notice.

Conklin moved in step with him, following his lead. "You're standing on something that belongs to me," he said. "Let me have it."

"If you say so, Mr. Conklin."

St. Germain burrowed in the neutral ground between them, the metal so cold he felt white heat in his palm. Suddenly, Conklin stepped on the bar, pinning his hand, and the gun barrel crashed into his head.

"You shouldn't strain yourself thinking," Conklin said sternly. "You figured you could break my knees and get back your gun. I can read minds, Larr, the easy ones." The revolver came down again and the cylinder collided with St. Germain's cheek. "Pick yourself out of the snow. You're disgracing your uniform."

St. Germain touched numb fingers to his jaw. Mashed bone stretched the skin where swelling soon would begin; if he stayed cool enough to get out of this alive, he'd be sipping soup through a straw for months. He pulled himself up against the Chevy. More than the pain he was troubled by an unfamiliar feeling in his guts, which he suspected was the onset of panic.

Conklin bent for the gun belt and slung it over his shoulder. He went to the corner of the house and raised his binoculars toward the cove where Jeffcoat waited in the Brown Bomber. "Tell your partner he's invited, too, Larr."

The panicky feeling spilled over and St. Germain hooked his fingers in the door handle to keep from sliding off the car. "The hell are you talking about?" he tried.

Conklin walked back smartly with the pistol at his knees, then brought it up without warning. St. Germain heard himself cry out loud as his body jerked back. He ran his tongue behind his lips, snagging a jagged nub where a tooth had shattered. He tried to say something, but the frosted air sent a shiver of pain through his body and he clamped a hand over his mouth and turned away so the boy wouldn't see.

"Do it now," Conklin said.

St. Germain stumbled to the side of the house, saw himself doing it as if he were being forced to act in a pornographic movie. Conklin scarcely watched him; he dug his instep under the rod and levered it into his grip, then swung it around his head in widening circles with the cool hiss of an iron whip. St. Germain went all the way into the yard. He waved his arms till an engine coughed across the water and the Brown Bomber moved out of the trees, its bobbing lights probing the tortured route to Sturgeon Cove Road.

5

Jeffcoat navigated cautiously, working the pedals with both feet. The Brown Bomber was unpredictable in snow and one of its balding tires seemed to have gone soft, so that each time he hit the brakes he had to tug the wheel to keep the road. Twice in the first quarter-mile he checked his hair in the mirror. If St. Germain wasn't kidding about photographers (and with the lieutenant's reputation as a publicity hound he saw no reason to believe that he was), it wouldn't hurt to be all spiffed up when they brought Conklin in. Tomorrow he would sneak off duty half an hour early for a few beers with Manny Lockwood, an old high school buddy who worked in the *Free Press* circulation department and who would know enough to save a dozen papers for him if he made the front page.

A sign put where it was most likely to be missed showed the way to the Conklin place. He came down hard on the brakes and backed up to make the turn. No need to rush. From what little he had seen from his vantage point across the cove, St. Germain was well in control. Probably had the boy cuffed in the backseat of the turbocharger. Else why had he signaled so slowly, almost as though he were waving him away.

Jeffcoat lined up his wheels with the double row of ruts. Steering with one finger, he let gravity bring him toward the lake. The last house before the road bent from the shore was splashed brownish red. In the drive was St. Germain's cruiser beside a dusty van. He flicked on his brights and saw the lieutenant leaning against the side doors, motionless, boredom coming in for the kill. Or was it just a pose, getting it right for the cameras waiting for them at headquarters?

"Quiet here," Jeffcoat said out the window. "What did you want me for, a wake-up call?"

St. Germain didn't answer, didn't move. He was looking toward the Brown Bomber without acknowledging that it was there, as cool in his own way, Jeffcoat thought, as John Wayne watching the cavalry arrive after all the Indians were dead.

"Where is he?" Jeffcoat asked.

St. Germain started to say something, but the words were slurred and low.

"What's that, Loot?" Jeffcoat said. "I didn't catch—"

St. Germain stepped away from the van. As he came into the Brown Bomber's light, Jeffcoat began breathing through his mouth, bunching great gulps of air. "My God," he said and hurried out. "What happened to you? Your face—"

Then something crashed into him from behind, hit him so hard that he would have gone headfirst into the van if St. Germain hadn't blocked him with his body, kept him on his feet with arms that seemed exhausted by the effort. At his back a voice warned, "Keep hugging. Either one takes his hand off the other, you're both dead and buried."

Above a sudden silence Jeffcoat heard only his accelerated breathing. His foot tangled in St. Germain's, nearly toppling them, and as they struggled for balance he felt a hand on his revolver. His own hand came down to swipe it away, but froze at the unmistakable pressure of a gun at his spine, the same disembodied voice saying, "I guess you don't believe me."

The .38's report filled his head, dissolved into ringing louder than the shot. He moved closer to St. Germain, to collapse in his arms when the pain and darkness overtook him. He felt metal in his body, could have described its path into his chest. But then the voice was saying, "If you sweethearts can tear yourselves apart, we've got things to do." The hand was on his shoulder, prying him away from St. Germain, and he realized that the bullet had gone into the air, the terror and the message it was meant to convey so real that he'd have crawled into his grave if someone had seconded the notion he was dead.

The boy came around and stood at the edge of the light. There wasn't much to him, Jeffcoat decided, but the big guns magnified what there was. When he stuffed one in his pants, it was as though he were cutting himself down to size. Jeffcoat started to relax.

"Careful," St. Germain was saying, the words not very distinct. "You don't want that to go off now."

"I guess not." Conklin grinned and tilted the muzzle away from his crotch. "This your mascot?"

Jeffcoat didn't think it was funny. He slipped his hands from under St. Germain's shoulders and both men stumbled back.

"I asked—"

"Tell him who you are, Wally."

Jeffcoat spit in the snow. He barely looked at Conklin, as if to say he'd been through worse before.

"His name's Jeffcoat," St. Germain answered for him.

Conklin nodded and touched the deputy's gun to an imaginary hat brim. "You don't mind if I borrow this."

"What are you going to do with us?" Jeffcoat asked. He turned toward St. Germain, who was barely recognizable behind a purplish mask, and who blotted at his swollen face with a handkerchief.

Conklin shrugged. "I don't know. What do *you* guys want to do?" He backed against the Brown Bomber's grille, put his heel on the bumper and vaulted onto the hood, sitting with the chrome ornament between his legs. "What say we get out of here, go someplace we can have fun?"

Jeffcoat squinted into the high beams. The boy was so slight, so . . . ordinary, it seemed impossible he could have bloodied the lieutenant. He looked around, expecting to find the other Conklin hidden behind two more guns.

"You," Conklin said to St. Germain. "I want you in the driver's seat."

Jeffcoat stepped forward until the light was out of his eyes and he felt it blazing against his forehead. "It's my car," he said. "It's tricky if you're not used to it. If we're going anywhere, let me drive."

"You're the boss," Conklin laughed.

St. Germain went to the passenger's door. Jeffcoat watched for a signal, wishing they had worked out a code more articulate than flashing lights.

"You need a special invitation?" Conklin said.

Jeffcoat trudged after St. Germain and took the wheel, and then Conklin slithered behind them. Once, wire mesh had extended from the headrests to the ceiling, so that police dogs could be penned in back. But the partition had been removed two years before, when the coldest winter of the century took the fight out of the shepherds and sent them into semiretirement with the Tampa PD. Conklin pulled himself up against one of the old support posts and dropped the keys over Jeffcoat's shoulder. "You left these in the ignition," he said. "You should know better than that."

Jeffcoat's breathing had returned to normal. He felt calm, calmer than usual, the way he did when he had to address his Cabot Community College speech class, the tension building all week and then dissipating two words into his talk so that he wanted to hold the audience forever. He turned slightly toward St. Germain, who seemed lost in thought. No way the lieutenant didn't have something up his sleeve, something to make the skinny boy sorry he was born.

"Well," Conklin was saying, "what are we waiting for?"

"We're waiting for you to tell us where we're going," Jeffcoat answered.

"Just drive, huh?"

The Brown Bomber backed out of the yard and climbed away from the lakeshore. Overhead, the moon had taken all the light in the sky for itself. In its glow the pines threw ragged shadows that the heavy car tore up as the tires slipped out of the ruts.

"Hey," Conklin shouted. "Slow down."

Jeffcoat slammed the brakes and Conklin came forward so sharply that his chin smacked against the headrest. "Drive like you know how," he said. "I'm warning you."

Jeffcoat brought the car to the end of Sturgeon Cove Road and stopped under the sign. "Know where you want to go yet?"

"Keep straight." Conklin leaned back, rubbing his jaw against the back of his gun hand. "We want Smugglers Notch."

"Can't," St. Germain mumbled. "Road's closed . . . you should know. Won't be open till snow's gone, in May."

"*Don't* I know it," the boy said.

Jeffcoat held the cruiser with his foot off the brake, the rear wheels churning angry ribbons of slush. "Maybe you'd like to make sense before we ride all the way out there for nothing."

"It won't be for nothing." Conklin raised his gun hand until Jeffcoat caught sight of it in the mirror and the Brown Bomber lurched forward again.

The wheels gathered traction as the lane went to crushed rock, and Jeffcoat prodded the needle to thirty. St. Germain leaned back stiffly, not saying anything as he craned his bruised neck away from the headrest. Jeffcoat didn't need a signal to tell him what was on the lieutenant's mind. The thought was a shared one: soon they would be on Route 108 where it snaked around Spruce Peak through Smugglers Notch. Only there, a two-hour hike back to Stowe if they didn't freeze to death first, would Conklin feel safe enough to let them go.

"We ain't got all night," Conklin said.

Jeffcoat felt the boy's breath against his ear. "I thought you said to go slow."

"Kick it, it's getting late."

"Late for what?"

The Brown Bomber climbed a gentle rise and Jeffcoat touched the brakes again. A snowmobile burst across the road between gaunt hardhacks, leaving a trail of slushy droppings like a giant snail. Jeffcoat scanned the trees for another Skidoo, but saw only a blunt furrow in the snow. When he glanced into the rear seat, Conklin was pulling the second gun out of his pants and balancing it in his lap with the other.

"Late for you," the boy said.

"You're going to kill us there?"

St. Germain mumbled something that wasn't clear. To Jeffcoat it sounded like, "Don't waste . . . talking. Nuts."

"It's good a place as any," Conklin said. "We'll take this heap into the mountains as far as it'll get us and then go for a walk. I'll shoot you in a pretty spot and bury your bodies in the snow where they won't be found till spring. My brother doesn't live too far. He can pick me up and get rid of your cars while I beat it out of Vermont, which I was gonna do anyway. How's that sound to you? Be honest."

Jeffcoat put more pressure on the brakes. "What will you gain by killing us?"

"Satisfaction," Conklin said.

"The satisfaction of having every police officer in New England after you?"

Conklin thought about it for a while. "In the place where they kill the burnt offering," he said, "shall they kill the trespass offering; and the blood thereof shall he sprinkle round about upon the altar." He was smiling. "Leviticus. Chapter seven, verse two."

"You're right, Lieutenant," Jeffcoat said, spinning the wheel all the way to the left. "He's out of his skull."

Conklin fell across the seat as the Brown Bomber left the road. It skidded over a frozen ditch into sparse brush, Jeffcoat tromping down on the gas, bracing himself as a tree stump took off the muffler and the engine bellowed in pain. Then the ball joints shattered and, as the front end collapsed, a stone fence came out of the darkness and broadsided them.

St. Germain's face struck the window and he felt blood on his jaw again. Beside him Jeffcoat was pushing uselessly at his door. The inside panel had buckled, revealing sprung hinges behind the imitation leather. Conklin lay on the floor in back, the guns under his body as he struggled to his knees. St. Germain wrenched open his door and swung his feet into deep slush. "Slide out my side," he shouted to Jeffcoat, hoping he'd be understood.

He ran along the fence, feeling his way with his hand. Where a section of stone had crumbled, he climbed into a field enclosed by old growth timber. Wet snow dragged at his legs like frozen quicksand, and he tugged his pants around his hips and raised his knees higher. Without stopping he looked over his shoulder for Jeffcoat, but saw only his own shadow chasing him into the trees.

He opened his mouth for more air, but pain accompanied each breath till he clamped his jaws and again fed his burning lungs through his nostrils. Above the hammering in his chest he heard two quick shots. Using energy he hadn't known he had, he pumped his legs harder. The trees were less than a hundred feet off when he heard a third shot, heard it still when he staggered against the trunk of a red maple.

As his breathing grew less labored, he became aware of something advancing slowly in his direction. Deer, perhaps, or maybe one of the rare moose migrating through the valley en route to the Adirondacks. Then the rhythm of footsteps grew distinct and he moved around the maple, putting its gnarled bulk between himself and whoever was out there. He backed deeper into the trees. Crouched behind a rotted oak that was balanced between two boulders, he glimpsed a shadow meager enough to be either Jeffcoat's or the boy's. He raised himself till he saw a figure in the brown shirt of a Cabot County deputy and nearly went limp as the adrenaline drained from his blood.

"Wally," he cried, and jumped up from the log.

The figure in brown stopped moving, cocked an ear.

"Wally. Over here. Christ, am I glad to—"

Branches parted and St. Germain saw a cap two sizes too large, shirttails hanging loosely outside twill pants. Beaming, Conklin squeezed off a shot that went into a basswood behind St. Germain's head. He lunged forward with bullets probing the way.

St. Germain slipped, twisting around, and gashed his knee on a boulder. As he struggled to his feet, a shot ripped his left arm below the elbow and put him on his belly again. He picked himself up and dashed into the trees with the boy so close that he could hear the wind rattling in his throat. He was offering an easy target now; with every step he expected a slug in his back or, if he was lucky, not to feel the one that would shatter his head.

Another shot rang out. When he didn't hear the bullet thud, he realized Conklin had lost him and was shooting blindly. He hunched his shoulders, trying to make himself small, cursing the broadness that was his pride. As he snaked through the hardwoods, the forest opened on a brushy tangle where tree poachers had taken a chainsaw a decade before. Hiking up his pants, he hurtled into the undergrowth, snapping twigs like mortar fire at his heels.

Quit worrying about Jeffcoat, he told himself, for all the good it would do. If Conklin had his cap and shirt, no way he'd left him alive. Because the thought seemed to weigh him down, he tried to force it from his mind. Guilt kept it where it was. But Jeffcoat was dead, had to be, and there was nothing to be done for him now. And if he was wrong, then why in God's name wasn't Wally doing something for *him?* Funny idea, wishing Jeffcoat would pull his chestnuts out of the fire.

Woody debris had been collected in bales among the tree stumps. St. Germain dived into the largest one, clawing at branches and twigs and then pulling them in after him, wallowing like a beaver in a dam. Though he held his body still, his heart was loud enough to home in on, like a radiosonde programmed to self-destruct. He promised himself that if Conklin fired into the pile he would take a bullet without making a sound. The crackling of dried leaves dictated an immediate change in plan, and he burst out of his nest without seeing the family of raccoons whose foraging he had interrupted.

The undergrowth was thicker deep inside the old clear-cut. The perfect spot to lose himself was somewhere in here—if only he could find it. Looking, he went too far and the scrub returned to hardwood, a thin stand ending in a field where scattered cornstalks stood like minutemen against intruders from the woods. Still listening for the boy, he hurried into the corn, unwilling to ask himself what he hoped to find there.

A spurt of optimism came with his second wind. But the burning in his lungs relocated in his arm and then his whole body rebelled. He put his head down and ran harder, and when he took his bearings he was in sight of the lake, at a cove that gouged a craggy wedge from the cornfield. He stopped there with nothing left, turned his back on the water to take on the boy's guns with his fists. But then Conklin came out of the trees in a miler's graceful lope, and St. Germain dropped his challenge while it was still unannounced and began racing along the beach.

He had never been a runner, his size a drawback when speed was what counted. Now, with the boy gaining on him with fluid strides, it was everything. Reaching deep inside, St. Germain pushed himself along the water's edge, looking back over his shoulder like a swimmer sucking air with each stroke. Somewhere in the woods Conklin had lost Jeffcoat's hat, and the moonlight in the boy's face revealed a determination to match his own.

"Give it up," Conklin called out to him. "You can't win. Why knock yourself out for nothing?"

As though it were the answer to a trick question, St. Germain imagined Annie between soft sheets, summoning him to bed.

"Quick," Conklin was saying, "easy, over in a sec. . . . Be doing yourself a favor."

Maybe the boy was right. The idea alone was enough to sap his energy, and, angry with himself, St. Germain picked up the pace as best he could. A shot rang out well away, as if Conklin were firing out of range. Gambling that it wasn't a ruse, St. Germain slowed to look back once more and saw the boy drop behind, clutching a stitch in his side.

Drawing on unsuspected reserves, St. Germain set out for the shadows behind the cove. With Conklin weakening, he would take his chances in the trees again. He cruised toward the finish line, thinking less about the boy and his guns than of his own feet chafing in sodden shoes. But where the beach was funneled into a narrow strip of land, there was no forest rising out of the pebbly soil, only a stone outcrop extending into the shallows offshore.

Exhaustion bent him nearly double. He rested his hands on shaky knees and gulped air in spite of the pain, spotted the boy before he was able to start back for the cornfield. Without knowing it, Conklin had cut off his retreat, so that all that was left was to submerse himself in the blackness and hope the boy would go home before the frigid waters took their toll. Shielding his head against a freshening wind, he crept to the lake under the cover of the bedrock that rose out of the sand like a mossy wall. But when he stopped again to cup an ear for tiny waves lapping against the beach, he heard only his own forced breaths as they came back to him off the rippled crust that capped the still cove.

He tested the surface and brought his foot back quickly as a gray slab disintegrated under half his weight. Thirty feet away he tried again. The ice fractured, but didn't give, and he put down the other foot and moved cautiously from the land. Untracked snow muffled his steps, absorbed some of the shock of 200-pound footfalls. When he looked back, Conklin was studying footprints on the beach, then stuffing the guns in his pants and trying the ice, walking with his arms out from his sides like a highwire artist over a lethal drop.

Though he tried not to, St. Germain thought of Mackie Pike, who had spent fifty winters on the rock-solid ponds of the Northeast Kingdom carving the bluish blocks that were packed in sawdust and then shipped to the icehouses of the Carolinas and Georgia. Even on days when the temperature stood at 40 below, it was not rare for someone off by himself to fall through a thin spot over an inlet. The old ice cutter had told him he'd never worried much about it. If you let those things bother you, he had advised, better stay off the ice.

But St. Germain had no choice. He ran for the mouth of the cove, trying to step lightly. Another shot echoed behind him, closer than the last, the boy announcing that he was resuming the hunt in earnest. St. Germain tried to calculate how many bullets Conklin had left, but knew it didn't matter. One, not very well placed, would be enough to bring him down.

He twisted his ankle where the ice had buckled, and shook off the pain to catalogue with the rest. A quarter-mile out, a rocky promonotory marked the boundary of the cove. He swung around it blindly, praying for ice on the other side, picking up speed when the hard surface didn't evaporate beneath him. In the distance he made out the boxy silhouette of a dilapidated hut the size of an overgrown outhouse standing at the edge of land. As he neared the beach he saw a dozen like it and then many more, and decided that he had been running in a circle, hooking back toward the ice fishing village he had passed on his way to the Conklin place.

The boy was well behind when St. Germain stepped onto land again, weaving through a Main Street three feet wide, studying the shacks and losing himself in their comforting sameness. At a hut of brown particle board built on wooden runners he stopped for a second look and then forced open the door. His lighter caught the first time he tried it, showing a dented minnow bucket beside two round holes in the floor and not much else. He turned the pail upside down and squatted on it, resting as much of his weight as he dared against thin walls that groaned in the wind. His teeth began chattering and he played the Zippo to rummage in a rusted footlocker for a blanket or scrap of cloth to put between himself and the cold. The best he could do was a stack of year-old newspapers. He pulled off his shoes, stuffed the yellowing treasures inside, and warmed his numb toes in his hands.

Christ, but he was cold, colder than out on the lake. And the humiliation of what he was being put through by a boy not even old enough to drink—the kind who'd hang outside a liquor store begging you to buy a pint of wine for him to get sick all over himself—more chilling than that. He stood up to beat his arms against his chest and, when that generated little warmth, to chink up the spaces around a window of orange Plexiglas with the last of his newspaper. His stomach was demanding attention, too. The Zippo revealed a wall shelf stocked with a ketchup bottle plugged with green mold and a battered can of corned beef hash. He had no opener; along with his keys, Conklin had taken his Swiss army knife. Frustrated more than starved, he would have pounded his fists against the walls if the particle board looked as if it could stand up to the punishment.

He pulled the wadded newspaper from the wall, afraid of what he would find. The shore was cloaked in a low cloud nibbling on the moon as it swept over the lake. Then the cloud was swallowed by Burlington's distant brightness, and he saw the boy not a hundred feet away, peering behind a blue door and shutting it, opening another to look inside a hut with silver walls.

"Come out, come out, wherever you are," Conklin sang childishly.

St. Germain's throat caught as Conklin backed out and began moving down the street, methodically poking inside every shack.

"Chilly out here, Larr. Least you could do is invite me in out of the weather."

Whispered words told Conklin where he could go. St. Germain remained at the chink in the wall, searching his imagination for a plan and the strength to put it into effect. Another cloud buffeted the moon and he considered a dash through the darkness. But how far could he expect to get before the boy took up the chase again, and this time shot him down? No, he would make his stand here. With Conklin careless enough to lead with a gun, he wouldn't have much trouble wrenching the barrel away and turning it on him before the other came into play. . . .

Fantasy land, he told himself. If that was the best he could come up with, it was all over but the eulogies and the cortege with flashing domes.

Without a conscious command from his brain, St. Germain carried the bucket behind the shack and stood on the pitted bottom. A bent stovepipe protruded below the peak of the roof. Guessing that it would support him, he used it to hoist himself onto rough planks. He waited. After several minutes his leg fell asleep and he shifted his weight to his other side, not daring to raise his head. He tried to put himself in the boy's place, wishing the boy were in his, and was relieved when he could think of no reason to look on the roof. If he lay still, Conklin would miss him. If not, he wouldn't have to worry about a bullet in the back.

The clouds fell apart and metallic light rained down, leaving him naked and exposed. Watching his shadow swell in the snow, he pressed himself into the roof till he saw it shrivel again. A door slammed so hard that the vibrations stung his cheek, and then Conklin stepped into his narrow field of vision, close enough to tousle the spiky hair.

"Home free all," the boy said, tapping his gun against the brown slabs. "How about if I hide now and you try and find me?"

St. Germain squeezed harder against the planks. He ignored a splinter that pierced the skin under his eye, fascinated with the shadow that grew still smaller as though it reflected a shrinking body. His knee slipped, and the wood conducted a scraping sound that filled his head. But Conklin was laughing out loud and didn't hear.

"You want to play some more?" the boy said. "Fine by me. I've got nothing special for tonight." He hammered the door with his heel, and St. Germain heard the wood explode and the boy cursing as his foot snagged in the broken boards.

It was a piece of cake now. Conklin was stuck, perched on one leg as he tried to kick free, his back a vulnerable target. Just drop off the roof and drag him down, that was all, put him in a choke hold and forget to let go. But with only one good arm there were no guarantees, and St. Germain felt uncomfortable with the odds. He couldn't remember the last fight where his size hadn't made him a winner before the first punch was thrown.

"Hang on, Larr," Conklin called out as he struggled to extract his foot. "I'll be right after you."

Panic had St. Germain by the balls and he fought it with

short, silent breaths. He suspected that other men had conquered fear by developing antibodies with each exposure. But he had gone too long without really being afraid, and now, like an adult in the grip of a childhood disease, he was defenseless.

A low rumbling like approaching thunder percolated through the village, making St. Germain wonder what the boy had cooked up next. He looked down at Conklin bent over a rolled-up pants leg with his head tilted toward the sound. St. Germain recognized a light truck or four-wheel-drive vehicle pushing across the beach, no doubt Conklin's brother summoned to the hunt. But as the engine quit, the boy darted behind the shack, and there was only the certain beat of heavy boots plodding toward them.

"What're you doing in here?" a voice called out.

It was a man's voice, middle-aged or older, St. Germain decided, and in no mood to be trifled with.

A yellow beam pierced the dead street. It followed the flattened snow around the corner of the shack and found Conklin huddled against a wall.

"I said, what are you do—"

"What's it look like I'm doing, Gramps?"

The light traced shapeless contours, taking in the ruined door. "Looks like you're fixing to torch these shanties, like they done last week up to North Hero."

St. Germain saw a man in a wool jacket like the one Conklin had worn, with tufts of white hair sprouting from under a billed cap of the same checked cloth. An older version of the boy, who should know better than to go easy on him.

"Go away, old man," Conklin said. "You've got no business bothering me."

"I'll say I have." The flashlight settled below Conklin's eyes. "These shanties belong to me, to me and my friends. If you don't get your ass out of here, you'll see what a bother I can be, all right."

St. Germain wanted to applaud. He moved closer to the edge and saw Conklin's fingers playing impatiently on the gun.

"Now get," the old man said.

Conklin seemed to relax. St. Germain couldn't. Trapped behind an invisible barrier, he watched powerlessly while the boy began to bring the weapon around, freezing—as everyone did—when another voice reached them in the night.

"Millard? Millard, who are you talking to?"

It was a woman asking, a woman about the same age as the man, St. Germain guessed, and angrier with Millard than Millard was with the boy. Conklin tucked the revolver against the small of his back. He moved away from the shack, showing his empty palms like a child seeking approval for clean hands.

"It's no one, Peg," Millard called back. "Just some little bastard out to burn the shanties."

St. Germain peered over the village, trying to track the voice to its destination.

"Hold your water," Conklin said. "I'm not trashing anybody's property. I'm looking for a friend, that's all."

"A friend?" Millard stifled a laugh. "What would your friend be wanting in a place like this?"

Conklin walked around the white-haired man, scanning the shacks one last time. "Playing hide-and-seek," he said. "Prett' soon it's my turn to hide."

St. Germain watched Millard shepherd the boy down the street until they were lost in the gloom.

"*Millard?*" The woman did not sound pleased, did not sound as if she ever were. "What in Heaven's name was that about?"

"Now, Peg, don't get all—"

The rest was lost in the whine of the transmission as the heavy vehicle retreated across the beach.

St. Germain pushed himself up on his elbows. He could see almost to the end of the village now and Conklin was nowhere in sight. It seemed unlikely that Millard had offered him a ride, yet why had he gone to the trouble of flushing the boy out only to leave him there? St. Germain thought it over, glad for the excuse not to move. He lay back, hearing only a whistling in his nose and the occasional moan he was unable to suppress. Sick of the sound of himself, he clambered down and ducked inside the brown hut. He stood at the chink in the wall, watching moonlight dilute the night. For no reason that he could think of, he put his badge in his pocket and went outside again, walked slowly down the center of the street.

6

Marlow tilted the remote at the man with the perfect smile, listening with a sense of accomplishment as the perfect baritone fell silent by degrees. On the next ring he reached for the phone. "Marlow, here," he said without taking his eyes off the picture.

"Sheriff," the voice at the other end said, "it's Ed."

"Yes, Ed."

"Sorry to be disturbing you at home, but we got a call I thought you'd want to know about. Chittenden sheriff's says the Brown Bomber's been found off the road in some woods near Malletts Bay. That's on the lake, north of Burl—"

Marlow took aim at the screen again. When the perfect smile refused to fade, he carried the phone across the bare floor and slammed the TV with the side of his hand. "I know where it is," he said, backing through the darkened room. "Did they tell you anything about Jeffcoat?"

"They say he's hurt."

"How bad?"

"Don't know. Hurt's all they have on him."

"What about Larry?"

"Didn't say anything. I don't think they know he's there. Fact is, they were asking what one of our cars was doing in their county without their being told."

"I'm starting to understand," Marlow said. "Call Vann and Gray, wake 'em if you've got to, and have 'em meet me at the office. Tell 'em we're going out to see what we can do for Jeffcoat and to help Larry, whether he needs it or doesn't. Then call 'em both back and remind them to hurry. Will you do that, Ed?"

Marlow replaced the receiver and bent to lace his shoes. When he sat up again, his wife was standing over his easy chair with his gun belt and his coat. "There's been some trouble, Martha," he murmured, an actor running through his lines for the thousandth time. "I don't know when I'll be getting back. Be a good idea if you didn't lose any sleep waiting."

The woman tugged a flannel dressing gown across her bony shoulders. "I'll keep a pot of coffee on," she said where her part came in.

When he pulled into the lot, Marlow recognized Artemis Gray's Buick beside the loading platform. A red Trans Am raced in on two wheels, and Dick Vann slid out, fastening the collar button on his uniform shirt.

"Fancy piece of driving," Marlow said. "Why don't you save it for the road?"

"Ed said, 'On the double.' " Dick Vann was a dark-haired man three years older, a couple of inches shorter, and twenty pounds lighter than the lieutenant who had supplanted him as the sheriff's favorite. Marlow made it no secret that he liked his deputies big, as if sheer size were enough to keep the populace of Cabot County in line, and during St. Germain's rookie year Vann had gone in seriously for weight lifting, attempting to regain his place in the sheriff's esteem by outbulking the new man. Fifteen pounds of knotty muscle had attached itself to his upper arms and thighs, where he needed it the least, giving him the muscle-bound stoop that Marlow believed projected a Neanderthal image the department could do without. Telling no one but his wife, Vann twice had taken the exam for appointment to the state police and was waiting for word from

Montpelier. "When I heard about Wally," he said, "I wasn't going to screw around getting here."

"Wally and Larry, both," Marlow said. "I sent them to Chittenden County to pick up Becky Beausoleil's killer."

"Wally? For a job like that? No wonder things got loused . . ." Seeing Marlow's eyes narrow, he caught himself. "Cancel that, John, it was uncalled for. What happened?"

Marlow prodded the big man up the concrete stairs. "Don't know yet. Chittenden authorities've got only sketchy details."

Art Gray, wearing a green shooter's vest over wide-wale corduroy pants, was waiting for them in the corridor. At thirty-five, he was the veteran of Marlow's staff, an officer of few aspirations save putting in the twenty-two years remaining to collect his pension.

"This is swell," Marlow said, taking the green wool between his thumb and forefinger. "Did you think I was inviting you to gun skeet?"

"Ed caught me as I was about to drive the baby-sitter home," Gray said without apology. "Bonnie and I'd been to the movies, and I didn't have time to change."

Marlow let the cloth slip from his hand. "Doesn't matter." He was holding the door with his heel, and now he kicked it all the way open. "You fellows ever been to Malletts Bay?"

"Nope," Vann said.

"Same here."

"We're looking for a place called Sturgeon Cove," Marlow said. "I'll lead."

Dick Vann's new Trans Am was a distant second as Marlow set the pace across the interstate. Instinct, luck, and a Chittenden County map brought him toward the shore. As he hunted for the Conklin place, his headlights picked a black Ford Escort out of the pigweed and mustard, and on the opposite shoulder a green-and-white tow truck. Marlow was wading through the brush before his deputies had braked their cars.

The Brown Bomber was flush against a stone wall, the undercarriage dug into the snow. Two men stood a respectful distance away, as if they expected it to start moving again. One was wearing a loden coat with horn buttons over stiff new blue jeans, the other in the soiled uniform of a Malletts Bay wrecking service.

"Are you a doctor?" Marlow asked the man in the loden coat.

"He doesn't need a doc. You from the county?"

Marlow walked into the dim glow feeding off the Brown Bomber's dying battery. The man in the loden coat stepped after him, saying, "You took your sweet time getting here."

Vann moved quickly to head him off. "He's the Cabot County sheriff. We're his deputies. The officer there, so's he."

When Gray and Vann caught up, Marlow was fifteen feet from the Brown Bomber, looking into a depression in the weeds. Jeffcoat, staring back through filmy eyes, was sprawled on his back with his left hand across his bare chest. A trickle of blood had congealed beneath his nostrils; more blood darkened his chin. Between his parted fingers a ragged splotch above the nipple marked the exit of a bullet that had flattened after it was fired high into his back. Marlow reached inside the car and killed the lights. When he turned around, the deputies had backed away and were standing with the others.

"I'm Gordon Hall," the man in the loden coat told them. "These woods belong to my dad, most of them. I was driving by when I saw the cruiser off the road and went in for a look. I phoned Malletts Bay police and they said they'd call the county. But all that's come by is the wrecker, and there's not a whole lot he can do for anybody, is there?"

Marlow walked off to stand closer to Jeffcoat. "Shot in the back," he said mostly to himself, "his gun and half his uniform gone, not a trace of Larry or his car. How could something like this—"

Shadows flickering in the trees turned the officers toward the road. A car with noisy lifters pulled onto the shoulder, spinning its wheels over the frozen ditch.

"I'd better turn my flasher on before somebody runs into me," the tow truck driver said.

Three men passed him coming into the woods. They were dressed in brown uniforms identical to Marlow's save for Chittenden County insignias on the sleeves.

"Dave Aubuchon, Chittenden sheriff's," said the officer in front. He was a stocky man with a prizefighter's zippered eyebrows, wearing captain's bars in need of polishing. "Hear one of your men's hurt bad here."

"Real bad," Marlow said. "He's dead."

"Heard that, too, but didn't want to believe it. What went down? We were never told you had officers in the county."

"I sent two. They were going to touch base with your office, then come out to make an arrest in a murder case."

"First I learn of it," Aubuchon said. "That wouldn't be the Beausoleil killing?"

Marlow looked at him sharply. "Why, what do you know about it?"

"Nothing you don't, nothing I didn't read in the papers. And we were never contacted by your men."

"Damn your soul, Larry," Marlow said under his breath.

"What's that?"

"I said I don't understand how this could've happened."

Aubuchon inched away until he was close to Jeffcoat's body. He played a flashlight into the weeds and centered it on the deputy's face. The tow truck's flashers went on suddenly, casting his own features alternately sallow and ruddy. "Same suspect do both killings?" he asked.

"It'd seem that way."

"Who is he?"

"A Malletts Bay man," Marlow said. "Paul Conklin."

"That one," another Chittenden officer said, and thumbed his nose. A metal plaque on his chest read NICHOLS.

Marlow didn't acknowledge him right away. He stood between Aubuchon and Jeffcoat's body until the captain flicked off his light. Then he asked, "Know him?"

"Who doesn't?" Nichols said. "The little prick's been making trouble for women since his arms were long enough to reach his fly. He's got a juvenile sheet long as *your* arm, and ours have been tied because of his age. You say you want him for murder. What I can't figure is what took him so long."

"Can you show us where he lives, lend us a couple of men?" Brighter lights swept away the yellow. Marlow spoke faster, heading off an interruption. "My chief deputy's still out here somewhere."

"I'll come with you," Aubuchon said. "Nichols, you too. Bob," he told the third officer, "stay with the body till the state police show."

He switched on the flashlight again and picked his way back to his car. "The Conklin place is a mile off," he said to Marlow. "We've been there often enough to know."

A Fanny Allen Hospital ambulance was waiting next to the tow truck. Aubuchon whispered something to a man holding a doctor's black bag and Marlow saw both of them point into the brush. The man nodded, drawing on a cigarette, and opened the rear doors. When he came out again a moment later, he had traded the bag for a collapsible litter.

Vann and Gray slid into the sheriff's car beside their boss. "Shit," Marlow said softly. "I told Larry over and over how important it was for him to contact the Chittenden deputies before he moved on Conklin. I don't see how he could have disobeyed a simple order like that."

Aubuchon revved his engine and then swung around the ambulance with the Cabot car in his exhaust.

"If we don't find Larry at Conklin's," Marlow told his deputies, "I want you to come back here and scour the woods, if you have to light matches to keep from bumping into the trees." A hail of gravel swept the windshield, putting a crack in the glass that lengthened with every jolt. Marlow came off the gas and dropped back ten feet. "And be glad that's all you have to do. I've got to go looking for a priest who still makes house calls."

The sheriff's car regained the lost ground on its own, and Marlow hit his brakes again. "Dick . . . Art, it's been three years," he said, "but either of you have a smoke?" Then Aubuchon stopped so suddenly that Marlow had to swerve into the brush to avoid rear-ending the Chittenden cruiser.

"Look by that house," Art Gray said, pointing to a reddish bungalow on the lake. "There's the turbocharger, in the yard."

The Cabot officers were standing around St. Germain's cruiser by the time Aubuchon's men stepped into the drive. Marlow stuck his head in the open window and pulled away, looking pale and drawn. "Nothing," he said. His eye caught the blue van. "This the Conklin place?"

"Uh-huh." Aubuchon moved on the bungalow ahead of the others, hesitating at the porch steps to stare up at the windows. "Doesn't look like anybody's home," he whispered, "but you never know who likes to sit in the dark, keeping an eye out for company." He drew his revolver and rubbed the barrel as though he were warming it up. "Nichols, you go around back and drop anyone who comes out that's not in brown. Sheriff Marlow, you and your men come with me."

Marlow, his hand against Aubuchon's back, had reached the porch when the stillness was spoiled by a vehicle moving in the slush. Everyone looked across the yard and then went back down the stairs. Squeezing between the Chittenden car and the trees was a four-wheel-drive Wrangler with red flake paint and silver mud flaps. A white-haired man in a wool cap was fine-tuning the heater impatiently. A woman in bib ski pants, trying hard to look fifty again, shared the passenger seat with a boy young enough to be her grandson.

"But this was where you told us you live," she said loud enough for the men in the yard to hear. "Now you say you don't?"

"Keep going," the boy told the man in the wool cap. "Just keep on go—"

"Looks like you've got visitors, Paul," the man said.

Art Gray was first to reach the Wrangler. Ignoring the woman's startled cry, he jabbed the muzzle of his gun against Paul Conklin's forehead. A reddening circle was visible between the eyebrows as the boy recoiled from the cold metal.

"You don't want your brains, such as they are, all over these nice people," Gray said, "you'll come out quietly with your hands on top of your head."

Conklin turned to the elderly couple. "Mr. and Mrs. Sullivan, I do want to thank you for the lift," he said before the deputy hauled him out by the shirtfront and flung him into the snow, held him there with a foot against the back of the neck until Vann had cuffed him and taken away his guns.

"What did you do with the other officer?" Marlow asked when Conklin had been dragged to his feet. "Where's Lieutenant St. Germain?"

"Don't know who you're talking about," Conklin said.

Gray kneed the boy in the groin. Conklin fell across his feet, and the deputy pulled away as if he had stepped in something smelly and kicked him in the ribs. "Where is he?"

"Big fellow?" Conklin gasped. "Blond, with muscles he doesn't know what to do with, thinks he's hot shit?"

Gray drew back his foot again.

"I took him down a few notches," the boy said, "and when I saw he wasn't a keeper anymore, I had to let him go."

A camera crew from Boston had the choice spot on the loading dock while radio and the newspapers staked out their turf in the lot. Marlow drove slowly, nudging reporters out of the way like a pilgrim passing through a herd of sacred cows. He slid out of the car with Conklin manacled to his wrist and prodded him up the steps. An ash blonde from the Boston station got to them first in gray Reeboks her viewers never would see. Harsh lights that were her own worst enemy seemed fascinated with a facial tuck in need of freshening. She shoved a microphone under Marlow's nose and he brushed it aside with a mechanical "No comment," yanked at the chain and pulled the boy inside.

They waited in the corridor until the deputies had filtered through the mob. Vann stayed at the door to keep the news hounds at bay, while Gray brought Conklin to a bullpen cell. With an unlit Marlboro between his lips, Marlow hurried to the communications room and pressed the dispatcher's shoulders. "Any word on St. Germain?" he asked.

Ed took off his earphones and swiveled around in his seat. "Damn, but you gave me a start," he said. ". . . What's that you asked?"

"Have you heard anything new on Larry?"

The dispatcher nodded. "Not ten minutes ago Chittenden sheriff's called to say he'd been admitted to Tragg Memorial Hospital in Burlington. Fellow driving home from a poker game found him sort of wandering by the side of the road in Malletts Bay and brought him."

"Admitted with what?"

Ed shrugged. "With a whole lot of things is the way it sounded. He's been shot in the arm and beat up pretty bad, his jaw broke and a handful of teeth hammered loose. Maybe some internal damages, too. But the docs told Chittenden sheriff's he wasn't in any danger."

Marlow took the Marlboro in his fingers and glowered at it before lighting it from a butt in the dispatcher's ashtray. "I'm heading back there now," he said. "You learn anything else, I want to hear about it right off."

* * *

A trail of blood showed the way into a tiled emergency room where a man with a hatchet on a belt loop held two extra fingers in his left hand. A doctor and three nurses were trying to get him to sit down as they worked feverishly over him. "I brung 'em so you could sew 'em back on for me," the man said, "but I forgot the needle and thread." More than a minute went by before one of the nurses turned away and saw Marlow staring down the cigarette machine beside the admissions desk.

"You must be here to visit the officer they brought in earlier," she said.

"Yes, ma'am, I am."

"He's up in . . . 302. If you hurry, you might be able to get in a few words with him before."

"Before what?" Marlow asked.

But the nurse had gone back to the man with seven fingers in his hand and didn't seem to hear.

He came off the elevator into a corridor with burnished rails against the walls. Red arrows in the linoleum pointed him toward a nurses' station where a girl too young to drink was dropping colored capsules into paper cups he thought would make handy shot glasses.

"Room 302?" he asked.

"Keep going around the L," she said, pouring another, "and it's on your left."

An old man with no teeth or legs lay plugged into an IV unit close to the door. Marlow tiptoed past him toward a bed cloaked in stained curtains. "Larry," he whispered. "Larry, you in there?" The old man rolled over in his sleep, licking his lips lasciviously. Marlow felt for the opening in the cloth and stuck his head in.

St. Germain, wearing a hospital gown three sizes too small, was propped up in bed with a blue sling immobilizing his arm. His face was discolored, swollen so badly that the shock of blond hair was Marlow's only point of reference. Marlow wondered how his own face looked. "How you doing?" he asked.

St. Germain turned toward him as if he had never seen him before.

"That's okay," Marlow said. "Don't try to say anything, we'll have plenty of time to talk later." He pulled the curtains behind him and stood beside the bed. "Looks like you went up against a meat grinder."

St. Germain touched a gray panel hanging from the bed railing and the mattress flattened, lowering him gently. Marlow squeezed his arm and said, "You might feel better knowing Conklin's cooling his heels in a cell. The arraignment's tomorrow morning."

St. Germain's jaw tightened. "What about Wally?" he whispered.

Marlow studied a picture on the wall, a covered bridge over the Connecticut River at the peak of autumn. Where he expected to find an artist's signature it read, *Fujicolor.* "The doctors tell me you'll be your old self in no time," he said. "That overgrown carcass of yours must still be under warranty."

"Wally," St. Germain said hoarsely.

Marlow shook his head, and St. Germain pulled his arm away and let himself all the way down.

"My God, Larry," Marlow said, "what the hell happened out there?"

Then light washed over Marlow's shoulder and a man on the short side of thirty came inside the curtain wearing a green scrub suit and a smile of professional disdain. "Mr. St. Germain isn't supposed to see any visitors yet," he said.

"Doctor, I'm Sheriff John Marlow of Cabot County. The patient is my chief deputy. I know it's past visiting hours, but—"

"I'm going to ask you to leave," the man in the scrub suit said, "so we can wire Mr. St. Germain's jaw."

"I'd like a few more minutes with him. There are things I need to know."

"Come back in the morning and take all the time you want. I've got to do this now."

"Same here," Marlow said and turned away. "Larry, if you can just tell me where—"

Marlow's back seemed to agitate the doctor. "I must insist that you go. If you don't, I'll have to ask the guard to escort you out. You're not in Cabot County now."

A woman's voice brittle with worry was calling from somewhere in the corridor. "John, John, is that you? I came as soon as I heard. Is Larry—"

The voice grew louder until the opening in the curtains framed Annie St. Germain trying on a brave smile like an understudy about to go onstage before she had learned her lines.

"Who's next?" the doctor sniffed. "His cousins from Detroit?"

"Good to see you, Ann," Marlow said. "He's in here and looking reasonably healthy, considering." He moved aside to let the woman have the place closest to the bed.

"I really *must* insist . . ."

Marlow stepped on the doctor's toe as he backed him against the wall. "Let her have him for now," he said. "Once you're done, you know damn well he won't be able to make an intelligible sound for weeks."

The doctor adjusted a stethoscope around his neck, groping for his dignity. Marlow stifled the urge to ask if he was searching for his heart. "Tell me," Marlow said, "how is he?"

"I might find out if you'd let me at him. I still haven't had a decent look—"

Marlow put a finger to his lips and craned his neck toward the curtain. Inside, Annie was nearly finished with her protestations of love and concern.

"How do you feel?" he heard her ask.

"Wally's dead."

"That can't be. I'm sure he's in another room somewhere."

St. Germain whispered something that Marlow didn't catch.

"You came all the way out here with Wally Jeffcoat?" Annie said. "Why?"

"The Beausoleil murder . . . make the arrest."

"But what went wrong?"

". . . My fault."

"I really can't allow this to go on any longer," the doctor said.

"Why was it your f—"

"I'm going for the guard, to have you both removed right now."

". . . Coward," was all Marlow heard over the clatter of indignant footfalls.

The doctor came out stuffing rubber gloves inside his scrub suit. He went into the solarium and circled behind Marlow, who was chatting amiably with an overweight man in a rent-a-cop's blue tunic. "You can go in," he said, "but only for a few minutes. He really must get some rest."

Annie looked away from a blackened window. "How is he?"

"Strong as an ox or two. You'll have to take my word for it, though. He doesn't seem that way now and won't for some time."

As Annie and Marlow walked past the elevators, a bell sounded and a green arrow lit up above the doors. Ray Beausoleil stepped out, looking rumpled and drained. "I came as soon as I heard. I had to see him."

"He's down the hall," Marlow said. "But don't expect a lot of conversation. His jaw's just been wired."

Beausoleil squeezed ahead and marched inside 302. He tore back the nearest curtain, stared at the legless old man as if his worst nightmare had been realized, and went quickly to the bed at the window. "Lieutenant St. Germain," he said, offering his hand, "I want to express my profound appreciation to the man who brought in my daughter's killer at no little cost to himself."

St. Germain rubbed his jaw. He looked at the outstretched hand, but didn't reach for it.

Beausoleil stood closer to the bed. "I understand how you feel. I suppose I was a bit out of line at the sheriff's office. But you can't . . . you should never have to know what I was going through. Losing Becky that way, it was like someone had twisted a screwdriver in my heart. I hope . . ."

"Hey, can't you let a fellow catch some sleep in here?" The words were sloppy, sibilant, muffled by the curtain nearest the door.

Beausoleil paid no attention. "I hope you'll find it in *your* heart to forget what I said that day."

St. Germain rubbed his jaw some more.

"Be reasonable," Beausoleil said. "I'm offering to apologize. What more do you—"

Annie stepped through the curtain. "His partner was killed making the arrest and . . ." She brought him away from the bed speaking softly into his ear. "He doesn't believe he's entitled to any praise. He blames himself for what happened."

"Who are you?" Beausoleil asked.

"The lieutenant's . . . Mrs. St. Germain."

Beausoleil's voice rose, filling a vacuum. "That's preposterous. The man's a hero. He tracked down my daughter's killer when no one else was even looking in the right place and made the arrest disregarding his own safety. I want everyone to know how he handled this. There'll be a news conference in Montpelier. I'll put the word out all over."

Annie shook her head. "That's the last thing he wants."

"Leave everything to me. I know what he needs, what it will

take to restore his spirits." He glanced inside the curtain again. "I'll be seeing you soon, Lieutenant, when you're feeling more yourself. In the meantime, keep your chin up."

On the way out, Beausoleil bumped into Marlow leaning against the windowsill. "That's a fine boy you have here, Sheriff," he said. "A real go-getter. Count on me to make sure there isn't a citizen of this state who doesn't find out exactly what he's done."

On a cold, wet morning forty rookies from the state police academy assembled on the walks around St. Ignatius's Roman Catholic Church at the eastern end of Main Street, between the public library and the firehouse. Others milled about the adjacent schoolyard where workmen had mounted loudspeakers on the backboards and now were setting up rows of folding chairs, trying to keep up with a crowd that already was spilling over into the street. Inside the sanctuary, the governor, county commissioners, and brass from police departments throughout the state filled the cramped pews while family and friends of Wally Jeffcoat stood beneath stained-glass windows showing the stations of the cross. St. Germain and Marlow sat stiffly in the front row in their dress uniforms. Across the aisle a slender woman entirely in black, her small features puffy with tears, clung to two toddlers who were too excited to keep still.

Annie couldn't take her eyes off them. "Nobody told me Wally was married."

"Me either," St. Germain said through clenched teeth.

"She's very pretty."

"Her name's Lenore," Marlow said. "From Vergennes, originally. They would have been together five years next month."

"And I certainly didn't hear anything about children."

"Those were his brother's kids," Marlow said. "Wally adopted them after the parents were killed in a car crash in Plattsburgh."

"God," St. Germain whispered, "he had a whole life I wasn't even aware of."

At the altar the priest stared out over the flag-draped coffin. "Deputy Jeffcoat was someone special among a company of men whose profession marks them as unique because of the dedication of their lives in the service of us all."

Annie pulled a tissue from her pocketbook and dabbed at her eyes. Someone coughed in back, and then Art Gray was moving toward the altar. He adjusted the microphone, tapped it and blew into it. He said, "Wally was a cop's cop. To him, being a policeman was more than just a job." Gray cleared his throat. "He always cared about the guys and everybody loved Wally."

"Hearing it," Marlow said under his breath, "you'd almost think Art had been civil to Wally when he was alive."

"Why did you have him deliver the eulogy?" Annie asked.

"The widow wanted Larry to represent the men. She didn't know he can hardly talk. When we get to Precious Blood, though, it'll be Larry who gives her the flag from the coffin."

St. Germain's head snapped toward Marlow. "I don't want . . . I can't do that, John."

"You will, though, won't you?"

"I wouldn't feel right about it. I hardly knew him."

"You knew him as well as anyone," Marlow said. "You were there when he died."

Marlow and St. Germain followed pallbearers from eight law enforcement agencies who brought the casket past a uniformed honor guard and placed it inside the hearse. Then a half-mile procession of motorcycles and cruisers led the way to *La Cimitière du Sang Précieux.*

"The priest will say a short prayer at the grave and you'll fold the flag and present it to the widow," Marlow said. "I'm going to give her the department's medal of valor."

"I can't. Don't ask me."

"You're putting your foot down on this?"

St. Germain nodded vigorously.

"I'll get Dick Vann," Marlow said. "But I'd sure like to know what's gotten into you."

After the ceremony Marlow walked to the crowd of mourners where St. Germain was holding hands with Annie. "I almost forgot," he said. "In light of what happened, the county's giving you an expenses-paid vacation to Florida. You can go to the Keys like you planned and take all the time you want to get back your health. Everything's on us. How does that sound?"

"We're very grateful," Annie said.

"We'll stay here." St. Germain looked as if he had taken a body blow. ". . . Use up the time I've got coming and . . . it's all I need."

7

St. Germain tossed the newspaper into Annie's lap and shut off the TV. "Think I'll get lost for a few hours."

Annie looked at the front page, said nothing.

"Did you hear?"

"Yes, I heard. I've heard it every afternoon at four for the last two weeks. Care to tell me where you're going?"

"Out."

"Oh." Not real angry, not pleased either. "Now I see."

St. Germain went to the door. He put on a green Goretex parka, down mittens, and the fur-lined uniform cap from which he had removed his shield so that the outline stood out darkly against the faded cloth.

"Damn it, Larry, why are you being so mysterious?"

"Just be gone a short while," he said, and kissed her lightly.

"What do you want for supper? Can you at least tell me that?"

St. Germain touched his fingers to his jaw, grimaced. "Cream of mushroom."

She watched him go to the car. December had come with hip-deep snow, and he waded between the drifts with high steps that were almost dainty, as if nothing could be worse than cold feet. Nothing except for him to look awkward or uncertain, anything less than the perfect physical specimen in control of whatever came his way. And which, because he came close to pulling it off, was what made him so maddeningly attractive and, most of the time, impossible to live with. He took her Subaru, the four-wheel-drive job, plowed out of the yard, and was gone. Annie went back to the TV and watched the tail end of the soap opera she had been drowsing through. Maybe it wasn't a bad idea for him to have someplace to go each day, before his mind started to turn flabby, like hers. . . .

She busied herself with the carpet sweeper, lugging it clumsily over the floor. No, she would be the first to admit, she wasn't the world's greatest housekeeper. But maid service hadn't been part of the deal when she had agreed to come back. For three years they'd been married—it hadn't been part of the deal then either—and then one day they weren't. Why, she still wasn't sure. There had been a few casual affairs, one with Dick Vann that Larry didn't know about and never would. But those were symptoms, hardly the cause of their breakup. Most of it she blamed on police work—Larry so wrapped up in the department that living with him was like rooming with a large pet unable to express itself except to demand affection (though not often enough) and food. When she had moved back eight months after the divorce was final, her mother had wanted to know how she could live with a man she wasn't married to, a stranger. She had no answer for that. Larry had promised to change, of course, but she'd known better than to believe he could. More likely, she simply had missed him, missed his playfullness and the rock-hard body and the way he'd force himself on her when she didn't even know she wanted him—so that she had come to believe he understood her better than she did herself and was keeping her most intimate secrets from her for perverse reasons of his own. And for a while Larry *had* seemed to be opening up, to be there for her. But then Wally Jeffcoat had gone down and with him the lines of communication between her and Larry, and now when she asked him what was troubling him, he would point to his jaw and shake his head. The words came easily enough when it suited him, though, the time she smacked up the Subaru, or when the house looked like it was starting to fall apart from the inside out. She wondered where he went each afternoon, if he was with another woman. Okay— if that was what it took to bring him out of his funk, to make him happier than she knew how—but that didn't mean she had to like it.

She dropped the sweeper, slipped into her coat, and ran out to the yard. Larry had left the keys in the turbocharger with the usual warning that she wasn't to go near it except in the most extreme emergency. She slid onto the seat, brushing aside the touring skis they had taken into the country after the last blizzard. She twisted the key and shifted carefully into drive. The engine growled, but the car scarcely budged. Damn you, Larry, she thought, and then remembered to release the emergency brake.

She steered away from the house, following the Subaru's narrow tread. When she came to the highway, she looked both ways, and seeing no sign of him went to the interstate. She turned west automatically and shaded her eyes against the remaining sun. She kept the turbocharger at an even sixty, hoping none of John's deputies spotted her, so she wouldn't have to hand them an improbable story that would get back to Larry before he was even home.

A woman in a blue Ford gawked at her from the fast lane and she hunched over the wheel. Up ahead she thought she made out the snubbed silhouette of the Subaru, but as she came up she saw that it was a Mazda, 50,000 miles too new and the wrong color, and she pushed the turbocharger to seventy and moved away from traffic. Where the interstate started its climb into the mountains, she spotted another foreign compact, and this time there was no mistaking its battered rear end. She came off the gas with a prayer that Larry wasn't looking in the mirror, not letting herself relax until the sun dipped below the distant Adirondacks.

The Subaru was headed for Burlington. If Larry had a lady there, he'd kept the secret well; it was news to her if he knew anyone in the city. The boy who had shot Wally was supposed to live somewhere nearby. But what would bring Larry all the way out here now that the boy was locked up in jail?

They bypassed Burlington for a broken road toward the lake. She dropped back until she nearly lost sight of the Subaru, then picked out its high beams playing against the maples at the edge of the blacktop. She braked and killed her lights, straining against the gloom as Larry stepped out. He opened the trunk, dropped something she couldn't see in the snow and crouched down. When he stood up again he began walking in the woods with his legs wide apart, swinging them out from his hips as if he'd wet his pants.

Snowshoes . . . Larry was going for a hike in his old, warped Bearpaws. But why all the secrecy and why here, when there was more snow than anyone could want behind the cabin? Watching him disappear behind a tumbledown stone fence, she slid her skis out of the cruiser. Her boots were in the back seat along with cans of the blue wax and the red. What was the color of the day, she wondered, for spying on your ex-husband? She carried the gear through a gap in the stones and fastened the bindings.

The snow was soft and dry, untracked save for the faint crosshatch of the Bearpaws. With calves still aching from Sunday's trek, she moved cumbersomely. She forced herself to pole harder, trying to work out the soreness, but had to slow down when she came up on Larry. Head down, he was taking short, choppy strides, in too much of a hurry to enjoy himself. What had brought him to these black and lonely fields? Hardly the exercise, she thought. He hadn't been home from the hospital ten days when he'd thrown away his sling and begun pedaling to California and back on the stationary bicycle in the living room. Whatever it was, he was searching in the wrong place. For she saw it hiding in the brooding silence that made him a greater mystery to himself than she ever had been, and whose rare breaches bound them more closely together even as they forced his awful secrets deeper inside.

She glided through a dying sugar bush, avoiding the twisted roots that protruded like trip wires through the snow. When she looked for Larry again, he was gone. The Bearpaws had left a trail even she could follow, but the trees stood too close together to ski between and she plodded into brush that snagged her clothes, tore a pocket. In the first light of the moon through sparse clouds, she spotted him at a pile of brush. He examined the debris and then kicked at it, falling as the Bearpaw caught in the twigs. Without dusting himself off, he adjusted the strap around his shoe and went deeper into the woods.

Where the pines were rooted farther apart, Annie got back into her skis. She found him in a field of corn stubble, tilting his head as if he were reading the wind. He whirled around without warning and she froze against a tree. His face was a blur that she would have emptied her wallet for a good look at. He turned and trudged out of the field, and when she dared follow he was almost at the lake. Conceding him another fifty yards, she stopped to pull off a mitten and wipe her nose with the back of her hand.

A shield of ice pressed down on the water, the deep snow on top so inviting that she gladly would have trailed him to the far shore. Instead, he kept to the beach where there was barely enough cover to keep from damaging the Bearpaws. For no reason she could see, he picked up the pace, so that it seemed he was running away. Not from her, though—no way he suspected she was there. She dug her poles faster, struggling to keep up.

The beach ended in a rocky wall from which frozen ground-water hung in yellowish veils. Standing in its shadow, Annie watched him move confidently over the ice, then stop to glance over his shoulder, stop and look back again. She waited till he was at the mouth of the cove, then tugged her knit hat down over her ears and poled onto the lake. She enjoyed the chase, this game of Fox and Hounds with Larry—or would have if his pain weren't so obvious.

A wooded outcrop wandered away from the land and she lost him again on the other side. The temptation was to let him play by himself while she explored the bay from shore to shore. But a knot tightening in her stomach was a reminder that they weren't playing, and she pistoned her arms in time with her legs, her heels rising and falling mechanically, until she came around the promonotory and stopped as suddenly as if all her strength had been drained.

Ice fishing shanties, more than she ever had seen in one place before, were clustered on the lake like a boomtown thrown up overnight. Weak light seeped from narrow windows and came back brighter from pickup trucks circled inward like an idling wagon train. She scented woodsmoke and kerosene that was palpable in sooty curls trapped beneath the clouds. Why, she wanted to know, did Larry come to Lake Champlain when his own neat shack was waiting so close to the cabin? And why hadn't he told her where he went? And why the long hike instead of parking on the ice like everyone else? And why, come to think of it, had he never brought home any fish?

She was about to call out to him when he skirted the lights, making for another beach where a lone shanty listed despondently on broken runners. He leaned the Bearpaws against a wall and entered where the door should have been. When he came out a moment later, she knew better than to come near. He was reaching for the stovepipe, sweeping his hands against rough boards. In the other she made out the sullen glint of his new gun, a heavy .44 John had let him have while his service revolver lay tagged in an evidence locker. He hauled himself onto the roof and lay flat, fingering the strange gun as he pondered its capabilities. Then his face was illuminated in a flash from the muzzle and she saw him drop to the snow. A man dressed all in army surplus came out of the shack closest to her with a bucket of silvery fish. "It's five-thirty, you can set your watch by it," he said in her direction. "The nut's by the old shanty, shooting again."

She began poling to the shore. Her face was damp with nervous sweat, her clothes cold against her skin with the sweeter perspiration of physical exertion. "Larry?"

He cringed, then walked away as if he had heard nothing.

"Larry St. Germain, stop right there."

To her surprise, he did, jamming the gun in his parka. "How'd you know I was here?" His face was still a blur.

She stepped onto the beach, dropped her poles as she came up to him.

"You followed me." He held his jaw rigid, moving his lips like a second-rate ventriloquist."Why?"

"Did it ever occur to you I might be worried by the way you've been acting, disappearing for hours every afternoon, not breathing a word what you were up to?"

"You shouldn't've come here."

Annie showed the back of her hand, fluttered it as if she was brushing away crumbs. "This is where the boy chased you that night, isn't it, the night he killed Wally Jeffcoat?"

"Let's go back to the car."

"Larry, answer me."

She blocked the way with her body, put a ski tip over the Bearpaws. "Are you going to tell me what you're doing?"

"Please," he said, "you have to trust me on this. I need you to . . . to . . ."

"To what?"

"To understand."

"But I don't understand. How can I when you won't tell me—"

"I was looking for something," he said.

"For something you lost that night?"

St. Germain nodded.

"In the dark? Did you think you'd find it in that pile of brush in the woods?"

"You saw me there?"

"I saw everything," she said. "Well, did you?"

"Part of it. I lost bits and pieces everywhere."

"Can't you just say what it was?" Letting the exasperation show, letting it work for her.

"My honor," he said. She moved her ski away and he backed off. "Wally'd be alive today, none of this would've happened if I hadn't let it."

"Nonsense. John told me everything, and there's no way anybody would have acted differently. You can't blame yourself."

"John wasn't there. If I hadn't waved Wally into the yard, if I'd've been thinking of something besides saving my own skin . . ." His face was drenched in sweat, wetter than hers. "The only reason Wally's dead is I'm gutless. That's the God's honest truth."

"You shouldn't say things like—"

"I'd never been in a spot like that, didn't know I could react so bad." The words rushed out as if they had broken through the wires that had kept them welled up. "Soon as Conklin had my gun, I knew I was a dead man, *knew* it, Ann, just like I knew there was nothing I could do about it. All that mattered was to keep breathing a second longer and then the second after that."

He knelt to tighten his snowshoes and began walking along the beach. She picked up her poles and pushed after him.

"Wally looked up to me. He was counting on me, and I let him down. I violated all the rules of police procedure . . . of being a man. That's something I'm going to have to live with. I only wish Conklin'd shot me right there."

"I don't believe you."

"You weren't there either."

She had no reply to that. They went silently to the edge of the trees, and then she said, "What good is it to come back every day and climb on top of that shanty and fire John's gun? To replay that night? You can't, you know. What happened, happened."

His lips worked feverishly, but he was out of words, and he moved ahead of her again with long strides. "It's not your problem," he finally said.

"Whose is it, then? 'For better or for worse, in sickness and in health.' Sound familiar?"

"Aren't you forgetting something?"

"Like what?"

"We're not married anymore."

"I didn't think it mattered. When you were on the roof with that gun and I didn't know if you were going to blow your brains out, do you think I was worried less because of something some judge said? Everything is the same to me."

"It's not, though. It hasn't been since you and Dick Vann."

She crossed her ski tips and tumbled in the thin snow, and he came over and held out his hand. She batted it away and rolled onto her side, straightened her skis without help and got up. "How long have you known?"

"Longer 'n I care to."

She forced herself to meet his gaze, to hold it. "Why didn't you say anything?"

"To you, Ann, or to Dick?" He whisked the snow off her back, slapped her harder than he had to. "Either one of you, the way I felt I'd likely 've ended up where Paul Conklin is now."

"And still you let me move in again."

"I was more miserable without you. That, or the same reason I did nothing when Conklin had the drop on me."

"Thanks a lot."

"*You're* pissed?"

She began poling again, keeping a few feet behind him, her anger used up before it had gotten very far. "Nervous," she said softly. "I was always afraid what you'd do if it came out."

"So was I. Guess the joke's on both of us."

"I still am. Can't we put it in the past with what happened here that night? Do I have to tell you how I feel, how badly I want your baby?"

"Breaking up, that was another of your ideas."

"So was coming back," she said.

He walked into the trees. She watched him slip out of the Bearpaws and then skied after him. "Are you telling me to go again? Do you want—"

"Want what?" he asked without looking at her.

"Nothing." He heard her sniffling, laughing at the same time. "Damn it, Larry, I was going to ask if you wanted a divorce."

The weave was flawless, the brown threads matched perfectly to the sleeve so that the hole was nearly invisible. St. Germain rolled down the cloth, wincing as the new stitches fell against the tender spot below the elbow, the shirt's scar on his own. He fastened the cuff and then the other one, and as he pinched the collar together was surprised to find an extra inch of cloth between his fingers. Well, he thought, maybe Annie was good with buttons, too. He strapped on the heavy gun. As he shut the locker, the weapon slapped against his thigh. He adjusted the holster until it rode against the point of his hip and went upstairs.

Marlow was standing with his back to the door, stooped over the low table beside the file cabinets. At St. Germain's "Morning, John," he spun around quickly and a stack of coffee filters sailed onto the floor like paper parachutes. St. Germain came inside with his forearm against the holster, holding the new gun in place. Marlow grabbed his hand and pumped it. "Hello, stranger," he said. "What kind of shape are you in these days?"

St. Germain debated it for a while. "The arm's fine. Got a sore spot where the bullet went in and a bigger one where it came out. But I hardly know they're there unless I'm looking for them."

"What about your jaw?" Marlow turned back to the coffee maker that lay on its side with the plug dangling from a torn electric cord.

St. Germain cupped his chin with the heel of his hand. "The wires didn't come off till last week. I'm still getting used to solid food again. First few days all I did was chew steak and Annie's ear off, till I got a charley horse and had to rub Ben-Gay on my face. It twinges if I gab too much. I just might take the hint."

"It's good to have you back, even if you are damaged goods," Marlow said, and there was an uncomfortable silence that lasted until he began retrieving the filters, blowing off the dust as he piled them beside the broken coffee machine. He slipped the plug from the cord and showed it to St. Germain. "What do you know about small appliance repair?"

"Nothing."

"Don't see how you'll ever make sheriff," he said, allowing a smile as an afterthought. "Well, maybe we can find something else for you to do. We've been falling farther behind every day you've been gone. You didn't return when you did, I don't know that we'd ever catch up."

"Catch up with who? Last month's speeders?"

Marlow didn't laugh. "You sure you're ready to go back on patrol? You still look a little peaked, if you don't mind my saying so."

"It's what I'm here for, John."

"I know that. Till you get your sea legs back, though, I'm putting you on limited duty."

"Doing what?" St. Germain's jaw clicked painfully.

"Breaking in the new fellow, for one," Marlow said. "We found a youngster to replace Wally, a Ewells Mills boy with two years at Castleton College who seems to thrive on starvation wages. I want you to show him the ropes."

St. Germain fought the urge to rub his jaw. "That's hardly the kind of action I was looking to get back to those weeks I was laid up."

"It has to be done," Marlow said. "I can't think of anybody who'd do it better."

"Why bother? Wally picked up everything on his own."

"Yes, and maybe that's how come he ended up the way he did." Marlow tore the plug from the cord and cleaned out the bits of copper wire. "It's what I want, so let's not argue. The kid's upstairs, banging his head against the accident reports."

In the bullpen an overweight young man with muscular arms ending in long and bony hands, about a two-octave span, sat at a pile of paperwork almost to his chin. He slid out of his chair and had started to rise when Marlow motioned him to stay where he was. "Vaughn Halvorsen, this is Lieutenant St. Germain, my chief deputy."

Again the young man stood, and this time he made it all the way up. To St. Germain he looked young enough to be *Wally's* kid brother.

"Good to have you on."

"The lieutenant's going to give you a refresher on reports and court papers and then walk you through some more of your duties."

"I can really use the help." Halvorsen's voice was brittle and reedy, and St. Germain supposed that it cracked when he was excited, which probably was often. "Some of these crashes have got me all bolixed up."

Marlow started into the corridor. St. Germain stopped him with a hand on his shoulder. "John, I'd like a word with you." They walked toward the water cooler, and St. Germain said, "Mind telling me what's going on?"

"Someone has to wet-nurse him. As long as you're not up to par—"

"Why not Dick, or Art, or any of the others? You don't know how bad I'm itching to get back to work . . . to real work."

"Soon," Marlow said. "For now, do this and quit bellyaching." He lowered his head and let the water run against his lips, swallowed some. "There've been changes since you were gone, Larry. Had to be."

"What changes?" St. Germain's hand flew to his throbbing jaw.

"We ran short-handed way too long and I had to divide your responsibilities among the men. Feel flattered it's taking four or five of them to do it all. But you can't expect me to bust them down the instant you come back, not without a mutiny." He bent for another sip. "Besides, in case you haven't stood in front of a mirror lately, it might not hurt to go slow for a while. Taking it easy after what you've been through is nothing to be ashamed of."

"Doing accident reports? Charging road hogs? That's for kids like Wally, who don't know which end of the gun the bullets come out."

"Don't they?"

St. Germain forgot what he was about to say. Massaging his jaw, he drifted away from Marlow, went back to the bullpen.

The pile of paper in front of Vaughn Halvorsen seemed to have climbed to his eyes. St. Germain moved a chair beside him and inspected the reports the rookie had completed on his own. "I can see you weren't a penmanship major at Castleton State," he said.

"No, sir. Animal husbandry."

St. Germain put down his pen. On second thought, Halvorsen was not likely to get excited about anything, wouldn't have the sense to focus his eyes if there was a gun pointed between them—and so probably would work out all right. "Never mind. Let me show you what you do with these and maybe we can be out of here sometime this afternoon, put in a few hours on patrol."

Forty-five minutes later, the pile looked higher. St. Germain loosened his tie and pushed the reports away. He said, "You'd better take some home with you, Halvorsen. Else you won't get finished before you're pensioned off."

"Whatever you say, sir. All right if I go in the hall for a drink?"

"You don't have to ask."

St. Germain pulled another report and was correcting it when Art Gray came inside the bullpen. A frayed gun belt hung over his shoulder, and the buckle was in his hand, and he was muttering. When he saw St. Germain, he began to smile. "Well, look who's here," he said. "How you doing, cowboy?"

St. Germain let the report fall from his fingers. "What's that supposed to mean?"

"Long time no—" Gray did a halfhearted double take. "Huh?"

"You think it's funny?"

Gray hunched his shoulders, showed his palms to the empty corner of the bullpen. He went to his locker and was rummaging inside when St. Germain walked away from the table and came up behind him. "You didn't answer the question, Art."

Gray turned to face him blankly. "You sure you're feeling okay?"

"That does it." St. Germain sent out a looping roundhouse that caught Gray under the ear. His head snapped back and collided with the locker door with a dull *thunk,* but he didn't go down. St. Germain reeled in his fist, examined it as if it were out of order, and never saw Gray's right. It landed high on his cheek, sending shafts of familiar pain into the knitting break in his jaw, and then they were grappling, toppling to the floor.

Art Gray grunted. "Marlow didn't say you'd got your brains scrambled, too."

Gray squirmed on top and St. Germain bucked him off, forced him onto his back and straddled him, digging both knees into his chest. He threw a short punch Gray trapped in his palm and another that got through to his heart. Gray exhaled hoarsely and grabbed St. Germain by the collar. Two buttons popped and St. Germain heard a ripping sound before a rabbit punch rattled his kidneys, and he knew that Annie would kill him if Art Gray didn't do it first. He chopped down and saw redness between his fingers. More, much more squirted from Gray's nose.

"Give," Gray said.

St. Germain held his punch. "Let's hear it again."

"Give up, chickenshit?" Laughing at him, Gray tossed a jab to the chin that St. Germain rolled with, but not far enough; another shot like that and he'd be spooning cream of mushroom again. He drew back his right. Before he could land it, heavy hands had him by the shoulders and were lifting him to his feet.

"Let go, damn it."

"Not till you start acting like adults."

St. Germain recognized Dick Vann's nasal tenor. He pivoted quickly with his hand still doubled into a fist. Rather than let it go to waste, he swung wildly, catching Vann in the midsection. He drove the stocky man into the barred doors, bringing his head up sharply into Vann's face as Gray jumped on his back and the three of them crashed into a cell.

"Big fucking hero," Vann said, kneeing him in the ribs. "Where were you when your partner was getting killed?"

St. Germain butted Vann again, and his forehead was bathed

in warmth as blood gushed from the other man's mouth. He was trying to elbow Gray off his shoulders when Marlow's "Quit it! Now!" echoed off the bars.

Marlow stormed inside the bullpen and pulled Gray from the pile. St. Germain stood up shakily, and then Vann pushed himself off the floor. He spit out some blood and put a finger in his mouth, jiggled an incisor like an overgrown child dreading a visit from the tooth fairy. In the doorway Vaughn Halvorsen took it all in, his chin as slack as if he had caught a punch.

"What happened here?" Marlow demanded.

"Nothing," Art Gray said, sinking into the seat behind the accident reports.

Marlow was steaming. "Larry, what were you idiots up to?"

St. Germain tapped his jaw and shook his head.

"Somebody had better answer, or I'll have the three of you swamping toilets in the holding pen at the courthouse till you do." He took a close look at Vann's face and pushed it away in disgust. "Dick, do you think I'm just pissing in the wind?"

Vann blotted a cracked lip on his sleeve. "When I came in, these two were going at it like a cat and a rat. I tried to pull them apart and got sucker-punched for my trouble."

"That how it happened, Art?"

Gray was cradling his head in his hands, in too much pain to talk.

"Larry?"

"They were laughing at—"

"If you have something to say, say it."

St. Germain lowered his eyes, studied his shoes.

"You'd better come with me," Marlow said, "because I've got plenty to say to you." With a last look at the others he nudged St. Germain outside, and they went to the water fountain, where St. Germain washed blood off his hands. In the bullpen Gray was saying loud enough for everyone to hear, "You ought to be more particular about the company you keep,

Halvorsen, if you don't want to end up like Wally Jeffcoat did."

Downstairs, Marlow went to his desk for a Band-Aid. He tore the wrapper with his teeth and plastered the flesh-colored strip an inch below St. Germain's hairline. "You enjoy getting the stuffing knocked out of you? Is this something you plan to do on a regular basis?"

"I had them where I wanted them, John." Grinning, St. Germain made a fist for Marlow's benefit. "If you hadn't ordered everyone to a neutral corner, you'd've really seen something."

"It never fails to amaze me how a head as big as yours comes equipped with such limited capacity for reason." A red smudge colored the end of Marlow's nose, and he flicked at it like it was a fly, then wet a finger with his tongue and rubbed it away. "You're hardly in a position to throw your weight around, so what do you do? Right off, you mix it up with my best men."

St. Germain flattened his hand and used it to feel behind him for a slatted chair. On the way, he remembered to stop grinning.

"Dick and Art might not have had much use for Wally Jeffcoat," Marlow said, "but they've gauged the mood of the men when they act like he's the most sainted officer in the history of the department. This is no time for you to be picking fights."

St. Germain kneaded his arm where the bullet had gone through. "They're jerks. Who gives a damn what they think?"

"I won't quarrel with that," Marlow said. "But, to be blunt, you've lost a lot of respect here. I don't know that you'll ever get it back."

"All the guys came to see me in the hospital. It never occurred to me they blamed . . ." He rolled up the sleeve. A fresh bruise was blending into the redness of the scar, and he covered it again quickly. "Maybe it'd be best if I go back to the cabin till things blow over, till I'm feeling more myself." He shut his eyes, thinking about it. "I'd like that."

"If you were feeling any more yourself, the building would

have come down during that wrestling match in the bullpen. No, now that you've put in an appearance, I want you every day. And I expect you to find a way to get along with Dick and Art if you have to kiss their butts to do it."

He felt let down, cheated of something that should always have been his. He put his feet flat on the floor, held onto the chair. "I'm still entitled to some vacation time. I think it'd be best if I took it now."

"You're entitled to nothing. Conklin's prelim comes up in three weeks and we have to start prepping your testimony."

St. Germain mopped his forehead with his sleeve, saw crimson streaks in the moisture. "Nobody said anything . . ."

"Then let me. Old Jess Whitehead has taken Conklin's case, and Ray Beausoleil says their best shot is to make your professionalism, or the lack of it, the cornerstone of their defense. They're going to try to show it was a screw-up on your part that brought on Wally's death. And if they eat you up on the stand on this one, your testimony in Becky's killing won't be worth diddly."

St. Germain forced a bitter laugh. "Shouldn't be much of a problem for them, should it?"

"I wouldn't know. But if a jury comes back with anything less than guilty of first-degree murder, Wally died for nothing." He leaned across the desk. "Or do you want to fight about that, too?"

Annie sat under the floor lamp with her sewing box emptied all around her, pushing small, precise stitches into a pair of brown trousers. When St. Germain walked in, she held the pose and then stood up, her lips catching his cheek as he went by. "I'm getting pretty good at this," she said, lifting the pants by a leg, "don't you think?"

St. Germain hung his coat on the door and put his hat up after it, stepped deliberately into the light.

"What happened to your forehead?" She tried to keep cool, dropping her voice a notch with every word. Still under control, she reached into a pocket for a tissue to brush away the dried blood, and when she looked at him again she lost it. "Oh, no," she blurted, "your shirt. I worked so hard. . . ."

St. Germain went to the couch, fell back on its thin cushion. "Sorry, Ann."

She sat beside him and went to work on his face. "You just got out of a sickbed. John didn't put you on something dangerous right away, did he?"

"Dangerous enough. He let me come back. The men hate my guts because of what happened to Wally." He tore off the Band-Aid himself. "And I don't blame them."

"You're being ridiculous," she said, dabbing at the wound. "How can they think like that after what you went through? How many would have done as well in the same situation?" She tried to measure the effect of her argument, but he hardly seemed to be listening. "What did John say you should do?"

"He despises me as much as any of them."

"*John* does? Now I know you're imagining things."

"He doesn't want me around. He'd ask for my badge if he didn't need me in uniform for my testimony against Conklin. Soon everyone'll know."

"If he's undercut your authority, how can he expect you to win back the men's respect?"

"He doesn't. I'm a kiddie cop now, breaking in rookies." St. Germain stripped off his shirt. "Any way you can salvage this?"

She spread the shredded cloth under the light and then dropped it. "Use it for a rag. Well, what are you going to do?" she asked impatiently.

St. Germain picked the shirt up off the floor. He wadded it into a ball and tossed it in the fireplace, watched the orange flames come alive as they started to eat at the patched sleeve.

"Doesn't matter," he said. "I never looked good in brown anyhow."

In his tailored robes and silver-blue hair Chittenden District Judge Burton L. Leeds reminded St. Germain of nothing so much as a TV evangelist offering eternal salvation on easy terms. These seemed to include quiet in his court, and when it was slow in coming he banged his gavel a dozen times. He rustled his papers and poured ice water from a copper pitcher, slipped on eyeglasses with unstylish black frames from the long years he had spent clerking before a new administration swept him onto the bench. "Pursuant to Chapter 26," he intoned in a rumbling lament, a preacher whose ratings would never be high, "sections ten through fourteen of the Vermont General Laws . . ."

St. Germain looked anxiously around, as though he were expecting someone to take his ticket. The only other courtroom he had seen the inside of was the one in Tremont Center with its club chairs, scuffed linoleum, and incandescent lighting from the demolished Coolidge Street School. The Burlington court had hardwood balustrades and was as vast and imposing as "The People's Court." Across the aisle, dressed in slacks and a sports coat that his attorney must have picked for him, picked out of the children's department, Paul Conklin was doodling on a yellow legal pad. With his ears protruding from a brand-new haircut and his wrists from sleeves too short for his arms, he looked about fifteen years old. From time to time he glanced back at his brother in the first row of seats, winking and making faces when he thought no one was looking. Jess Whitehead sat confidently beside him, a seventy-year-old country lawyer in an $800 Armani suit.

"The purpose of this hearing is not to determine the guilt or innocence of the accused, but to find out if enough evidence exists to bind him over to the grand jury whose function it is

to decide if he should stand trial. The defense will call no witnesses, but may question the state's witnesses if it desires."
Leeds addressed the table in front of St. Germain's side of the
courtroom. "Mr. Corcoran, are you ready to proceed?"

Thomas Corcoran, the assistant state's attorney for Chittenden County, popped out of his chair like a groundhog scurrying
to check the weather and relaxing only when he didn't spot his
shadow. "Yes, I am, your honor."

"Mr. Whitehead?"

"Ready, your honor."

The way Leeds looked from one attorney to the other, he
could have been explaining the mandatory eight-count rule in
the event of a knockdown and the necessity of defending oneself
at all times. Then he nodded toward a bailiff who stood before
the bench and called Gordon Hall, the Malletts Bay man who
had discovered Jeffcoat's body.

Hall spoke in a scratchy voice like a soft tire on a gravel road.
As he recounted coming upon the wreck of the Brown Bomber,
St. Germain looked over again at Conklin. The boy was scrib-
bling enthusiastically on his pad as though he had just the questions Jess Whitehead would need when he went up against the
witness. But when he tore off the page he tilted it toward his
brother, and St. Germain saw a rough drawing of Judge Leeds
with a pointed beard and devil's horns sprouting from his razor-
cut hair.

After Hall had finished his story, there were no questions
from the defense. St. Germain decided that both sides were
treating the early testimony as part of a feeling-out process, the
first round in a tactical battle that would not be decided with
a quick knockout—as Leeds seemed to have warned. Then the
bailiff called Dr. Paul Rosenthal, the Chittenden County medical examiner, who approached with one arm held straight
down, the hand curled slightly, toting an invisible black bag. It
was this hand, the right, that he placed on a worn leather Bible

and muttered the few words that gained him entry to the witness stand.

Without prodding, Dr. Rosenthal told the court that at the time of his death Walter Jeffcoat was a twenty-four-year-old white male in generally good health except for small, premature fatty streaks present in the coronary arteries.

"The fatal wound was made by a .38-caliber bullet, through and through—"

"Through and through?" Corcoran seemed delighted at the opportunity to interject himself into the narrative. "Would you explain . . . ?"

"The bullet passed completely through the decedent's body," Rosenthal said without acknowledging the interruption. "It left a clean wound in the upper back and a larger, jagged one where it exited above the left nipple. The angle indicates that Deputy Jeffcoat was erect at the time he was shot, but slightly bent over, perhaps running. The bullet cut the spinal column between the third and fourth thoracic vertebrae and also penetrated the right ventricle of the heart, the intraventricular septum and the left ventricle, blew it apart."

"And the cause of death?"

"The damaged heart, loss of blood. The spinal injury would probably not have proved fatal, but means that Deputy Jeffcoat would not have had much quality to his life had he survived."

Corcoran had a few more questions, which seemed to St. Germain to serve no purpose other than to show off his grasp of pathology. Corcoran then excused the witness.

"Just a minute." Jess Whitehead rose slowly with knees in need of lubrication, but approached the stand on the balls of his feet. "Dr. Rosenthal, you describe the fatal bullet as being of .38-caliber, yet you say the wound was through and through? How can you be sure what kind of slug . . . ?"

Rosenthal did not look at the attorney. He gave no indication that he had heard the question until his lips began to move.

"The Vermont state police recovered a bullet from a mound of detritus beside the stone fence where Deputy Jeffcoat was found. The bullet had flattened on its path through the body and on impact with the soil, but was not so badly marred that it could not be subjected to ballistics comparisons. These indicated it was fired from a .38-caliber Smith and Wesson Chief's Special belonging to Lieutenant St. Germain."

"Objection." Corcoran jumped to his feet. "The witness has not been shown to be a qualified ballistics expert."

Jess Whitehead was already on his way back to the defense table. "No further questions," he said.

Paul Conklin scribbled urgently on both sides of a yellow sheet of paper. St. Germain, watching him, nearly missed hearing the bailiff call his name. He pressed his holster against his thigh as he went to the witness stand. Although he had testified in thousands of court cases (the great majority of times against suspected speeders), he listened to the oath as if he had never considered its implications before and answered hesitantly, wary of a trap, when asked if he would tell only the truth.

Corcoran was beaming like an old friend who couldn't have been more pleased to see him. "Your name, sir?"

"Lawrence St. Germain, Lieutenant, Cabot County sheriff's department. Badge number—"

"That won't be necessary, Lieutenant."

The questions came one on top of the other, like swells buoying a man in a life vest even as they threatened to pull him under. St. Germain answered mechanically, his eyes sweeping the courtroom. He picked out Marlow sitting with Ray Beausoleil, trading comments as they monitored his testimony, Beausoleil shaking his head unhappily like a theatrical producer at a cattle call.

"On the night in question," Corcoran was saying, "what brought you and Deputy Jeffcoat to Sturgeon Cove?"

"We'd gone there regarding an investigation in which we had

reason to believe Mr. Conklin might be involved." St. Germain answered as he had been coached, avoiding specific mention of Becky Beausoleil's killing which a judge in Cabot County was due to take up in two weeks. "It was decided that I would go to the Conklin house and that Deputy Jeffcoat would back me up."

"And what happened when you arrived?"

"I parked in the drive and got out and looked around, and at first it didn't seem anyone was home. But as I came back in the yard Conklin must've sneaked up from behind and pulled . . ." St. Germain shifted his gaze to the last row, to a figure in black that he recognized as Lenore Jeffcoat. "And . . . and he disarmed me, and when I . . . when Deputy Jeffcoat followed me, Conklin took his weapon away, too, and ordered both of us into his—that's Deputy Jeffcoat's cruiser . . ."

Corcoran glanced over his shoulder and moved closer to the stand to block St. Germain's view. "Where were you in relation to the others in the car?" he asked.

"I was in the passenger's seat, in front, and Wall—and Deputy Jeffcoat had the wheel. Conklin was in back. He was holding our guns."

"And what did he say?"

"Conklin?"

Corcoran was still searching for the best place to park himself. "That's right."

"He told Wally to start driving to Smugglers Notch." St. Germain stopped trying to look around him and focused on the state's attorney's vest buttons. "He said he wanted to shoot us where our bodies wouldn't be found till spring."

"Did you make it there?"

"No." Corcoran had positioned himself slightly to the left of the witness stand, and St. Germain got another look at Marlow and Ray Beausoleil. They had stopped talking and were watching him as if this were the performance they had come to see.

"Why not?"

"As we were riding out of Malletts Bay," St. Germain said, "Deputy Jeffcoat swung the car off the road and we crashed."

"He deliberately—"

"Yes, and I jumped out my side and ran off and I thought Wally was behind me, but then I heard a shot and I knew . . ." He brushed some dampness from his lip and sought out Corcoran's vest buttons again. "And I was pretty sure Conklin was firing at him. And then he was shooting at me, chasing me, and we ran for a long, long time before I finally . . . before he gave up."

The rest of it was painless, Corcoran inquiring into the nature of his injuries and the length of his hospital stay and rehabilitation and the current state of his health. Asked about his arm, St. Germain started to roll up his sleeve until Jess Whitehead offered an objection and Leeds ruled it wasn't necessary for the court to view the wound. Then the jurist announced that they would break for lunch. Almost as an afterthought Corcoran said that when they returned he would have no more questions.

St. Germain remained seated until Leeds leaned over as he might have for a lost child. "The witness is excused until one-thirty," he said. "Have yourself a nice meal. It's on the county, you know." He looked at St. Germain over the top of his glasses. "A good stiff drink or two might also serve the interests of justice."

St. Germain stepped down from the stand, searching for Lenore Jeffcoat. The woman was already gone from the courtroom, however, and Corcoran ushered him up the aisle where Marlow was in conference again with Ray Beausoleil.

"Well," Corcoran asked, "how do you rate his testimony?"

Beausoleil held out his hand, tilting it from side to side. "You look like you're in a trance up there, Lieutenant," he said. "It's one thing to let the judge know how strongly you were affected by what happened to you and your partner, but you also have to tell your story firmly, with conviction."

"I . . . I'll try to do better this afternoon."

"You'll have to," Corcoran said. "Jess is like a barricuda when he senses an unsure witness. He doesn't come in for a quick kill, just keeps tearing pieces out till he's down to bare bone. I don't imagine it's a lot of fun to have that happen to you."

"Any advice for him?" Marlow asked.

"Try not to respond too specifically to anything you're asked," Beausoleil said. "Tell your story over again the way we discussed it, letting Jess break up the recitation with his questions. No matter what, don't react to Jess's sarcasm or invective, and never, for Heaven's sake, let him lead you around like a bull with a ring in his nose."

"And if I do all that . . .?"

"Maybe the Cabot sheriff's office won't come out of this smelling any worse than it did going in."

Neither Jess Whitehead's knees nor the rest of him appeared in need of lubricating for the start of the afternoon session. As the elderly lawyer approached the stand, St. Germain couldn't miss the three-martini lunch on his breath. Whitehead kept his chin tucked against his chest, as if the bright lights of the courtroom were too much for him. But when he posed his first serious question, St. Germain saw that his eyes were clear and alert, an almost translucent blue.

"Lieutenant, you stated that as you moved through the yard Mr. Conklin took away your service revolver. Yet there's been no mention of a weapon of his own initially in Mr. Conklin's possession. What I'm having trouble with is how he was able to get your gun away when he was unarmed himself."

"He . . . uh, came up on me and placed an object against my back which . . . he said was a shotgun, a 12-gauge shotgun, and relieved me of my gun belt."

"Did, in fact, Mr. Conklin have a shotgun?"

"No, sir."

"What was it that he was holding to your back?"

"It was, I believe, a metal rod, the heavy kind used in const—"

"Not a shotgun?"

"No." St. Germain looked toward the prosecution table and, as Corcoran had that morning, Jess Whitehead moved to block his view.

"Is it common procedure for members of the Cabot County sheriff's department to surrender their weapons so easily?"

Corcoran was quickly on his feet. "Objection."

"Let me couch the question in different terms," Whitehead said. "Are you under instruction always to give up your weapon in such a situation?"

"I don't know that there are strict guidelines. It's something I guess each officer has to decide for himself."

"So you're saying it was your choice to hand over your service revolver before determining what it was Mr. Conklin allegedly held in his hands."

St. Germain nodded.

"I didn't catch your answer, Lieutenant."

"Yes," St. Germain said.

"Now, if I may again refer back to your testimony of this morning . . ." Whitehead scarcely looked at him, as though his admission had made him unworthy. "You stated that Officer Jeffcoat had accompanied you to Malletts Bay in a back-up role. Which, I presume, means he was there to pull you out of trouble if trouble came up. Yet after your gun was taken away from you, he went openly into the yard and was disarmed himself. Why would he do something like that?"

St. Germain paused. So did Jess Whitehead, waiting him out, outlasting him.

"I signaled to him."

Whitehead pounced on it. "You signaled him into the yard

after your gun was gone, knowing he would be placed in the same unenviable situation?"

"Yes."

"Is that also common practice in Cabot County?"

"Object—"

"Was that part of the strategy you had worked out with Officer Jeffcoat before you came to Malletts Bay?"

"No."

"In point of fact, Lieutenant, didn't the original plan call for you to meet with Chittenden deputies so there would be sufficient manpower available in the event anything went wrong?"

"Yes."

"Then where were they?"

St. Germain stared in Marlow's direction and, as he had hoped, Whitehead moved between them. "I changed the plan," he said softly, as if it were their secret. "I didn't think they'd be needed."

"And that was a decision you had the authority to make on your own?"

"I . . . it was my decision. Yes."

"Just as it was your decision to signal Officer Jeffcoat to drive up when you had been disarmed and there was a gun pointed at you?"

Again St. Germain didn't answer right away. He looked to Corcoran, but got no help.

"Lieutenant?"

So it wasn't Conklin's actions that were at issue, but only his own. "You weren't there," he said.

"The question, Lieutenant St. Germain, is—"

"You could never understand the situation I was in. Conklin was out of his mind, dying to pull the trigger, hoping I'd give him reason to. He'd hurt me bad, had everything on his side. I needed time, a chance to figure out what to do. I don't remember waving to Wally, just him pulling up in his car, so I must've—But whatever I did, I thought I had to. Damn it, you would've done the same."

"The question," Whitehead said, "was whether it was your decision to signal—"

"Yes," St. Germain said, and sank back in his chair. "It was."

"And it was your decision also to run away, and to keep running when you heard shots, to let your partner go up empty-handed and alone against . . . How many guns and iron bars did you say it was, Lieutenant?"

"Objection."

"Objection sustained."

But St. Germain didn't care anymore. He was staring past Whitehead into the back row of seats, where Lenore Jeffcoat had gathered her things and was leaving the courtroom, delivering the first verdict on his testimony.

"Is that the standard of excellence demanded of officers in Cabot County?"

"Objection."

Judge Leeds removed his glasses and, holding them several inches from his face, centered the defense attorney in the thick frames. "Mr. Whitehead," he said, "I would advise you very strongly not to badger the witness. Now, Lieutenant, if you would like to respond to any of this, you may."

Even here he needed someone to fight his battles for him. He shook his head.

Then Leeds turned again to Whitehead. "If you think you can tone it down, I will let you resume your examination. But only if you allow the witness to answer the questions."

"I have just one more," Whitehead said. "Lieutenant St. Germain," he began calmly, "you've admitted to incompetence, to arrogance on top of it, to dereliction of duty, to the most craven behavior—"

"Objection," Corcoran bellowed.

"To deserting your partner, your friend, at a moment of grave danger—"

"Sustained."

"And having readily conceded that . . ." The calmness was already gone; he pounded his fist against his palm. "I'd like to ask what dismal revelations have yet to be made . . ."

"Mr. Whitehead," Leeds said.

"Whether it wouldn't be straining the imagination to suggest that your partner, who was in Malletts Bay for no purpose that has ever been shown, who was killed with your very own gun, was not also—"

"That's enough, Mr. Whitehead."

"—killed by your own hand."

Corcoran rushed toward the stand, a lifeguard to the rescue of a drowning man, but stopped, seeing that he was too late. Jess Whitehead limped back to the defense table as if his knees finally had given out. Leeds ordered a recess and called Whitehead into his chambers where he informed him that he was citing him for contempt and reporting him to the bar association. When they returned, Corcoran announced that he would present no additional witnesses.

Conklin threw down his pad and leaped out of his seat. "I've been brought to the gates of hell," he shouted. "What about my side?"

"This is not a trial, Mr. Conklin," Leeds said as Jess Whitehead pulled the boy down. "You'll get your chance to testify if the case goes before a jury." Then he gathered his papers and retired to chambers.

Half an hour went by before the jurist came back to the bench. Expressionlessly, as if it didn't matter much, he said, "I find the state has presented sufficient proof so that a reasonable person would conclude that Paul Conklin should be bound over to the grand jury for the murder of Walter Jeffcoat."

St. Germain, at the defense table, exhaled deeply, standing

suddenly as he looked behind and was unable to find Marlow and Beausoleil.

"You seem surprised, Lieutenant," Corcoran said as he collected his own papers.

"I wanted to speak with the sheriff and with Mr. Beausoleil, but they didn't stick around for the judge's decision."

"Well, there was hardly enough drama to keep them here, was there? In the fourteen years that I've been practicing law in this state I can't recall any murder case ever being thrown out at a probable cause hearing. I doubt they can either."

When St. Germain entered the bullpen the next morning, Vaughn Halvorsen was spit-shining his shoes at a desk from which blond wood gleamed through a scattering of accident reports. "G'morning, Vaughn, I see you've nearly cleaned your plate off."

The rookie looked up alertly, waiting for the punch line. He seemed disappointed when St. Germain had nothing more to offer. "Sheriff wants to see you."

St. Germain heard footsteps on the stairs and caught up with Marlow as he was entering his office.

"There's a few things we have to talk about," Marlow said. "Sit down."

St. Germain glanced at the slatted seat as if he had been invited to try out the electric chair. "If it's all the same, I'll stand."

"Suit yourself." Marlow went to his desk. "Ray Beausoleil has decided to recommend a plea bargain to Jess Whitehead. Conklin's going to be allowed to plead guilty to two counts of murder in exchange for concurrent life terms with eligibility for parole after twenty years."

St. Germain dropped into the chair, looking as though he could feel the current.

"He says he has no choice. After the performance you put on yesterday . . ."

"You're not trying to tell me anyone in their right mind believes I could've shot Wally?"

"I'm not a psychiatrist," Marlow said coldly. "But Ray says if he goes to trial Conklin stands an outside chance of winning in *voir dire*. Jess'll hold out for a panel of hilljacks who'd buy anything he tells them about a policeman, so long as it's bad. Except for the medical stuff, your testimony is about all we have going for us in both cases, and Ray thinks you're too vulnerable under cross-examination. Jess Whitehead can have you for breakfast any time he wants."

"Ray can go jump in the lake. I learned plenty about handling myself on the stand. Next time—"

"Show some sympathy for the man. This has got to be the toughest thing he's ever had to do. If Ray Beausoleil is suggesting Conklin should cop to life with parole, you can be sure it's the best we can get." He paused to shift the weight of the world to his other shoulder. "It was his daughter, Larry."

"And Wally was your deputy."

The softness went out of Marlow's face. He walked to the window, opened it, put his head out and sniffed cold air, but when he came back the lines were still pinched around his mouth.

St. Germain sat forward, preparing for a second jolt.

"You look like you're about to have a cow," Marlow snapped. "Anything else you want to get off your chest?"

"Just this." St. Germain unpinned his badge and tossed it on the desk. Watching it spin, he had to fight the urge to take it back. He forced himself out of the chair and began walking out of the office.

"Stop right there," Marlow ordered, and St. Germain took another step and then braced as rigidly as the newest rookie. "Don't go sanctimonious on me. You weren't any nicer to Wally than the others, and you don't resent him any the less for getting killed on your watch. But there's only one person to blame for what happened that night, and the responsibility is something you'd better start facing up to."

"My God, John, do you think I sleep easy anymore, that it isn't with me every minute?"

"That's bullshit. If you were half the man you pretend you are, you wouldn't be running away."

St. Germain's body sagged under its own weight. "I'm not even ten percent of him," he said. "Not five percent—if I ever was. Can't you see, I'm yellow."

"Feeling sorry for yourself, too, are you?"

St. Germain headed for the door again. "I don't have to take this, I don't work here anymore."

"No, you don't." Marlow palmed the badge, dropped it in a pocket. "One more thing."

St. Germain stopped again, as if Marlow might be calling him back, begging him. . . .

"The .44," Marlow said. "Hand it in, too. Any of my men catch you with a gun you're not licensed to carry, they might just want to lock you up."

8

Dear Mel,

As I am sure I do not have to remind you it is now eight months and two weeks and four days that I have been rotting here and still waiting for your second visit. Southern Vermont Correctional Facility is not my idea of a rest cure and it would help the time to pass quicker if I could see your ugly face more often. (Just kidding, you know me Mel.) Mom has had nothing to do with me since I got in this mess and the time Pa came the screws had to get between us, he was so POed, so you can see I am counting on you brother. It is only my sanity that is at stake.

This place is a nuthouse, a regular zoo. If they got 50 niggers in the whole state of Vermont then 75 of them are living with me in three tier. They are a real fun bunch, specially around Ramadan, which is one of their holidays (at least for the Muslims) when they do not hardly eat anything during the daytime, which makes them even touchier than usual. As a rule I try and stay out of their way. But there is not a lot of way to be staying out of here.

I suppose I should not be complaining so much about the niggers. Before there were Muslims I am told they used to serve *pork seven days a week till it was coming out your ears. Now the menu is more balanced, specially if you care for meat loaf cooked in ketchup and what I think is salisbury steak and lima beans for babies and like to wash it down with lime Kool-Aid and lime Jell-O for the dessert. Twice a week we get liver, which is a real treat when you are trying to cut it with a spoon, as they do not allow us knives, at least not in the dining hall. Up on the tier everybody has his own shiv and why they do not let us bring the liver to our cells and cut it there I do not know. Other things they do not allow in the dining hall are pepper, which the screws consider a weapon as it may be thrown in their eyes, and enough time to eat.*

Next to the niggers and the food what I like best about this place has got to be the faggots. I can still remember the time we found those sissies under the Route 7 bridge in Winooski and beat the living shit out of them and robbed their pants. Ha-ha. Here they got two different kinds of faggots and neither brand is like the ones under the bridge. The first stands six foot eight and weighs in the neighborhood of 300 pounds and can generally be found power lifting down to the gym. These ones I usually call sir and never turn my back on, specially in the showers. The other ones are maybe 90 pounds soaking wet and think shoe polish is to use for eyeliner and have to be kept in segregation, because if they are not all the other cons will be fighting to see who can get them to be their girlfriend. So as you can see the whole joint is really one goddamn fruit palace, with the single last exception of me.

Yesterday one of the sissies put his hand near a place of mine where it did not belong and when I began to bang his head on the floor he just laughed and said, "Beat me, kick me, make me want you," which is a disgusting thing to have to hear from anyone, specially another man. The screws pulled me off him, but did not write me up as they said they would have done the same if they were in my boots. One said I had better beat up

*any punk that tries that again or else I will have all of Southern
Vermont Correctional Facility on my back if I don't. As if I was
here three minutes and did not figure it out on my own.*

*Well, I do not want you to think there is only the bad and
none of the good too. I have been assigned to the prison farm
taking care of the flock of sheep. This is useful interesting work
that lets me get plenty of fresh air and sunshine and because it
is what they call a C grade job it is high paying as well, which
means I make 67.5 cents a day and so will have quite a pile put
away soon, won't I Mel? But what is more important, I am
getting valuable training that I can use when I am a free man
again in the early part of the Twenty-first century if some fucking
collie dog does not beat me out of a job.*

*Sundays are my favorites, as they serve ham and eggs for
breakfast and sometimes one of my sheep for supper. After
breakfast you can generally find me at the Protestant Center,
making my peace with Him. They are an okay bunch of guys
there, real Christians like me, and I believe our prayers are
reaching His ears. Remember what He says in Psalms, chapter
37, verse 4: "Delight thyself also in the Lord; and He shall give
thee the desires of thine heart."*

*Also on Sundays we get to see our prison volunteers who
understand how the sorry conditions show what a corrupt society
we live in. At least that is what they tell us. These volunteers are
girls from Bennington College, which is a college that costs a
fortune to go to for each term, and is a handy place for rich
folks to park their kids when they can not stand to live with them
any more. Many of the girls come to the prison without wearing
underwear (no shit Mel, I mean it) and if this is the best they
can do to prove they support the cons it is all right by me.*

*But I do not want you getting the wrong idea that all they have
for sex here is faggots and college girls you can only cop a feel
off of and pulling on your own pud. On Sunday afternoons the
prisoners who are lucky enough to have relatives who give a shit*

about them get visitors, and when the weather is good enough, which is to say after mud season is over, they have picnics for maybe 400 cons and their families on the athletic field. You would like these picnics Mel. The cons' wives know to bring a picnic basket full of home-cooked goodies. And while this is considered a great treat after the crap we are forced to eat, what the men are interested in mostly is having a nice table cloth to feast on. You heard me right, a table cloth. What they do is they put an extra large cloth over a picnic table with enough food on it so it won't blow away and when the screws are not looking the cons crawl under the table and toss the pork at their wives and this goes on all afternoon. So Mel, when you come visit I would appreciate it if you would try and bring a table cloth and a girl (a blonde one with big jugs, but not too fat if you can help it) and tell the screws she is our sister and then leave us alone under the table cause if there is one thing I miss most of all at Southern Vermont Correctional Facility for sure it is fucking girls.

On the other hand if you cannot find a girl I would not object to crawling under the table with you so we can switch clothes and then I can walk out with the rest of the visitors, which is something that happens more often than you would believe. I think you might enjoy the change of scenery for a while. There is no shortage of dope here, or bootleg whiskey, although from time to time a batch of it will make you blind. And if you get assigned to a job in the textile shop you will even be able to stay warm in the winter, as it is not unusual for the cons to steal wool (from my sheep) to stuff inside their clothes for an extra lining and make some profit as well. For every three sweaters the cons are supposed to be sewing it is my bet they swipe another to trade among the men. Plus you would learn a valuable trade, such as dressmaking. That's right Mel, dressmaking!!! The other day one of the cons was caught turning a long sweater into a dress on his sewing machine and when the screws asked what he was doing he said that he was making an evening gown for his girl-

friend, who is one of the sissies I was telling you about before. When the screws took away the dress the con was so POed that he smashed the sewing machine and, of course, was put in the segregation building as a result. And so now he is living next door to his girlfriend and I hope the two of them are happy together.

Also there are plenty of things to do at night such as joining the chapter of the Alcoholics Anonymous. These meetings are very well attended, as the members of this club are always shit-faced and can be counted on to know where you can get a drink and who is making bootleg. Another popular activity is seeing the jailhouse lawyers. These are cons who have been in stir so long they have become regular legal eagles that can tell you how you can beat your case on appeal, though if they are so smart it is a mystery to me what they are still doing here. I talked to one who told me if I never entered a guilty plea I would have a good chance of getting a new trial under what is called the Necessity Defense. This is an old English law, maybe 200 years old, that is from the days when sailors got shipwrecked and would find themselves in a lifeboat with nothing to eat except each other and they would kill a man and polish him off just to stay alive and when they got back to England they would be tried for murder and then let go when they explained they had to kill the one sailor to save all the others. I do not see where this applies to my case exactly but may give it a try if nothing better comes up.

On the whole though, like the comedian with the big beezer used to say, "I would rather be in Philadelphia." It is hard as hell trying to get any sleep here as half the men are either trying to saw through the bars or hang themselves from them at any given hour of the night and the lights never go off in three tier. If you can sleep through all the snoring and moaning and 30 toilets flushing at the same time I suppose you can sleep through anything. But the worst of it is that three fourths of the cons are out of their fucking minds and every one of them has got to be a homicidal maniac. The other day two of the men got in a fight over a Hustler centerfold (not the girl Mel, but the lousy picture) and the next thing you know they were duking it out in the yard. One of these characters was a Muslim and the other was a white guy and so you knew there was going to be bad trouble. The warden wanted to head things off so he called them to his office for a peace conference where the Muslim admitted swiping the beaver shot from the white guy and the warden must have figured that was the end of it. But the other Muslims decided their honor had been insulted and they put the word out that they wanted a Jihad, or some shit that sounds like that. Next time the white guy showed up in the yard he had two shivs and was wearing a piece of aluminum from the machine shop under his shirt like a suit of fucking armor. For all the good it did him when three of the Muslims piped him and then cut his throat and held him down till he bled to death like a stuck hog. When the screws arrived they asked did anyone see what happened. Eight hundred cons in the yard and everyone must have been watching an eclipse of the sun or something cause no one had seen a damn thing.

Which reminds me, do you ever see my friend Lieutenant Lawrence St. Germain of the Cabot County sheriff's? Except I hear he is not a lieutenant any more, or even a pig, but instead is just working at a sugar shack down to Peacham collecting the sap from the trees. I think this is a better line of work for him, as he is such a big sap himself. If you should bump into him, you might tell him I said so.

A couple other things to tell the big sap are that one of these days I will be out of here and I do not mean in 20 years. (With your help Mel, it won't have to be even 20 weeks.) And when I am on the outside we have some unfinished business between us, him and me. Tell him I apologize and am sorry for killing his friend, the little pig, when I meant to be killing him instead. I mean this from the bottom of my heart.

Other than what I have already written you about I do not

have much more griping to do. As I said before what I hate most about this place is the lack of nookie and you can be sure that is the first thing I will look into when I am a free man again. I have been thinking a lot about girls in the time I have to myself (as what else is there to think about?) and have developed some interesting ideas on how to get them and make time with them as I did with that Rebecca bitch who I swear had the hots for my body but was playing hard to get. I only wish you were there to see it.

Well, enough about me for now as I am sure I have talked your ear off to the point where you must be rubbing your eyes. I am looking forward to your visit one of these Sundays so we can make plans for my getting the fuck out of this insane asylum before something awful happens to me. (Don't worry, I do not mean that I am about to turn queer.) Pay the man what he asks for delivering this and tip him good too, as his nephew (although he is a baby stabber and worse) is one of my few buddies in the joint and I could not have got this letter to you without his help. If the prison censors ever saw what I was writing they would black out so much that all you would see is the following:

> *Love,*
> *Your brother Paulie*
> *Paul A. Conklin #996213*
> *Drawer F*
> *East Shaftsbury, Vt. 05154*

9

Annie crouched in the shadow of the Subaru, strapping on her new Michigan snowshoes. She stamped them against the hard ground till they felt almost comfortable and stepped over the track left by Larry's Bearpaws. The Michigans, narrower and with a stubby tail, fit inside like a tennis racket brought up in a fisherman's net. Annie lifted her foot and studied the webbed imprint, then took off after him.

Two days of light rain followed by an Alberta Clipper had left the snow dry and crusted, and she tailed St. Germain easily into the trees. Where the pines descended into a hardwood stand she was slowed by the thickening underbrush. Not far ahead she could see him at a towering maple, examining it like a safecracker at a reinforced door. "What do we do with it now that it's ours?" she called out. "Drag it home?"

Startled, he turned around, didn't take his eyes off her until she was standing beside him. "*You* might," he said. "But the way I've been doing it all my life is more like this." A wicker backpack slid from his shoulders and he rummaged inside. He came out with a hand drill and placed the bit at eye level against the gnarled bark, slowly turned the crank. The drill bored into the wood, but then slipped out, leaving a yellow scratch half a foot long.

"Damn." He let himself smile with embarrassment. "I must be out of practice." He clenched the tip of his thumb between his teeth and pulled his hand out of his glove, put the drill against the trunk again and spun the crank. When he had gouged a hole three inches deep he moved around the maple and dug another and another one after that.

"Look here," he said, pointing to clear blobs of liquid oozing from the holes. "Sap's starting to rise already." He scraped away the snow till he had uncovered green tubing that snaked through the sugar bush like the plan of an English garden. Brass taps dangled from short lengths of plastic, feeding into the main line, and he picked up one and pressed it to the tree. "Get my hammer, will you?"

Annie removed a scarred mallet from the wicker pack, and St. Germain used it to pound the taps firmly into the holes. "If these aren't in tight enough, the sap'll drip down the trunk and what the beetles don't want'll be wasted," he said.

"This is sort of fun, know it?"

"Nothing's fun for four bucks an hour." St. Germain smiled anyway. "For me, the fun went out of this when they quit using buckets to collect the sap and a team and a sledge to haul them out of the woods."

"I mean it's fun just being out early in the morning . . ." She watched as he made sure the taps were secure and then wielded the drill against another tree. "A sledge and a *what?*"

"You heard me. How else are you going to get several hundred buckets out of the woods in one trip? This way won't ever make the picture on a bank calendar, but I have to admit it's lots quicker than using horses. These tubes empty into bulk tanks we haul down to the sugar house in a truck."

Annie walked up to the tree he was working on. "It doesn't seem like you're getting much," she said. "Hardly enough to put over a single pancake."

"The sap doesn't really start to run till we have nights where the temperature stays below freezing followed by warm afternoons. Weatherman's predicting a thaw for the weekend. That's why Old Man Norton wants me to check the tubes and put the taps in quick."

"I like this, I like it here in the woods with you." She took off a mitten and dipped her finger in the sap and touched it to her lips. "Phoo, this stuff hardly tastes like maple syrup at all."

St. Germain laughed at her. "My God, Ann, don't they teach you flatlanders anything at UVM? Syrup doesn't come out of a tree, sap does. If you get one gallon of maple syrup for every forty gallons of sap, you're doing fine. It's why the stuff goes for ten dollars to the quart in the tourist traps."

"Where did you learn so much about maple syrup?"

"Family secret, passed down from generation to generation since St. Germains still lived up to the Laurentian Mountains." He started to laugh again. "In caves, probably."

"Well, aren't you going to tell me? I'm family, too—" She caught herself, waiting for his reprimand, but he didn't miss a beat with the mallet.

"There's not a lot to learn. This is not exactly a high-tech occupation, you know. Norton rents six sugar bushes and for the past couple of weeks we've been out patching the gravity lines that bring the sap to the tanks."

"How do you know if the sap is any good? Couldn't you be wasting your time?"

"Every few years there *is* a lousy run. But this sap is light, with a high sugar content, which means a short, sweet run." He checked the taps and dragged the pack to the next tree. "Norton's laid in fifteen cords of softwood slabs for boiling down the sap. Hemlock and spruce for a hot fire, a flashy fire, which you want if you're going to produce the finest-grade syrup."

Annie stood close behind him. "You seem so . . . so relaxed, like when we first met." As he picked up the drill again, she snatched it away and wrapped her arms around his neck. "It must be contagious," she sighed.

"These trees aren't my worry," he said. "If the thaw never comes or the tubes rot out, I'm not going to lose any sleep. Four-dollar jobs are not in short supply."

"That's not what I meant. Since you left the sheriff's department it's like ten tons have been lifted off your back and you don't even know it."

"You'd be surprised what I know." St. Germain broke free of her embrace, put the drill to the tree and turned the crank. "It's a sensation that . . . well, if I haven't said anything it's 'cause I can't make up my mind yet whether it agrees with me. Sometimes I feel like a diver who's come up too quick for air."

She handed him the mallet. "I never should have mentioned it."

"Why not?" he said. "I do feel less tense now that I'm a civilian again, if that counts for anything. But hell, Annie, I'm not thirty-one years old yet and I can't make a career of hiding in the woods." He hammered lightly at a tap, then pulled it out of the tree and inspected it and replaced it with one from the pack. "I mean I could, I suppose. But what kind of life would we have to look forward to?"

"A longer one than we had before."

He seemed to be thinking it over. "If we didn't starve, or die of cabin fever."

"Are you ready for a full-time job again?"

He shrugged. "Not right now, while I'm still enjoying myself. But don't get the idea I'm not trying to figure out what comes after I get tired of pretending I'm some sort of rustic."

"I'm glad," she said. "There are so many things you can do, important things, if you set your mind to them."

He put down the hammer and looked back at her. "Still miss the city, do you?"

"No . . . not the way you mean."

"Then what are you getting at?"

"I . . . tell me some more about the syrup. Tell me why it costs so much."

"There's a variety of reasons," he said. "The law of supply and demand, the current taste for sweet things. But the most important is that the sugar maples are dying all over and no one seems to know why." He pounded the tap into place and checked the tube for leaks. "The trees in this sugar bush are half a century old, came up right after the hurricane of 1938 tore down whole forests. They should be at maximum production now, but Norton tells me he's getting half the sap he did five years ago."

He looked over his shoulder again. "Why are you so interested all of a sudden in—"

"Go on."

"Some of these trees, you could say they're in critical condition. That's why we don't tap them all. Taking the sap puts stress on a maple just like drawing blood does to a person. I read somewhere that in the last six or seven years Quebec's lost two million tap holes. The scientists don't know if it's overproduction, bugs, brutal winters, or what. Acid rain's what I think."

"So you wouldn't have a future in this even if you could buy the woods for yourself?"

"No way. A few more years and, short of a miracle, the industry's going belly up."

"Well," she said, "I hope you'll be looking for work that pays more than four dollars an hour, lots more."

"Ann, it's such a nice day, must we—"

". . . Because we're going to need it. In about three quarters of a year, we're going to need more money than you ever thought about."

"Money for what?" he said. "And why precisely—Do we have some huge bill coming due then?"

"No," Annie said. "I am."

"You're . . . you mean with a baby?" He struck the tap off center, bending it, then knocked it out of the tree and swiveled around to see her nodding, glowing. "Why didn't you say something before?"

"I didn't know before. I only went to the doctor yesterday." She was trying not to laugh. "Poor Larry, do you feel taken advantage of?"

"By you, Ann?" He kissed her. "Or the baby?"

"Take your pick," she said, "seeing as how you were hardly consulted."

"If anyone's been taken advantage of, it's you, letting me drag you around in the cold." He paused to let a smile take over from his look of astonishment, then pulled off his other glove and took her cheeks in his hands. "You shouldn't be tromping through the wilderness in your condition," he said suddenly. "Let's go back to the cabin. I can finish here later."

"Don't be silly. I don't have to start taking it easy for months." She let him kiss her again, then moved away. "Before this goes any further, we have a number of things to get straight between us."

"Is that a proposal? Because if it is, I accept." He didn't let her answer. "Now that that's settled, you've got no more claim to that alimony you say you'd never ask for."

"Nothing's settled." She studied his smile, decided it was real. "I wouldn't ask 'cause you can't get blood from a turnip, or whatever. And no way am I marrying a man who goes off to work every morning on snowshoes. You said it's going to be a short sap run. When will you start looking for a real job?"

He was gazing back through the trees, longingly, so that she thought he had lost interest, but the smile seemed a permanent part of him. "Well, how about that?" he said like a sportscaster calling a line drive over the wall. "A baby."

Twin serpents coiled around a herald staff glared menacingly from a silver badge. Two more clung to a patch on a dark brown

sleeve. St. Germain shuffled around in his stocking feet, showing off a tight seat and thighs. "Think you can find any more
to let out?"

"If I'd have known you were going back to basic brown, I
wouldn't have let you burn up your lieutenant's uniform," Annie said, "just sewn these patches over your stripes."

The trouser legs brushed against the floor as his entire body
seemed to sag. "Stand up straight," she ordered. She took two
pins from her mouth and pushed them through a fold of cloth.
". . . Except this is nicer looking, tapered, much more striking.
You really look smart in it."

"Knock it off, Ann. I know how I look, like a night watchman you wouldn't trust to carry a gun." He hiked the pants
higher on his hips. "Be glad it's only for six months. The management trainee program at Stowe starts the first Monday
after Labor Day. I'm lucky they found this for me, to tide us
over."

"An ambulance driver." She made a face and hid it behind
a sneeze. "It's not exactly what I had in mind when I said you
needed something to keep you out of the woods."

"Paramedic, if you please," he said, smoothing a yellow patch
on his breast pocket. "But even with the fancy title there's not
a lot of glamour to it, less when I think of how many of the
other drivers would give their eyeteeth to be cops. And the
only perk is that I can drive as fast as I want, go through red
lights when I'm pulling someone off the mountain."

"Is the job all broken legs?" she asked. "Ski season is over
in another four or five weeks."

He stepped out of the pants and handed them to her, watched
her hem the legs proudly. It was amazing, he thought, what
impending motherhood had accomplished after all the sorry
scenes played out trying to domesticate her. "A lot of the ski
lodges on Mount Mansfield operate tennis camps during the
summer, and there's no shortage of middle-age hackers who're

convinced they'll make the Davis Cup squad if they just put out harder. From what I've been told it's strictly sprained knees and coronaries till the first serious blizzard."

"Very exciting."

"Yeah," he said dejectedly.

She looked up from her sewing. "I'm glad it's dull. If it wasn't, come September you'd find an excuse for staying in this uniform."

"Well, there could be some excitement. Stowe ambulances are equipped with radios that are glued to the police band. I'll be monitoring all the Cabot sheriff's calls."

"Since when is that exciting?"

"If any of the guys request a paramedic, guess who rolls. It's hard to say how they'll react when they see me. I'm sure none of them want to be reminded about Wally Jeffcoat."

She looped the thread around a finger, knotted it. "Do you?"

"Not really," he said unself-consciously. Annie noticed that he didn't turn away or drop his voice. "But I can deal with it better than before."

"You're finally coming around to see where it wasn't your fault?"

"No, just learning to accept what happened. The man in this clown suit, he might not be so noble as the sheriff's lieutenant of last year, but I don't know that he's a worse human being."

"If John's men can't see it, if they make a crack, let them walk to the hospital."

"I hadn't thought of that."

Annie handed back the pants and he held them to his waist and then pulled them on. "How do I look now?" he asked without checking the mirror.

"Great, like the proverbial million dollars."

"Do I?"

Annie nodded. "Would I lie?"

"Marry me, then. It's probably your only chance at a million.

Besides, I don't want our kid going through life with two last names and a hyphen."

"I'll think about it."

"You've been thinking about it long enough. When are you going to say yes?"

Annie thought about it some more. "The day I see you off to work in a white shirt and tie," she said, "and a suit with nothing to read on the pockets."

10

The snitch, whose name was Cleve Holmes, was a thirty-four-year-old short eyes one month out of segregation, a four-time loser with no friends in the general population, the kind of inmate who could be trusted if any of them could. He said, "From what I been able to pick up, there's gonna be a break Thursday night. Someone's making smoke bombs out of oily rags from the textile shop that they are gonna set off by the basketball courts to, like, divert the guards. Then they are gonna try the wall on the other side of the yard, behind the batting cage. They have some kind of ladder rigged together. It's all I know."

Warden Evander Graham wanted names, the time the men planned to breach the wall.

"I can't tell you any of that," Holmes said. "This is all you're getting, 'cause it's all I have got. You said you'd do something for me. . . ."

Graham returned the short eyes to segregation. In the morning he would make a call to the superintendent of prisons requesting an emergency transfer to the medium-security Northern Vermont Facility. Holmes had earned it. If word of what he had done leaked out, he would be dead—or wish he was—within an hour of leaving his cell.

Graham bent back the top page of his desk calendar. Thursday was the second, four days after Easter, when up to half of his guards were guaranteed to be down with the Blue Flu. But there was still a chance of avoiding an embarrassing call for assistance to the state police. Monday, when the staff was at full strength again, he would issue an alert for any unusual activity in the blocks. If he could keep troopers—and the newspapers—out of this, so much the better. For another few days he might not lose too much sleep.

Raising the blinds, Graham looked out at four hundred cons divided into desultory bunches on an athletic field ringed by a cratered cinder track. Worn grass lay in flattened patches under late March snow, and few of the men ventured far from the eastern wall that got whatever sun filtered through the gloom. Graham studied them with a bitterness all his own. In the eighty-six years of its existence there had been nine successful breaks from Southern Vermont Correctional Facility involving a total of thirty-four men, the majority of whom were recaptured within twelve hours of gaining their freedom. Five of the escapes had come during his tour as warden; one more and he would be out on his ass, or back rattling keys on the tier. The thought of it made him go to his desk for the office bottle. But the lock had been jimmied and the drawer was empty.

When Vermont's only maximum security penetentiary was erected during the first term of President Theodore Roosevelt, it had been considered escape-proof, the last word in keeping men humanely in cages. Four cell blocks like spokes on a copper hub radiated from a domed building housing administration, factories, and mess hall. Walls eighteen feet high and three feet thick enclosed the blocks, each of which was two hundred feet long. Because convict lore held the walls to be impregnable, each of the nine breaks had been made by inmates who stowed away in vehicles paying regular calls at the institution—garbage trucks, delivery wagons, ambulances, in one case a hearse. So there was no doubt in Graham's mind that Cleve Holmes had handed him a load of shit. He would spend the Easter weekend not sleeping as well as he had expected, trying to figure out what was going down.

Sunday, in a classroom under the green dome of administration, thirty-seven-year-old Archie Walker, doing fifteen years for the attempted murder of the sister of the woman whose testimony had put Holmes in prison, was delivering an Easter sermon to the Fellowship of Christian Convicts. Due to the shortage of staff, the services were under the nominal leadership of the Protestant chaplain's clerk, Jefferson Stark, twenty-eight, a trusty in the ninth year of a life term for first-degree murder.

"Brothers," Walker said, "as promised we have a holiday treat for you. Mr. Conklin is going to lead a discussion of an inspiring and uplifting reading from the Book of Psalms."

Paul Conklin slid out of his chair with attached desk and went to the front of the room. Clutched against his chest was a mo-rocco-bound King James Bible, a gift from his brother at their reunion two Sundays before. Conklin opened the heavy volume to a page marked with a leather tassel and then gazed at his audience. Besides Walker and Stark only one other prisoner had spurned the visitors' room for Easter Bible class—Michael Munson—a night-time burglar from Poughkeepsie, New York.

"Today's portion is going to be short, but I think you'll find it relevant." Conklin coughed ostentatiously into his fist. "It's from the One hundred and forty-fourth Psalm, verse seven."

"You call that a portion?" Munson said. "It's two fucking sentences."

Stark rapped bruised knuckles against his desk. "*If* the brother will let Mr. Conklin go on."

Munson glowered at the trusty as Conklin lowered his head over the page. " 'Send thine hand from above,' " he read. " 'Rid me and deliver me out of great waters, from the hand of strange children.' " He slammed the book shut. "Now," he said, "does anybody know what that means?"

"Has something to do with you pray hard enough and really mean it, God'll take care of you no matter what you done before and what kind of mess you're in now," Stark said thoughtfully. "Doesn't it?"

"Cut the shit, Conklin," Munson said. "You know why we're here, and it's not for Sunday school. Do you have the blades or not?"

Archie Walker raised his hand. When Conklin acknowledged him, he pushed out of his seat and stood at attention like a schoolboy begging favor from a teacher. "What it says, I believe, is we pull this off we don't have to do any more hard time listening to such assholes as Mr. Munson."

"Could be you're taking it too literally," Conklin said. "Let's have another look in here." He opened the Bible again and ran his fingertips against the inside of the cover. Using his thumbnail, he peeled back the yellow paper glued to the leather and four thin strips of metal clattered onto the lectern. "Well, maybe not," he laughed. "Send out thine hands, guys. Deliverance is surely on the way."

The men gathered around and Conklin gave each a blade. "What the Lord has wrought is a Pro-Kraft hacksaw, the best made. Cuts through iron, case-hardened steel, you name it, except the vault at Fort Knox, Kentucky."

Munson tilted his at the window and squinted at the lettering etched in the metal. He was a short, swarthy man, a hairy man even in the moments after he shaved, and the carbonized steel was the same dark blue as his cheeks. "These are Nestor blades. You promised the Pro-Krafts."

"These are as good," Conklin said quickly. "Better."

"Nothing's as good as Pro-Krafts," Munson said, and Conklin felt for the reassuring weight of his Bible. "You fucked up. Do it some more and the one thing I'm sure these cookie cutters will slice through is your neck. . . . Damn kid," he muttered. "I never should've—"

"From the hand of strange children." Conklin was looking at Walker, for four years three tier's light heavyweight clean and jerk champion. Walker began to laugh, a dry chuckle that filled out into a roar that he turned on Munson until the burglar went back to his seat. "You do remember what we're bringing you along for?" Conklin asked.

"Yeah," Munson said. "I remember."

Stark pocketed his blade, started to pace anxiously in front of the door. "Let's get going."

"What's your hurry?" Conklin said, allowing a laugh of his own. "With Graham checking for smoke bombs, or looking under the food trucks to see who's hitching out on an axle, we've got all the time in the world."

"Not me," Stark said. "I wasted enough time in the joint already."

Conklin rubbed his palm against the cool Morocco binding, then put down the book reluctantly. "Okay, school's out," he said. "Now let's see what you learned." He opened the door and looked both ways, as if he were afraid of being run down in heavy traffic. The corridor was deserted. Empty cans, a drop cloth stiff with paint, and a ladder had been stored at the far end, blocking access to a steel door secured with a Yale lock. The men tore through the rubbish and then stood back as Munson used a pick fashioned from a nail file to open the padlock.

"What'd I tell you?" Conklin gloated as the door swung wide. "We just follow the plan, with everybody doing his own bit, and we're out of here."

Their eyes adjusted to the darkness of a stairwell cluttered with furniture that had been carted out of the classroom forty years before, scarred desks and chairs and shattered blackboards gray with obscene graffiti. Stark cleared his throat and spit yellow phlegm on the steps. "'S nice here," he said. "Quiet and peaceful."

"Maybe you ought to stay," Munson said. "No one'd miss you. And if they did, I doubt they'd give a big enough shit to start looking."

"Brother Munson," Walker said, "how is it that you always seem to be having your period?" Walker moved on the burglar, who reached quickly inside his shirt.

Conklin stepped between them with his arms spread. "You want to tear each other apart, be my guest. Only try and hold off a little longer, 'cause me and Stark need both of you till we're over the wall."

"Why do we have to take his crap?" Stark asked. "Who wants him?"

Conklin slapped the Yale lock into the trusty's palm. "You do."

Stark dropped the lock as if it were red hot and it bounced down the stairs, echoing so loudly that Conklin had to fight the urge to run after it. "Where do we go from here?" Stark asked.

Conklin unbuttoned his shirt and came out with a hand-drawn map. "You can thank my brother for this, too. It's amazing, the stuff you find in the public library." He glanced down the stairs toward a landing where the lock was still rattling and then nudged the others toward the next flight up. "This way," he said. "I'm pretty sure."

"You're *what*?" Munson said.

The same look from the three of them silenced him. They climbed a second flight, to a landing guarded by another steel door. "Where are we now?" Walker asked.

"Should be right outside the chapel," Conklin said. "It hasn't been used in years. Lousy atheists. If they let us hold services in there like they're supposed to, we wouldn't have to go through so much shit."

Munson moved through the others and examined the door. "You fucked up, wise guy. We can't get through this."

"Why not?" Stark asked. "Can't you pick the lock?"

"The door's bolted shut. Without tools there's no way to take it off its hinges."

Conklin seemed unconcerned. "Archie, did you hear what the man said?"

"Yeah, I heard." The weight lifter doubled his right hand into a fist. He drove it into the wall to the left of the door and a large block of plaster fell out and broke apart on the landing.

"What this is an illustration of," Conklin said, crumbling a morsel of plaster in his fingers, "is the power of God, or Archie Walker." He laughed again. "Or maybe just shoddy construction."

But the other cons weren't listening. They were tearing at the hole, using their blades to slice through a steel mesh grid until they had opened a space big enough for even Walker to crawl through. Conklin tied a handkerchief around his neck and pulled it up over his face. "Jesse Fucking James," he said, and waved away the gritty powder that hung in the opening and squeezed through first.

The all-faith chapel at Southern Vermont Correctional Facility had been off limits since the early 1960s, when interest in prison religious life had dwindled to a record low. It was a large room with a high vaulted ceiling and two dozen oak pews pushed into a corner and buried beneath cardboard boxes filled with prayer books and hymnals. Conklin sat down on a bench that stood away from the others. "We'll relax for a while," he said, "rest up till it starts getting dark. Nobody'd think of looking for us here."

"What if they do?" Stark asked. "What then?"

Conklin pushed some of the dust off the pew. "Sit down, Jeff," he said. "First of all, the screws won't know we're missing for another three, four hours, till evening count. Then Graham'll be so busy eating his heart out for not personally crawling under the bread truck or checking all the visitors at the gate, he won't know where to begin. But I wouldn't worry even if they started now. They probably don't know this place exists."

"Only thing that worries me," Stark said, "is where we go from here."

The chapel seemed hollow, a punishment cell the size of a theater. Light entered from a barred window behind the low podium that had served as a pulpit. Conklin hurried to the window and scraped away nearly three decades' grime, confirming that they were at the third-floor level of the administration building, which overlooked the yard where cons in weathered denim marched around the track beside women wearing gaudy hats and children with vacant, frightened eyes.

"Look at those fish," someone said, "like they're on Fifth Avenue."

"I am looking," Munson said, "and that goddam Easter parade is all I see. This place is a dead end."

Conklin returned to the bench and lay against the shiny spot where Stark had been sitting, put his feet up. "You're too antsy, Munson. Look close to the building, look straight down. All we got to do is saw the bars, drop to the second-floor roof, and follow it around the dome. If we can do that—and I'd like to hear one reason we can't—we're good as gone."

Munson touched his blade to his thumb. "I have one."

"What's eating you now?" Conklin said, the aggravation building, sounding like he wanted to hide it but couldn't. "Still don't like the view?"

"The bars are two inches thick. With these lousy Nestor saws there's no guarantee we can slice through before they discover we aren't in our cells."

Conklin sat up. He walked back to the window with short, even steps, trying to look unconcerned, just strolling, picking up the pace in spite of himself. Walker and Stark moved aside, and he stood close to Munson as the burglar smashed the glass with a Bible and brushed in the shards, then scraped his blade against the pitted bars.

"Check it out," Munson said, "hardly makes a scratch. If we're going out this window before they're ready to parole us, we've got to get on it now."

Stark's thick eyebrows wriggled across his forehead seeming to burrow into a crevice above his nose. "He know his business?"

"Only one way to find out," Conklin said. "Archie, you start."

It took Walker forty minutes to saw through the center bar and another quarter-hour to open a second groove two feet below the break, ruining his blade in the process. Stark replaced him and in half an hour doubled the depth of the bottom cut before the carbonized steel was worn smooth.

"Okay, we're just about done," Conklin said. "Munson, you take over. I'll finish up."

"No, now's your turn."

Conklin turned to Walker for support, but the weight lifter was busy studying his fingernails. He produced his own blade, holding it out like a pass as he came over the podium. He fit the blue metal against the bar, dragged it back and forth with little visible result when it snapped in his hand. "Sorry about that," he said. "My fault."

"You could get us killed, being sorry," Munson said. He snatched up the pieces and flung them across the chapel, then dipped inside his pocket faster than anyone could move. "It's a good thing I don't pay you much mind." His hand came out wrapped around his blade. "I've got to wonder why anyone does."

He slipped on dark glasses that he adjusted over his eyes like goggles. The others hovered close by as he began sliding the blade through the bar, pausing to gauge the depth of the groove with a fingertip. With smooth, sure strokes he enlarged the space like a woodsman whittling a miniature tree till the bar seemed to balance on an invisible point. Then he took off his glasses, and Walker tugged at the bar, working it back and forth until the metal gave out.

Munson dragged a carton of prayer books under the window and squeezed his torso through the space in the bars. "It's big enough for me." He slid back inside and glared at Conklin. "And for him. I don't know about you, though, Walker. It's something else you might want to take up with the boy genius."

Conklin looked up in surprise, like an actor called onstage before he had memorized his lines. What was going on at the window had seemed of no special importance because he wasn't at the center of it, not like the good time at Malletts Bay when he had the big sheriff's lieutenant twitching like a puppet on a thousand strings. Now he shoved through the men, reclaiming the spotlight. "Go ahead, Archie," he said. "You'll see."

Walker ground bits of broken glass with his heel until Munson jumped down from the box, then stuck his head into the opening. As he squirmed outside, his broad shoulders snagged on the jagged nubs of the bar. "Shit," he said. "It hurts."

"Yeah, but you can pull yourself out, can't you?" Conklin asked.

Walker grimaced and sucked air between clenched teeth. "In or out, I'm stuck."

"Crawl out of there, quick," Munson said. He pulled at Walker's hips and the weightlifter inched inside, bleeding from under the left arm.

"You like to tore my ribs out, Munson."

"Someone could have seen you."

Walker lifted his shirt and examined two gashes running freely with blood. "Like who? The yard's empty, everybody gone home or back to the blocks. Or didn't you notice?"

Conklin circled around the pair. If Munson got off putting his head in the lion's jaws, who was he to ruin his good time? He stepped onto the carton for a grandstand view and glanced out the window. "Shut up, Archie," he said suddenly. "He's right. I don't know where Graham found screws to spare, but there's a bunch coming into the yard."

"I didn't see them. What are they doing there this hour?"

"Trailing a work crew cleaning up after the Easter crowd."

Conklin went back to the pew and sat with a prayer book in his lap, returning to the window four times before he said, "Time to blow."

"Thought I'd never hear it," Walker said.

"Same here," said Stark.

"Munson, you have an opinion?"

The burglar climbed onto the box again. "Yeah, let's go."

"You feeling all right?" Conklin said. "Everything's okay?"

"Yeah, why?"

"How come you're so agreeable?" Conklin opened the prayer book over the bottom of the broken bar. He boosted himself onto the sill, slithered out, and sat with his legs dangling. Light from a ripening moon lent substance to the second-story roof that jutted from the base of the dome twelve feet below. If he dropped straight down, he would land without injuring himself. A miscalculation would bounce him into the yard with a fractured leg or two for his trouble. "Archie," he whispered. "Archie, give me a hand."

He felt the weightlifter's grip under his arms and then Walker was lowering him down the side of the building. "Okay, *now,*" he said, and the big man let go and he fell against the dome and rode it down, turning his ankle slightly in a mound of pebbles. When he looked back up, Stark had poked his head out and was surveying the landing area. "It's a cinch," he called to the trusty. "Archie'll help."

Stark was gazing past him, looking anywhere but the narrow roof. "I . . . I got a thing about high places. Let Munson go next." He ducked away, then reappeared at the window, wide-eyed and trembling. "I'll murder you, you don't put me down," he shouted.

Conklin heard someone say, "Either you do this yourself, or we dump you on your head. Which one's it going to be?"

Again Stark vanished, and then Conklin saw his feet between the bars. His arms were wedged against the window frame. Walker hacked at them one at a time and then the trusty was falling with a shout so loud that Conklin flattened himself against the roof. He counted to twenty before raising his head, but saw no one looking back from the yard. Beside him, checking for broken bones, was Jefferson Stark.

"Am I alive?" the trusty asked him.

"Uh-uh," Conklin said. "You died and went to heaven."

It was Munson's turn. He climbed onto the sill and dropped without hesitating and landed on his feet. Walker followed, holding his breath, coming down hard, rolling to the edge of the roof where Munson stopped him with his legs. Walker stood up and dusted himself off with one hand. In the other was a prayer book. "Here," he said to Conklin, "I brought something for you to read."

Conklin batted playfully at the volume. It dropped into the yard and the four of them dove for the pebbles.

"Are you trying to get everyone shot on purpose?" Munson asked. "Or is this so easy you want to make it more challenging?"

"It was an accident," Conklin said.

"If you don't watch out, you could have another for your very own."

"Shut up," Stark said to the burglar. "He's going to get us off this roof."

"Not for a while," Conklin said, subdued. "One of the cons in the work detail must've seen the book. He's coming by."

They watched as an inmate wearing a vest criss-crossed with reflective tape dragged a broom into the shadow of the dome, glancing up at the chapel and back toward his crew and then stuffing the prayer book in his shirt. "Guys here'd steal anything," Conklin said. "Rip off candy from a—"

"The hell with him," Munson said. "Do you know a way off of here, or don't you?"

"Like I said, we go behind the dome and . . ." Conklin unfolded the map, and Walker held his cigarette lighter over it. "And then across the A block roof to the wall above the main visitors' entrance. There should be . . . there's a drain pipe there that runs down to the street."

"And guards in the tower waiting for anyone dumb enough to try."

"Maybe they'll be there tomorrow," Conklin said, sure of himself again. "And definitely on Thursday, when everybody'll be geared up for the big crash-out. But tonight Graham's lucky if he has enough screws around to keep from talking to himself, let alone put a full shift in the towers."

The work crew gathered its implements and went back into the cellblocks, and then Conklin began walking the men around the dome. "The beauty of it," he said, "is the screws don't check around the visitors' entrance even when there's a full complement on duty. Who'd try a break *there?*"

They came around the dome, and Conklin held up suddenly, ran his hand along a ledge he seemed surprised to find.

"What are we stopping for?"

"The cellblock, it's higher than the map . . . than I thought it was. Somebody give me a boost."

Walker made a sling of his hands and catapulted Conklin onto the roof. "What do you see?"

Conklin got to his knees and peered along the top of the cellblock. "Clear sailing all the way." He took Stark's wrist and helped him up, but when he offered his hand again Munson spurned it and vaulted onto the roof unassisted. "I forgot," Conklin said without sarcasm. "You're a pro."

As Conklin and Stark reached down for Walker, Munson crept along the roof. "Shit," he said, "there's no place to take cover, not even a shadow."

"No screws watching either," Conklin said.

They kept to the center of the roof, where someone standing in the yard would be unable to see them. Duck-walking, it took ten minutes to move the two hundred feet from the dome to the perimeter wall, plowing through slushy snow.

"The promised land," Walker said, raising his head. "I can smell it."

A three-foot gap separated the end of the cellblock from the wall, and Conklin jumped it easily. Stark's knees buckled as he looked down into a shaft piled deep with refuse. Shutting his eyes, he froze.

"You don't move fast," Walker said to him, "I'm going to tip you over and run across your back."

Conklin took the trusty's hand and, with Walker pushing, dragged him onto the wall. First Walker and then Munson leaped for the railing of the catwalk that normally was patrolled by guards carrying Uzi machine guns. Conklin, peering over the side at the visitors' entrance directly below, suddenly stood and began running.

"Get down," Munson shouted. "What do you think you're doing?"

"Looking for the drainpipe. It's supposed to be here."

Munson sprinted after him and brought him down with an ankle tackle, then crawled with him to the edge of the wall. "There it is," the burglar said.

"Where?"

"In the street." Munson spit the words. He pointed to a section of rusted pipe that had fallen from the top of the wall, leaving the bottom fifteen feet still attached.

"Well, I never promised it would be that easy," Conklin said.

"Fucking idiot." Munson crawled back to the others. "Walker, Stark, let me have your shirts."

"You crazy?" Walker said. "It's cold."

"It'll be damn colder spending what's left of your life on this roof. The drain's no good the way it is. I'm going to try and hook up a rope." He laughed without using his mouth. "Like Holmes told the warden we would . . ."

"He *is* crazy," Stark said.

"Give it anyway." Munson hurried out of his own shirt, but the others toyed with their buttons until Conklin handed over his faded chambray and the burglar knotted the sleeves in his. Then Stark and Walker stripped down to their T-shirts and Munson fashioned a cloth chain six feet long and cast it off the wall.

"It reach the pipe?" Walker asked.

"Almost." Munson looped the end that had been his shirt around the railing and gave the other to Walker. "Put your weight against it, see if it'll hold."

Walker wrapped the rope around his waist and pulled. "Good enough," he reported.

Munson inspected each of the knots again, then slid the rope above the drainpipe and dropped over the side. "See you on the ground," he said.

The others crowded the rail like two-dollar punters as the burglar shinnied down. He maneuvered to the spout, caught it with his feet and lowered himself cautiously, landing in a puddle capped with a veneer of dirty ice. From the shadow of the wall he watched Conklin descend hand over hand as easily as he had and transfer to the drainpipe, pausing only to secure his grip.

"You're in the wrong line of work," he said when Conklin was beside him. "You ever think of taking up an honest trade, burgling?"

Stark was still bent over the rail, his colorless knuckles fused with the cold metal. "You go next," he said to Walker.

"Uh-uh. No stragglers. We leave you behind, got to saw your tongue off first."

Stark took a deep breath and held it. Slowly, like a man emerging from a narcotic haze, or seeking one, he released his hand and tugged hard at the rope, searching for a reprieve in a weak knot. Sadly, he dipped under the railing and sat on the wall.

"Get going, damn you," Munson barked.

Stark didn't move until he felt Walker's heel against his back. "Your choice," the weight lifter said, adding pressure.

Stark forced himself over the side. Wind swirling along the face of the wall swept him away from the drainpipe and he kicked futilely, not quitting even as the pendulum swung back. He crashed against the aluminum column and latched on, slid down gracefully.

Walker, right behind, was reaching for the pipe when the revving of sirens shattered the night and the wall was washed in unfocused light. On the street a motor roared to life, growing louder as it warmed.

"Hurry, Archie," Conklin said.

Walker squeezed the spout tight enough to pinch it shut. As he clambered down, the center section groaned and then twisted away from the wall and he shook loose and crashed to the street.

Conklin was first at his side. "Jesus, you pulled the lousy thing down with you. You okay?"

Walker nodded. He tried to get up, but fell back on his haunches. "My hip . . ."

Conklin wrapped the weight lifter's arm over his shoulder and Stark took the other. They walked him to the gutter, where Munson crouched against the curb as if his feet were in starting blocks.

"You said there'd be a car," the burglar shouted over the siren's hysterical wail. "What does your great plan call for now?"

He glared at Conklin in the spasmodic light bouncing off the wall. The idiot, the fucking idiot, was giggling, laughing in his face. Munson forced himself to turn away. He would be happy to make good on his threat to cut Conklin's throat if it wasn't more urgent to find a way to save his own neck, give up without getting himself shot like the rest of them. He was heading toward the visitors' entrance with his hands already at his shoulders when machine-gun fire chased him back to the curb. A van rolled out of the dark and a boy in a Red Sox windbreaker and condescending smirk slid open the side doors. "What took you so long?" he asked. "I been waiting here all night, it seems like."

"Just drive, Mel," Conklin said as everyone piled in. "You don't shut your hole, I'll knock your teeth out, I swear."

11

They sped through streets of government cottages, an elementary school walled like a practice penitentiary. Beyond the schoolyard stubby hills swelled under the pavement and Munson cranked down his window and bathed in sweet air.

"What do you think of the plan now?" Conklin asked.

"They kill us in the truck, we're just as dead as if it happened on the wall," Munson said. "I'll reserve judgment."

"Shit, you're no fun."

"Where we heading?" Stark asked.

"Massachusetts."

"Good thing," Stark said. "Jenny, that's my second ex's sister, is expecting me in Boston, Tuesday. If I don't show, Graham'll have to put me in segregation, I'll be in such deep crap."

Only Conklin laughed. "Archie, you got plans for the immediate future?"

"A couple scores to settle. After that, if I can float it, about a ten-day drunk."

"Munson, what about you, what've you got lined up?"

The burglar stuck his head outside, tilted his face into the breeze.

"Answer the man, why don't you?" Stark said.

"Yeah," Walker echoed, "we're all curious what a miserable

soul like you does on the outside besides break in people's houses at night and scare the shit out of them."

"I'm going up to Quebec and lose myself," the burglar said so low the others scarcely could hear him. "Try a regular job."

"I'll bet," Stark said, grinning. "What do you even know about Canada, besides they got a shortage of second-story men?"

"I know it's plenty damn far from Massachusetts, which is the first place they'll look for us. We're better off going north."

"So you can sneak into Canada?" Walker said.

"So we all can."

"It's a bullshit idea. . . ." Walker paused, debating whether he had made his point, and what it was supposed to be. "What have we got in Canada?" He looked to Conklin for support. "Don't tell me you're in it for the clean living, too."

"No," Conklin said. "The pussy. If we can make it to Boston, I know a—"

Sirens shrill with self-importance ended debate. Red lights sizzled against the blacktop like a fuse, and Mel's foot faltered and sought out the brake. A convoy of state, Shaftsbury, and Bennington County police cars erupted in the oncoming lane and the van dipped onto the shoulder submissively as the cruisers continued toward the prison, gathering speed. In back, Walker cheered.

"*If* we can," Munson was saying. "There's a million cops between here and Boston and all of them on the alert for four men without shirts. I say north."

"Vermont's open country clean to the border," Stark said. "Not one decent city to lose ourselves in."

"It's why no one'd think of—"

"Sounds like you're outvoted," Walker said.

Munson swung around in his seat. "Walker, you'd eat the nuts out of Conklin's shit. He was your punk in three tier, we all know it. You don't have a vote."

"What's that supposed to mean?" Conklin snapped, the anger forced, as if it were demanded of him.

"You heard me."

"Ah, you're cuckoo." He caught his brother's eyes in the mirror, held them there. "Anyhow, we're going to Massachusetts. Got it, Mel?"

They took 7A past woodsheds hung with ancient band saws, sleighs left to rot in muddy fields as planters for yellow weeds. At Shaftsbury, where a limestone shelf thrust out of the shoulder, an elderly couple filled a string of bleach jugs with spring water from a pipe in a rock and labored back to their pickup truck like Chinese peasants. Farther south, small gas stations that once had been train depots stood abandoned again beside rusted tracks. As the van emerged from a Boston & Maine underpass, the moon lit a silver obelisk that seemed higher than the nearest mountain.

"The fuck's that?" Stark asked.

"The Bennington Battle Monument," Munson said. "You'll be out of the state in twenty minutes."

Mel switched on the radio, toyed with the dial.

"Seeing if we made the news?" his brother asked.

"Nope, looking for some music. They got shitty stations here, know it?"

"Shut that thing off, Mel, I'm telling you."

Walker felt soreness under his arm and discovered reddish streaks down the side of his T-shirt. "We can't go into Massachusetts like this, we're not dressed for it. We need shirts." When no one took up his cause, he said, "All of us do."

"We need more than that," Munson said. "Jackets, and pants that don't yell for attention like this prison issue we've got on now. And food, pretty soon." He leaned across the hump between the seats. "How much money do you have?" he asked Mel.

"Few bucks. It's all I could scrape up."

"That's great. Add money to the list."

"You're forgetting something else," Conklin said. "Goes right on top."

"I am?"

"Pussy."

Munson, having rehearsed his surrender at the prison, made it. "Okay, that too."

"You heard him." Conklin looked at the mirror until he saw his brother nod. "I wouldn't want to do anything without Mr. Munson's permission." He pulled himself onto the engine hump and rubbed a clear spot of his own in the windshield. "Take a right here," he said at the intersection with Route 9 in downtown Bennington.

"I thought you wanted to go south."

"Don't think, Mel. Do it."

The van turned west onto a business street built around a bank with an outdoor vault alarm over the door. Munson wondered if it might not be an antique and wished he had the chance to go up against it. The staid block yielded to a strip of car lots and fast food restaurants darkened by the holiday, but a convenience store on the edge of the city lived up to a neon promise that it never closed.

Conklin ordered his brother into the lot. "You bring the—"

"In the glove compartment."

Conklin hit the dashboard with the heel of his hand, and an old .32, the grip wrapped in rubber bands, tumbled into Munson's lap. Conklin snatched it up and buffed the cylinder on his pants. "It loaded?"

"What do you think?" Mel said.

Conklin stepped over Walker. He opened the side door and paused with one leg out. "You guys never did give me your shirt sizes." He stuffed the gun in his pants. "Keep the engine running, I won't be long."

He walked around the lone car on the lot. A trash receptacle overflowing with food wrappers and bottles stood outside glass doors that chimed as he entered. A blond girl with a self-conscious smile and braces on her bottom teeth looked up from a romance novel and said hello. To Conklin she appeared to be about fourteen years old, fourteen and good enough to die for.

He went up the aisles and filled his arms with food—three loaves of bread, packaged meat, cheese, mustard and pickles—dumped it on the counter and hurried back for more. The girl turned the page, watching him, wanting to laugh but trying not to show the braces. So he wouldn't see her staring dumbly, she said, "Are you having an Easter picnic tonight?"

Conklin left potato chips and four sixpacks beside the cash register and went to the soda cooler. "You could say that."

"The only thing you forgot are napkins."

"Yeah, right."

"We're running a special on the Marcals, two boxes for—"

"I better stock up." The girl pointed him into the next aisle and he emptied the shelf, brought eight packages to the counter and dropped them on top of everything else.

"Wow, this is huge," she said. "Why didn't you go to the Grand Union?"

"I was driving by and saw you through the window and you looked so lonely and all that I—"

The girl squinted toward a ruler on the door, the half-feet delineated in different colors, that the manager had instructed her to use if she had to describe a troublemaker for the police.

Conklin followed her gaze. "Anyway, I'm not from around here. I didn't know where to find a supermarket and this is the first place I saw."

She decided that he was five-foot-nine and just a pest, with a face nothing would ever get her to remember. She punched more numbers into the register that didn't hum or seem to do anything.

"How much?" Conklin asked when she was done.

"Eighty-one twenty-seven. It's got to be a record. No one runs up an eighty-one-dollar order."

He patted his pockets. "Damn, I must've left my wallet in my other pants."

She frowned at him, her mouth slightly ajar, not caring if he looked all he wanted at the braces as long as he got the message. "You mean I've got to void this? It's only my fourth night working here. I hardly know how to work the register."

"Maybe you won't have to." Conklin grabbed her arm, and the girl yanked away. "I like you," he said. "What's your name?"

"You'd better go, mister. I'm calling the cops."

Conklin pulled the .32. "I don't like you that much. Get over here."

There were tears in her eyes, but he didn't hear sobs. She went around the counter and he marched her outside, showing her off as if he had won her trading horses with the Sioux. "Hey, guys," he said. "Look what I got."

Mel snickered. "A blonde. Since when is that your type?"

"Stuff's all the same." He shoved her in the truck and Walker slid over to make room. "I almost forgot," he said, and ran back to the store. "The food."

He was searching behind the counter for paper bags when the door chimed and two gray-haired women in Stratton Mountain ski parkas went straight for the ice cream freezer and brought over a half-gallon. "Hot enough for you ladies?" he said, and waited for smiles that didn't come.

One of the women put a twenty down. "How much?"

He scraped frost from the carton and found the price, made change from the register. "I'm all out of fives," he said, "Mind singles?"

The woman was fumbling in her bag. She handed him a coupon. "With this?"

"Why didn't you say something before?" He tore the coupon and pushed back the twenty with the ice cream. "The cherry vanilla's on me today," he said. "Now scram."

Looking over their shoulders, the women walked out to a green Dodge. Conklin filled three bags and emptied the register and caught up with the van as Mel was backing off the lot.

Walker shook out all the bags. "One thing you're still forgetting."

"What's that?" Conklin asked as his brother slammed the brakes.

"Shirts."

The girl was hunched between Walker and Stark, trying to look like she wasn't there. Conklin offered a beer and she surprised him by twisting off the cap and taking a long gulp. "What's your name?" he asked.

"Brenda Jarvis."

"Brenda . . . Brenda . . . That's not from the old testament, is it?"

"What? No, I don't think so." She squeezed smaller as Conklin sat next to her. "You robbed the store, didn't you? What are you going to do with me?"

"Don't look so scared." He patted her knee innocently. "We're just going for a ride in the mountains, have that picnic."

"You'll let me go then?"

He showed her the good smile. "How old are you, Brenda?"

"Nineteen."

"You don't look nineteen. But it's good you're older, probably been around the block a few times."

"What? I don't understand."

"We just broke out of prison, been there a long time." He opened a bottle for himself. "I'm sure I'm speaking for the rest of the guys when I say beer's not all we missed."

Her face was wet with tears, but still she didn't whimper. He wondered what it would take to hear her really cry. Maybe after they were done with her he would scare her some more with the gun, shoot her if she was going to be stubborn about it.

They stayed with 9 till they were in the country again, and then Conklin directed his brother southeast over hidden farm roads. When they returned to 7, he slid over the engine hump and tapped Munson on the shoulder. "You ride in back now, I want to sit with Mel."

The burglar swung reluctantly out of the seat and stepped over Stark's legs to the vacant spot by the girl. Walker made him a sandwich, and he sniffed at it with a sick face. Through the rear window he made out the worn summits of the Taconic range falling away from the highway to showcase the moon. He shut his eyes and stretched out, his feet tangling in Walker's. "It's too damn crowded in here," he grumbled.

"Won't kill you," Conklin said.

"There's no reason for us to be uncomfortable." He wedged an ankle under the girl's and was able to spread his legs a few inches apart. "What do we need *her* for? She's just taking up room . . . and groceries."

"You heard why. Course, if you've got things you'd rather do . . ."

"Yeah," Mel said, "don't worry about her being bored and lonely."

He saw the girl watching him hopefully. But if she thought she was the issue she was mistaken. Under different circumstances he wasn't certain that he would not be lining up for a chance at her, staking his claim to a portion of her misery. "Our job is to put ourselves as far from here as we can," he said, "not waste time with her."

"You call that wasting time?" Conklin laughed.

Munson bit into his sandwich. "Fucking idiot," he said with his mouth full.

"Stop the truck, Mel. Stop right now. I've taken all the shit I'm gonna."

The van slowed. They went another half-mile before they found a muck lane through bushes still dappled with snow and followed it to a pool of black water, a quarry edged in blocks of flawed marble. Munson felt the girl tense against his body and was paralyzed by the softness of her breasts, enjoyed it almost as much as seeing Conklin seethe.

"It's time we settled this like men."

"The problem," Munson said, "is you're not much of a man." He looked at Walker, but the weight lifter was busy with the beer, and the point was lost on him. "And a fistfight and a gangbang aren't going to make you one."

"Get out," Conklin said.

Munson searched for a likely peacemaker, but only Stark was not hostile to his cause. "Better do it," he whispered. "If he doesn't get his way, you know we'll be here all night."

Munson went out to a clearing littered with plastic sixpack yokes and ashes from clandestine fires. Conklin was waiting under birches twinned from a scorched trunk, looking slight and unprepared. Munson struck a boxer's left-hand lead, and the boy backed off and darted behind the trees.

"What are you trying to prove?" Munson said. "You don't know how to fight."

"That's what another tough guy thought." Conklin dashed into a puddle of light from the van's single high beam. With his audience pressed against the windshield, he drew the .32 and held it away from his body. "It's *my* choice of weapons, and I pick guns. Where's yours, Munson?"

The burglar dropped his hands. "You're still an idiot," he said, and walked away.

The bullet caught him in the thigh before he heard the shot. He went down too quickly to break his fall, aware only of the pain and the girl shrieking, the screams ending in a strangled cry as a hand was clamped over her mouth. Conklin ran like a spaniel after a duck and stood over him with the gun. As Munson was pushing himself up, a second bullet tore his other leg from under him and he flopped in the dirt.

"You're out of your mi—"

Conklin put the revolver flush against the burglar's head. "Say something?"

"My God," Munson gasped, "show a little mercy. What are we arguing about?"

The words repelled him, their shape on his lips as awful as the event they were meant to forestall. But he tortured his brain for more like them, for whatever it was the boy wanted to hear. If his life was to be ransomed from the meager self-respect that he had carried away from prison, he was prepared to sacrifice all he had.

"You listening?" Conklin called to the others. "Hear what he's saying?" He twisted the muzzle in Munson's ear. "Go on."

"If I said anything to . . . to offend you, I apologize, really I do. It was just . . ." Munson propped himself up into a sitting position and touched his wounds. His kneecap was gone and he ran his hand desperately over his pants leg trying to find it. Then Conklin spun the cylinder and the burglar recoiled and toppled onto his side. "It's just I was nervous . . . plenty scared myself and, you know, I had to—"

"You had to take it out on someone so you picked on me 'cause I'm the youngest. And 'cause you were jealous of my plan, and my map, and my gang, and how I put it all together. That right, Munson?"

"Yeah, it's right."

"Now you're sorry, aren't you?"

". . . Sorry."

"So sorry you'd jump Brenda's bones just to get on our good side, wouldn't you?"

Munson nodded.

"If she'd let you. I don't think she's so sweet on you anymore, Munson. You don't look real suave."

The burglar kept nodding, a blank check for the boy.

"And you'd like me to take you to a doctor so you don't bleed to death here, which looks like it's starting to happen. That right, too?"

Munson's head didn't stop.

"What? I didn't hear."

"I said yes."

"Yes, *please*, Munson. Say that."

". . . Please."

"Okay, I'm not going to be a hardass about it. Get in the truck and we'll find you a hospital."

Munson pushed against the ground, but fell back again. "I . . . can't, I . . ."

"You better start moving," Conklin said. "Mel's getting itchy to hit the road."

"Can't get up . . ."

"Then crawl."

Munson, starting to slip into shock, saw only the gun and the boy behind it. He was aware of the others, but the public loss of his dignity seemed a fair price for an end to his pain. He imagined himself tossing a handful of soil in the boy's eyes and then kneeing him in the crotch, choking the life out of him the way he'd seen it done in a thousand movies. Then Conklin motioned to him with the .32, and he wriggled onto his belly and clawed at the earth. "Can't move," he said. "My legs . . ."

Conklin seemed to be studying the problem with him. "You're smart, you'll find a way."

Munson lowered his head. He dragged himself along the ground, seizing greedily at each handful of earth that inched him closer to the truck. His fingers were bleeding, his mouth sour with limestone grit. The side door opened. An arm reached out to him, and he put his chin in the mud and slithered toward it. But when he looked up again, Conklin was standing over him, blocking the way.

"Know something, Munson? You were right all along."

"Wha—?"

Conklin grinned, giving him the happy look again. "It *is* too crowded," he said, and emptied the gun in the burglar's head.

Conklin heard the girl scream, but only for an instant. He walked around Munson's body, making sure every part of him was dead, then flipped him onto his back. The truck started and wheeled around, the headlights tracing shimmering parabolas that converged on the man in the dirt. A look of surprise had congealed on his mouth. It was tempered with embarrassment, as though he were ashamed anyone should see him like that.

"He dead?" Mel asked.

"No, he's faking it." Conklin patted down the burglar's pockets, but found nothing he wanted. "'Course he's dead. Think I missed?"

"What do we do with him now?"

Conklin leaned into the light, examining the drag marks in the wet earth. He shrugged. "Throw him in the water."

Mel knelt over the body and straightened the limbs. He saw a spot of blood on his own pale skin and daintily nudged his sleeves up over his elbows. He was waiting for his brother to tell him what to do, but Conklin seemed absorbed with something by the pool. "You're the one that shot him," Mel said. "Ain't you going to help?"

"Hold your horses," Conklin said. "If we drop him in the way he is, he'll float around like the duck in your tub. What we want to do is weight him down, anchor him on the bottom."

"You mean like with rocks?"

Conklin shivered. Suspecting a failure of nerve, he rubbed his hands against the gooseflesh on his arms and was relieved to find he was cold from the night air. He went inside the truck. The girl was wedged between Walker and Stark, whose hand was still over her face, the snub nose protruding under his thumb. "I'll take her now, Jeff," he said. "Go out and play with my brother."

He squatted in the trusty's place and reached across to Walker. "Archie, make me a bologna and cheese, hold the mayo." The weight lifter was surrounded by empty beer bottles and made no indication that he had heard. "If you're not too busy . . ."

Half a sandwich was clamped in Conklin's teeth as he dragged the girl outside, shoved her toward the body. "What do you think of him now?" he asked, chewing. "Hot stuff, ain't he? Hot stuff, except he's cold."

She began to sob. The show of emotion excited him, but he took little pleasure from it, less as he considered the reason for her tears. He gave her back to Stark and went over to talk to his brother. With the trusty's help Mel had constructed a small cairn beside the burglar and was working on a second one.

"I didn't say you should build him the Lincoln Memorial." Conklin kicked over the pile of stones and stuffed the smallest inside the dead man's pockets. The larger ones went in Munson's pants. Mel took a shoulder and they dragged the body to the edge of the pool.

"It's not what you would call a Christian burial," Conklin said. "But, tell you the truth, I don't believe Mr. Munson was a real Christian."

He dug his foot under the burglar's hips and levered him over the edge. The body dropped into the water without making much of a splash and went under, jackknifed at the waist.

Mel brushed his hands on his pants. "I guess that's that," he said.

"Well, maybe one more thing." Conklin unzipped his pants and stood over the water. Mel smiled and began to walk away, not getting very far before he heard his brother yell, "*Shit,*" the word echoing off marble slabs that rose like giant stairs over the quarry. Conklin pointed into the center of the pool where Munson bobbed face down at the heart of a Chinese puzzle of ripples.

"What do we do with him now?" Mel asked.

Conklin skimmed a flat stone across the surface, barely missing the body. "Pretend he's doing the dead man's float. We wasted enough time on him already."

Stark brought the girl over with an arm bent behind her back. He made her promise that she wouldn't run away and then let go, and she took off for the trees. The trusty caught up before she had gotten very far and ran alongside her, saying, "Faster, faster." Tiring of the game, he tripped her up and walked her back to Conklin.

"What are you going to do with me?" she asked.

"You know what, Brenda."

The girl backed off as far as Stark let her. She glanced into the van where Walker was staring back through the windshield. "All . . . all of you?"

"First time around," Conklin said. "We'll see who wants to be your boyfriend, get it narrowed down."

She hit out at him with her free hand, slapping punches that connected with his cheek. When he didn't react except to laugh, she tried to kick him in the shins. Then she began to scream. Conklin listened, rubbing his face. He liked that, liked it lots better than all the bleating over Munson. But then it looked like she never was going to stop and he had to tell her, "Shut up, Brenda. Will you please shut up?"

The girl screamed louder.

"Mel," Conklin said, "turn the radio on. See if you can drown her out before she breaks my eardrums."

"I was wondering when you were gonna ask."

Conklin went away from the girl. He wanted to look at Munson again, but wouldn't give him the satisfaction. He saw his brother in the driver's seat leaning over the dashboard. Then

Mel came outside looking like the messenger who gets killed bringing the bad news.

"Now what's the matter?" his brother asked. "Don't they have the kind of music puts you in a romantic mood?"

"I didn't hear music. They got Graham on, talking about how you crashed out."

Conklin strutted into the light. "That right?"

"Uh-huh. And then a couple of old biddies telling the reporter how you were gonna kill them."

"What biddies?"

"From the convenience store. They said you kidnapped the clerk and you were gonna snatch them, too, but they ran out before you could."

"I'd like to hear them say that to my face," Conklin said. "Those dumb shits, I wouldn't take them if they begged me."

"They weren't so dumb. They were watching you all the time, getting an eyeful till you jumped in a blue Chevy van—in case that sounds familiar. They said it went west out of town, and now half of Vermont's looking for it."

"I don't believe that."

"Well, you better. The reporter said they got roadblocks set up all across the southern part of the state and how it's only a matter of time before they find us 'cause the border's sealed off with Massachusetts and New York."

"Jeff," Conklin said calmly, "put Brenda in the truck. We'll make time for her later."

"What are we gonna do?"

Conklin looked around the quarry. "We could spend the night here," he said, thinking out loud, "but they'd find us for sure in the morning. It'd be better if we get new wheels before it's light, take them north, maybe all the way to Canada." He walked to the edge of the pool and watched the body drifting lazily in the black water. "Got to give you credit, Munson," he said. "You were right about that, too."

12

Annie arched her back, stamped her fingerprints in the springy flesh of his shoulders. "Don't," she whispered with her lips against his ear. "Please, don't."

"Somebody could be dying."

"I'll die if you . . . please, Larry . . . don't."

His hand came back to her. She locked her ankles around him, hips rolling again with the steady chug of his body. She opened her eyes and was glad for the darkness that hid their different kinds of disappointment. The phone went silent. She felt herself come alive, responding, matching her rhythms to his. But then the ringing filled her head again and Larry groped for the receiver. She shoved him away. What had begun in such perfect intimacy had degenerated into a wrestling match. She wondered what she saw in such a lug.

"No, nothing special," she heard him say, and not even a wink in her direction. "Why, what's doing?"

Her nerves were jangling. She craved a joint, but was in no condition to roll one. She turned her back—his favorite love-making technique, wasn't it?—and listened. This had better be good, she thought. This had better be a major catastrophe for the whole village of Stowe, or sure as hell it was going to be one for Larry St. Germain. Press her, and she would admit that she was jealous—of his job, of the immediacy she never seemed quite capable of inspiring in him. Not even the baby, her baby, would fill that corner of her emptiness. She switched on the lamp, but quickly turned it off. Excitement had entered his voice; she didn't want to have to see it on his face.

He put back the phone and reached for her. Screw you, she wanted to say, if you think I'm like a book you can put down and go back to where you left off. She shrugged off his hand and rolled to the edge of the mattress. Looking up at the clock, she saw it was close to eleven. Soon he would be heading out the door in that ridiculous uniform, leaving her to dangle so that she'd be lucky to be asleep before three. "Oh, crap," she said.

"What's that?"

"Nothing."

"Ann, you sore?"

"Sore?" she said. "Not at all. Actually, soreness would be nice for a change, a little exuberance on your part. Neglected, ignored, frustrated, that's how I feel. But sore, Larry—"

He didn't interrupt. Not really listening, he was using the time to marshal his facts. He put his hand out to her again, and she ducked under it and sat up against the headboard. "What did they want this time?" she asked.

"*They?*" He sounded surprised. This was not the question he had anticipated.

"The hospital. What's so important they had to call at such an hour?"

"It wasn't the hospital."

Great, she thought, just great. Soon she would be sharing him with the rest of the known world. "Who was it, then?"

"John."

She hesitated. Damn, but she needed that joint. *"John Marlow?"*

"Uh-huh."

"When he hasn't had the decency to look you up once to find out how you're doing?" She was furious, really getting into it now that she had an outlet for her hurt. "What's eating him? Don't tell me it's his conscience."

"He called to . . ." St. Germain cupped her breast to gauge her response to what he was going to say. "He wanted to let me know Paul Conklin busted out of prison tonight."

The gentle tapping in his hand accelerated into something violent.

"He . . . how could that have happened?" Relenting, she turned toward him. "They put him away in maximum security and threw away the key."

"He must've found it," St. Germain said, not smiling. "John says he got into the prison chapel that's been sealed off for a good quarter-century. From there he just had to saw some bars, run around a roof, and climb down the wall."

"I thought that sort of thing went out with George Raft movies."

"Evidently so did the prison administration. After they were discovered missing—"

"*They?*"

St. Germain nodded. "Four, all told. But the others are angels compared to Conklin." He reached over the side of the bed and pulled a quilt over their hips. "After they were found missing from their cells, the warden wasted hours searching the prison on the assumption they were still inside. When they didn't turn up, he requested state police with tracking dogs and a helicopter to shine its light in the yard. Even called in the Shaftsbury fire department. Had their pumper train floodlights on the wall till he got word a clerk had been kidnapped from a convenience store in Bennington and was spotted with some men in a dusty blue van."

Annie shuddered and tugged the quilt under her chin. "That doesn't explain why John called. He wants you to join the manhunt, doesn't he? Because you know Conklin as well as you do?"

St. Germain put his arm out and she pulled it around her, slid closer to him. "Just the opposite. He was thinking I'd hide under the bed if I heard about it on the news. He wanted me to understand I have nothing to worry about, that Conklin and his band of merry men are headed for the Massachusetts line and are odds-on favorites to be back in prison for morning count."

"You almost sound disappointed."

"Why should I give a damn where they are?" he said louder than he meant to. "It's not my job anymore."

"I'm glad," she said. "That awful boy . . . it's hard for me to think of him as just a boy after what he did, but . . . he still gives me the creeps. He isn't normal."

"I should hope not." St. Germain laughed halfheartedly. "Sorry, Ann, but I can't see what John's making a fuss about. Southern Vermont Correctional is a hundred and fifty miles away. The last place Conklin needs to show his face is Cabot County, where no one's forgotten him or what he's done."

"I suppose you're right."

"Of course I am," he said.

"Then why do you look as relaxed as I feel? That call bothered you, didn't it?"

St. Germain put a leg across hers, kissed her. He reached for the receiver again and took it off the hook. "Now where were we?" he said.

"Didn't it?"

He drew away, hovering over her. "I thought by now John's opinion of me would have started to change. But as far as he's concerned I'll always be something used up and soiled."

"Why must you care what he thinks?"

"Because I . . ." The answer, so simple until he had to articulate it, eluded him. "I do, though."

"And it's not only him. Why do you look to others to measure the kind of man you are? You make yourself unhappy trying to win the esteem of people who aren't nearly as good as you."

"I care what *you* think, Ann," he said. "And John may have shafted me, but you can't say he's not a decent sort."

"Forget John. I'm talking about the Dick Vanns and Art Grays, and even the Paul Conklins."

He laughed at her, amazed that he had managed it. "You're really reaching there."

"Am I? If Conklin had diminished you only in your own eyes, you could have dealt with that, told yourself you'd take it out on the next loony who raised a hand to anybody. What's bothering you is there's a single person who's found out you're human, who's not the least bit impressed with you. It's Conklin's approval you're after, not mine."

He had no answer for that, was glad when she started talking again.

"Larry, when are you going to grow up?" She pushed away from him. "I used to think it was being a cop that made you so . . . so brittle. I had it backwards; it's why you became one."

"Is it?" He was trying to sound interested while he tried to remember what it was he wanted to tell her. "But I'm not a cop anymore. I'm an ambulance driver and I've gotten to like it. And the best part of the job, the perk I didn't anticipate, is that Conklin's running around loose tonight and frankly, my dear, I don't give a shit, or whatever the expression is." He kissed her. "So where's the harm if I worry too much about what people think of me?"

She shook her head in defeat. "I just know it's not healthy."

He kissed her again. "You're getting yourself bent out of shape over nothing."

She took a deep breath. "I also know this," she began slowly, "that if ever again you do something reckless that might get you killed, I'll leave you. Even if it's not your fault, if the situation seeks you out I expect you to run away and be happy doing it—for me and for the baby. Things are different now. You can't put your warped notion of honor ahead of everything else anymore."

His mouth came down over hers, so that she felt he was forcing the words back inside. Then he whispered, "You've made your point. Can't we stop?"

Before she could reply he was floating over her again, so light, she thought, so tender. Stop, she wanted to say, when I haven't even gotten started? Instead she pulled him on top of her, answering to his body, the quilt around their ankles, thinking, Don't stop, don't stop, don't stop nooooo . . .

St. Germain squared the eight-pointed cap on his forehead, tucked a wisp of blond hair under the brim. He turned away from the mirror for a second opinion. "Well, how do I look?"

"I wouldn't worry about any of your customers refusing service, if that's what you're trying to find out."

"I'm serious, Ann. How do I look?"

"Good enough to . . . no, we've already done that." She giggled. Not like a little girl, not coy, he thought, but so inviting she'd have to boot him out of the cabin. "I'll keep your place warm," she promised, patting the bed.

"You're no help." He went back to the mirror.

"Busy night tonight?"

"Not likely. Working the graveyard shift is mostly traffic accidents and—"

"I wish you wouldn't call it that," she said. "You drive an ambulance, not a hearse."

"About half the time it's the same thing. Too many of the people I see, the only reason we bring them in is for the autopsy. Medical science is pretty much overmatched when it comes to raising the dead."

She grimaced. "Sounds like fun."

He walked over to the bed and kissed her, and she swept her

hand over the mattress. "The offer still stands, you know," she said.

"See you for breakfast."

"Drive carefully."

Ground fog seeped out of bare woods and tumbled along the road in ragged billows. He took his time to the interstate. If Annie had gotten on his case with unreasonable demands, it still wasn't asking too much of him to keep his car out of the trees. He wondered what was making her so jumpy, and decided that it had been the baby talking.

He pulled into the staff lot and parked away from the other cars, vaguely embarrassed that his plates did not carry the magical MD designation. In the emergency room two interns were standing at the coffee maker with a nurse known around the hospital as Miss Roundheels. Funny, he remembered telling her the one brief time they had spoken, you don't look like an Indian. Both doctors had bags under their eyes and stubbly cheeks. St. Germain knew they had been on duty for fifteen hours and were groggy from an assembly line of broken legs and ruined knees. Till dawn there would be little to keep them from catching some sleep unless someone racked himself up on Blood Alley, the lonely stretch of Route 100 looping into the mountains. He went down to the garage where 786, the Big Ford ambulance with the fuel-line problem, had just returned with the evening crew.

"What's doing out there?" he asked a man in a uniform identical to his save for a stethoscope spilling out of the hip pocket.

"Quiet as you could want. Couple of heart attacks in Moscow and Colbyville."

St. Germain looked under the hood. He kicked the tires. He polished some chrome and then climbed onto the seat, picked up a day-old *Free Press,* and kept busy with it for most of an hour.

Around one o'clock one of the interns came into the garage.

Steve Brownfield was a Stowe native who had gone off to Middlebury College and then Yale Medical School and had returned to Vermont to take over his father's family practice. "How's it going, Lieutenant?" he asked.

Though the intern was five years younger, it seemed to St. Germain that generations separated them, that Brownfield, with his future mapped out like a battle plan, had evaded the false starts that had put his own coming of age on indefinite hold. "That's Larry to you, Dr. Brownfield."

"Mind if I crawl in and cop some Zs?" the young doctor asked. "I'm whipped."

"What's wrong with the doctors' lounge? Bedbugs?"

Brownfield turned down the radio that monitored police and fire calls in a two-county area. "Uh-uh. Can't sleep without some static to soothe my frazzled nerves."

St. Germain smiled at him. "Dr. Greeley's in there tossing it at Roundheels, isn't he?"

Brownfield shut his eyes. "It was unpardonable, what we did, telling you she was a full-blooded Abenaki."

"Yes, it was," St. Germain said.

"Wake me if you hear anything good."

St. Germain went back to the *Free Press* and was rereading the front page when he homed in on a voice above the emergency clutter. Washington County was reporting an accident on Route 100 in Colbyville with a request for the nearest ambulance to bring two bodies to the morgue. St. Germain whispered into the microphone and poked the sleeping intern in the ribs. "Reveille, Dr. Brownfield," he said. "Got to run."

Brownfield brought his hand to his face, tried to coax the exhausted features into shape. "Something horrible, I take it."

"For the parties concerned," St. Germain said. "Myself included. Double fatal down to Colbyville." He slapped the newspaper into the doctor's lap. "Out. Sleep in your own bed. Maybe Greeley and Roundheels are done."

"They'll be at it till one or the other needs CPR. It's why interns look the way we do." He stretched, his fingers leaving smudges on the windshield. "Let's roll," he said. "I can use the fresh air."

St. Germain twisted the key and they coasted through the sleeping village. At the Route 108 light he came to a full stop and looked up the desolate Mountain Road. Past the covered footbridge over the Little River there was no traffic from Mount Mansfield or Smugglers Notch, which would remain snowbound for another month. He gunned the engine and ran through the gears, throwing Brownfield against the back of the seat. He switched on his flashing lights. "Keeps the blood flowing," he said to the doctor.

Beyond the bed-and-breakfast places, the farmhouses transformed into country inns, working barns intruded on picture-postcard Vermont. Brownfield opened the vents and let the cold air revive him. The ambulance swerved to avoid a porcupine plastered to the asphalt, and he reached for something to hold onto. "I'm starting to feel better already," he said weakly.

St. Germain nodded in agreement. "Great handling on these Fords."

Near Moscow the road dropped and straightened, and they ran by new factories growing out of rocky pastures. St. Germain pressed the needle close to eighty, then frowned and came off the gas. The exhilaration of pure speed, he had discovered, wore quickly when its purpose was the retrieval of dead meat; he'd been happier at the wheel of a cruiser halting traffic to allow a school bus to make a left turn. He killed the flashing lights. A mile ahead, red and blue beacons staved off the darkness.

"Looks like the local ghouls beat us to the merchandise," Brownfield said.

St. Germain flicked on his high beams. "Doesn't make sense.

The Washington dispatcher said the crash was in Colbyville. Those lights are Arnold's Crossing, and that's the Cabot County panhandle."

A couple of tan police cars blocked the northbound lanes. Squeezed between them was a Winnebago trailer and on either side a Cabot deputy. St. Germain recognized Dick Vann and Art Gray and approached them, riding his brake. Without pulling his head from the Winnebago, Vann waved the ambulance on.

St. Germain came even with the cruisers and stopped. "G'evening, Dick."

Vann whirled around, knocking his cap askew. "Why, if it isn't the . . . Hello, stranger."

St. Germain's fingers tightened around the wheel, but his face gave nothing away. Vann grunted. He adjusted his cap and leaned in the Winnebago again, and Art Gray walked over and rested his elbows inside St. Germain's window. "How've you been, Larry?" he said uncomfortably.

"Can't complain. What's all this?"

"John's got a bug up his ass about . . . you heard about Conklin yet?"

"Yeah."

"About him trying to make it to Malletts Bay by swinging through the county."

"I heard he was headed south."

Gray shrugged. He looked over his shoulder at the Winnebago, where a man with a white crewcut flicked a thick butt onto the pavement and steered through the roadblock. Then Vann came over and stood beside Gray, and St. Germain smelled cigar smoke on his clothes, saw two panatelas in his breast pocket. ". . . You know John," Gray was saying.

Thought I did once, St. Germain wanted to say. "That's why you're out at one in the A.M., looking in Winnebagos? You think Conklin's gone camping?"

Gray laughed in spite of himself, not stopping until Vann said, "You're the Conklin expert. You tell us."

St. Germain gave him a hard look. The deputy poked inside, showing lieutenant's bars on his collar. "This is what you're doing these days? Seems slow."

It occurred to St. Germain that verbal sparring bored him when it wasn't prelude to the real thing. He lifted his foot off the brake and started to move away.

Vann said, "But if it keeps you out of trouble . . ."

St. Germain stomped on the brake. "What's that supposed to mean?" He started to open the door, but then changed his mind. He hit the siren and Vann jumped back with his hands over his ears as the ambulance roared off.

"Those men seemed to resent you," Brownfield said. "Didn't they serve under you when you were with the sheriff's department?"

"Uh-huh." Still not giving anything away.

"They were so tense you could smell it. The big one, anyway."

"The job'll do that to you sometimes," St. Germain said. "They're under a lot of pressure."

"Is that why you switched careers?"

"Not really. I wasn't aware of the pressure till it was off of me and I was mostly missing it."

"You seem relaxed enough now."

"Well, it's taken some doing."

"I still don't understand about those two. Did you have reason to discipline them? Weren't they good officers?"

St. Germain drove two miles more and then turned to Brownfield. "Cabot County's finest," he said.

13

Driving home, McCallum couldn't get his mind off the services at St. Mark's. A new pastor had taken over the congregation, an earnest young man concerned about pornography and Nicaragua, although somewhat weak on Scripture. During the sermon he had seemed to be staring at McCallum as he explained that if God did not see fit to provide earthly rewards, you might as well kiss your portion of heaven good-bye. McCallum, feeling damned in the wood-paneled Buick station wagon that he had been babying for the better part of a decade, had been passed by the new pastor in a factory-fresh BMW. There was a jeweled stud in the young man's ear and a curious silver cross on a chain around his neck. When the light hit it a certain way, the cross looked almost like a small spoon.

After church McCallum had dozed while his daughter went around in a hat that cost what he used to bring home from a month at the plant. The egg hunt had to be canceled when the children refused to go out on the wet grass. Back at his daughter's, Jason, the youngest, came down with a tummy ache (no surprise, so did McCallum) and someone had to find a doctor, so Ruth volunteered to do the dishes. And now, if they were lucky, they would make Manchester Depot by 1:00 A.M. Next year, God willing he was still around, he would trade off with one of the younger guys and work on Easter.

Ruth said, "Please slow down, dear. What's your hurry?"

"My hurry is I would like to use my own bathroom and sleep in my own bed tonight." He clutched at his stomach. "Die there, too."

Ruth tittered. For the life of him, he couldn't see why she liked being talked to that way. He gave the car gas, and then they must have been back in Vermont because they were climbing into the Monadnocks. "Where are we?" Ruth asked. "I don't know this road."

"This is quicker, runs into 7," McCallum said, wondering if he could be right.

The blacktop leveled and he came quickly off the accelerator and flashed his brights. "What is it?" Ruth asked.

He pointed with his chin. "Looks like some kind of trouble."

A blue panel truck was stalled on a curve. Beside it a girl with long blond hair was pacing on a short rein.

"You're not going to stop for her," Ruth said. "It's getting on to midnight."

"It is," McCallum said. "And I am." As he brought the station wagon to a halt, he saw a birch sapling across the road in front of the van. He leaned out his window. "Can't you drive over that?"

The girl shook her head, kept tossing it as if once she got it moving she couldn't stop it on her own.

"What a strange child," Ruth said. "Why doesn't she say something? And if her truck won't go over the tree, she should pull around and go back the way she came instead of waiting like a dummy for an even bigger dummy like you."

But McCallum was already out of the station wagon, sizing up the downed log. "I don't see how this landed all the way out here," he said to the girl. He stood away from the branches and bent his knees the way his doctor had taught him to lift heavy objects. "Now you grab ahold, miss. It can't be heavy."

The girl didn't say anything, just looked at him, still swinging her head. McCallum heard steps behind him and turned to see a boy in a T-shirt and jeans walking around the curve. "Well, this must be your fellow. We shouldn't have any trouble moving it now."

"No trouble at all, old man," the boy said.

McCallum took an instant dislike to the boy. He backed off toward the station wagon. ". . . So I'll just let him take over."

"Hey, old man, not so fast."

The boy had produced a revolver and was pushing shells into the cylinder. McCallum saw two other men, one of them hobbling, leaning on his companion for support. A fourth man in a red baseball jacket dropped out of the van, carrying a tool chest and a sheaf of maps.

"That's a nice station wagon you have there," the boy said.

McCallum wasn't sure what was coming, but he knew it was bad, bad for him and for Ruth. He found himself looking toward the blond girl, starting to understand.

"I'd like to buy it from you."

McCallum said, "What do you want, my money? I only have a few dollars."

"Just the wagon," the boy said. "And I'll pay, name your price." He pulled a scrap of paper from his pocket and unfolded it. "Anybody have a pen?"

McCallum slid his new Papermate Deluxe Powerpoint out of his shirt. Then he raised his hands over his head.

"Tell you what, old man. If you promise you won't go for *your* gun, you can put your hands down. But only if you promise. . . . We got a deal?"

McCallum dropped his arms. One of the other men began to beat his hands against his sides. "Put a move on, Paul. How about it?"

Paul looked up, in no mood to be rushed. He printed a few

words and gave the paper to McCallum, who held it inches from his face. "What is this? My glasses are in the—"

"It's my IOU," the boy said. "Says I'll pay five thousand for your station wagon next time I run into you. That's fair, isn't it? Who else would give you so much for that old gas guzzler?"

"It's a woody," McCallum said.

"What?"

"A woody. That's real simulated wood paneling on the doors. It's worth more than five thousand."

"Will you stop playing games?" One of the others said to the boy. "We're freezing."

"Well, five thousand's all I'm paying. Now tell your mom to get out."

McCallum had been thinking again about St. Mark's, fairly certain of the message the new pastor would read into his one earthly pleasure being taken from him. Only now did he start to feel real anger toward the boy. "Ruth is my wife," he snapped.

"Tell her to shake her ass anyhow. She's got it parked in my wagon."

McCallum went back to the Buick and opened the passenger's door. He was trying to slide in over Ruth, reaching for the wheel, when he felt a heavy hand on his shoulder, and one of the other men, the big one with the bad hip, pulled him onto the road. Ruth slid out without having to be asked, and the boy lined them up against the van.

"What do you want from us?" Ruth asked.

"We already got that. You should be asking what we're going to do with you."

"What are—"

"Nothing, nothing you should worry about," the boy said.

He was laughing, trying to reassure them with a big grin. McCallum thought it was the ghastliest smile he ever had seen.

"We're going to Canada. Want to come?"

McCallum stood closer to his wife, digging in his heels.

"No? Well, we can't leave you in the middle of nowhere, couple of senior citizens like yourselves." The boy snapped his fingers and then looked up suddenly, as if the sound had startled him. "Say," he said, "what about this, what if we tie you up and you can, you know, work yourselves free and take off after we're gone?"

He reached into his pants and Ruth recoiled against the truck. "No opinion?" he said, and gave McCallum back his pen. "I'm going to take it for a yes. . . . Someone see if we've got any rope in the van."

Mel tossed a coil of nylon twine out the back, and Conklin put his arm through and slid it over his shoulder. Without having to touch his gun he prodded the couple into the darkness. "Don't look so down," he said. "It's not the end of the world."

They marched through the trees in single file, McCallum in the lead, reaching back for his wife's hand. The woman stumbled over a moss-covered rock, and as Conklin steadied her she began to mutter, " 'Yea, though I walk through the valley of the shadow of death I will fear no—' "

"You folks *Christians?*" the boy said.

"We attended Easter services this morning, if that's so amusing." McCallum sniffed.

"What denomination?"

"Congregational."

"I'm a Baptist myself. Where's your church?"

"We were visiting our daughter in Williamstown, Massachusetts," McCallum boasted. "Her husband's a professor at the college there. French literature." McCallum allowed himself an inner smile. If they could reach the boy, appeal to whatever religious convictions he seemed sure to have, he might forget about leaving them there, even drive them home if they found enough good things to say about the Baptists. "Ruth, that's Mrs. McCallum, had bypass surgery last autumn and—"

"I'm sorry."

". . . And I'm sure you understand the stress this is putting on her. It's getting cold, and if we have to stay out very long—"

"Good thing you mentioned it," the boy said. "How about we stop right here, you won't have so far to walk out of the woods? Pick any tree you like and I'll put the rope around you nice and loose. You'll probably beat me back to the road."

The way McCallum surveyed the forest, he could have been visiting a Christmas tree farm. Then he brought his wife to an oak that had lost its crown to lightning and they stood on opposite sides of the trunk. Though McCallum couldn't see his face, he had the uneasy feeling that the boy was grinning.

"Now turn around like you're hugging the tree."

McCallum did as he was told, his fingers finding Ruth's and linking with them. He heard her inhaling through her mouth, deep breaths, not letting herself get too worked up. Expecting to feel the rope, he looked over his shoulder—and then he wanted to laugh, to drop to his knees and thank God for the first true miracle he had witnessed. *The boy was rewinding the twine.* "Didn't you bring enough?" McCallum asked as if it was an old joke between them.

"This piece is plenty long. Problem is, it's all I have." The boy winked at him. "And you never can tell when you're going to need rope."

As McCallum was whispering his prayer of thanks, the boy drew the gun out of his waistband, put it to the back of Ruth's head and shot her once, McCallum wondering what the new pastor of St. Mark's would make of it as the bullet exited above her ear and splintered the rough bark of the oak. The smell of singed hair was in his nostrils before Ruth toppled across the roots. The boy blew smoke from the muzzle, though McCallum was certain there was no smoke, and then turned the gun on him. "I really can't spare the rope."

When Conklin walked out of the woods, the others were waiting outside the van. Stark stood closest to the girl, who had begun to cry again. Conklin tossed a blood-spattered jacket at Walker, and the weightlifter draped it around his shoulders. Then Conklin finished coiling the rope and gave it to his brother. "I won't be needing this after all," he said.

"Are they—"

Conklin nodded. "With Him," he said, and put new shells in the .32. "We got everything we want in the wagon?"

Mel leered at the girl. "Except her."

"Then put her there and let's get." He started up the van, backed it around the station wagon, and drove it into the trees along the same track he had brought the old couple. When he was out of sight of the road, he flung away the keys and trudged back with his chin against his chest.

"You all right?" his brother asked.

"I didn't think I'd feel so bad about it, but getting rid of the truck . . . it was like ditching an old friend." He motioned his brother into the station wagon. "I'll drive. I can use the practice."

"It's what I was afraid of," Stark whispered to the girl.

"Who said that?"

"Move," Walker said. "This is no time to be getting touchy."

Conklin put the wagon in gear and they glided around the curve. In the twenty-five minutes they had been there they hadn't seen another vehicle; now the lights from a small convoy beamed down on them. Two cars trooped over the summit of a bald hill behind a Dodge truck with a bug screen over the grille and a U-haul hitched to the rear. Conklin relaxed and pushed the Buick to sixty. "Nice pickup," he said. "No wonder those Congregationalists liked woodies."

"Where we headed now?" Walker asked.

"If the cops find the van, they've got to figure we're following 7." The words came quickly, as though he had thought it out well in advance. "What we'll do is swing east around the mountains and take 100 to Canada. If we run into troopers I know a road that . . . well, it isn't important 'cause we're not going to run into any."

"How can you be sure?"

"Long as we keep out of cities, we shouldn't see a single cop. And 100 stays in the country all the way to Waterbury."

They turned onto a road no busier than the one they were leaving. They picked up Route 9 again on the other side of Bennington and followed alongside the Roaring Branch where the stream sent brown meltwater over its bank. The Buick's high beams reflected off a sign that read, MOLLY STARK TRAIL, and Conklin said, "One of your exes, Jeff?"

Stark said, "Huh?" and everybody laughed, everybody but the girl. They climbed past Woodford and the blue chairs of the Prospect Mountain ski area swaying over barren slopes. At Wilmington Conklin waited five minutes for the red light in the center of town and then aimed the station wagon north on 100.

"Three, four hours tops, and we should be at the border," Conklin announced.

"And they'll let us in just like that?" Walker said. "You don't think someone'll want to know what we're doing coming into their country without luggage, or two shirts between us?"

"All they're interested in is if we're bringing money. When I show them what we have, they'll sell us their shirts."

"What about Brenda? What if she tells them where we got it from?"

Conklin looked in the mirror, made eye contact with the girl, who quickly looked away. "Take it up with her," he said.

Wilmington dissolved into a strip of motels with German-sounding names that extended past the Haystack Mountain lifts to Mount Snow. The highway ran between hardscrabble farms where uncapped silos towered above the fields like giant rain gauges. They rode for an hour with nothing to write home about, and then 100 spilled over the Sherburne Pass into the White River Valley, Mel dozing through the granite canyon of Granville Gulf. North of Warren the small towns came one on the heels of another, and Conklin slowed to forty.

Mel yawned, licked the sleep off his lips. "Where are we?"

"Coming into Waterbury. It's the one stretch I don't feel great about."

The highway traced deserted streets toward brick buildings on three sides of a grassy campus. "There's the laughing academy," Conklin said. "Had me there for thirty days."

Stark said, "I did sixty."

" 'Cause you're twice as nuts as me." Conklin glanced around the wagon as if he expected applause. When he checked the road again, the city was already behind them. He put his foot down harder on the gas but switched quickly to the brake.

Walker braced against the seat. "You trying to get us killed?"

"Trying not to. There's flashing lights up ahead. Could be troopers."

"We'd better turn around," Stark said, reaching for the girl.

"And go where?" Conklin placed the .32 across his lap. "I don't see this being anything we can't handle."

The Buick came up on a Washington County sheriff's cruiser. It was idling next to a tow truck whose hook was baited for a red Corvette wrapped neatly around a utility pole. An ambulance from a Stowe hospital seemed ready for a tug of war over the sports car. Washington deputies kept traffic away from a dark-haired man and a blond in a tan uniform kneeling over two bodies covered by sheets. Conklin slowed and squinted into the glare.

"Get a move on," Walker said. "This is no time to be rubbernecking."

Conklin stopped the wagon. "Mel," he said, "you see that big guy working on the stiff?"

Mel brought his hand over his eyes and looked out the driver's window. "I see the back of his head. And his ear. Why?"

"They look familiar to you?"

"I . . . nope, can't say they do. Who do you think it is?"

Conklin shrugged. He skirted the accident and brought the Buick to full speed. "Never mind," he said. "I'm hallucinating is all."

The girl swiveled around, watching the deputies as if her future were receding with them. She tried to crawl into the rear of the wagon, but Stark brought her back with his hand over her mouth. She bit at his palm, ground the web of skin between his forefinger and thumb, and he pulled away and let her yell. Mel switched on the radio. An easy listening station came on, and he made a face as pained as the girl's.

Conklin said, "See if you can get the news, find out what we're up to." He laughed at his own joke, kept it up as he began to pound his fist on the dash.

"What now?" his brother asked.

Conklin pointed at red and blue beams canvasing the highway. "Must be another fender bender."

The Buick's high beams washed away the colored lights. Instead of the crash scene Conklin anticipated, there were two police cars in the northbound lanes. A big officer with a cigar in his teeth, almost as big as the blonde at Colbyville, waved them into the narrow space between the cruisers and studied their license plate with his hand playing against his gun butt.

In the mirror Conklin saw Stark wrestle the girl across his lap and hold her there with a handkerchief stuffed inside her mouth. He rolled his window down an inch. "Some kind of accident?" he called out to the big officer. "We just saw a bad wreck down to—"

"I want you all to open your doors and step out of the car."

"Why, Officer?"

"Don't ask questions. Do it."

A second deputy walked up behind the big man. The cigar in his mouth was unlit and he took it out and cupped it in his hand. "I don't understand," Conklin said. He was eyeing the officers' guns in their holsters, trying not to stare. "Can't you tell us why?"

The second deputy whispered to his partner, who nodded as he came around to Conklin's door. "Now I'm ordering you—"

Conklin took the .32 in his right hand and angled it upward, squeezed the trigger as the culmination of the short, furtive motion. The slug blew out the window and tore into the big officer's shoulder, spinning him back. A second bullet caught him at the base of the skull, in the knotty lump above the hairline, destroying the spinal column where it entered the brain.

The other deputy dove to the pavement, tugging at his service revolver. As Conklin pushed open the door, the windshield disintegrated and the front seat was showered with glass. Conklin blinked blood out of his eyes, and the strength went out of him as he saw his brother slumped against the headrest with a piece gone from the bridge of his nose. Another bullet tore out the rest of the glass and Walker yelled and fell over the girl. Conklin got off a slug that went wide of the mark. The officer raised himself for a clear shot that also missed, then scrambled to his feet, still shooting. Conklin ducked under the dash. A bullet slammed into the radiator, and sweet-smelling steam leaked inside the car. Conklin heard a door open and then Stark's agonized gasp as a bullet sliced into his neck. Using his own door as a shield, Conklin got off two shots at the officer, the second one bringing him down. He ran to the fallen man, watched the breath bubble out of him through a hole high in his chest. He plugged the wound with his gun. As the deputy opened his eyes, he moved the muzzle away, put it to the man's lips and forced it between his teeth.

"Understand what I'm doing?" he said. "Do you?"

He waited. The officer's eyes flickered, and in that brief moment of comprehension Conklin put weight on the trigger. The back of the man's head skipped into the road like the rock skimmed over the quarry pool.

"That's for Mel, you fuck," he said.

He threw away the .32. A pump gun was mounted upright in one of the cruisers, and he brought it back over his shoulder like a hunter returning from the field. Stark had propped himself against the Buick's single fender skirt. The left side of his T-shirt was wet with blood from an opening in his throat. Conklin stood the weapon beside him and listened to his labored breathing.

"What now?" the trusty rasped.

"Sorry, Jeff. All you can do is make your peace with Him."

"Fuck that," Stark said. "I want—"

"That's no way to talk." Conklin slid inside the Buick. Droplets like red tears of rage stippled his brother's face, and he scrubbed each one away and then kissed him and placed the body across the seat. Out of the corner of his eye he saw the girl cowering against the tailgate. As he went for her, she began shrieking again.

"Knock it off, Brenda."

The girl screamed louder.

"God damn it, show some respect for the dead."

She shut up then, and he climbed into the rear seat for a look at Walker. A dark trickle was congealing against the weight lifter's cheek. Conklin traced it to a gash hidden in his eyebrow. Spreading the skin beneath the hair, he saw a metal nub embedded in a white ridge of bone. His fingers came away damp and sticky, and he wiped them on his pants.

"Let's go," he said to the girl. "I know a way . . ."

Brenda curled around the spare tire, crying to herself. Conklin crawled after her and pushed her out the rear.

"What do you want with me?" she sobbed. "Haven't you done enough already?"

"*Me?* I didn't do anything to anybody. It was those

cops. . . ." He shoved her ahead and went back to the cruiser in the weeds. The passenger's door was unlocked. "Flashy," he said, "but it'll do for now. Anyhow, I always wanted to drive one of these things. Get in."

The key was in the ignition. When he started the engine, the siren sounded, and he hit half the buttons on the console before the wailing died. Carefully, he tried his foot on the gas. The turbocharger sprinted along the shoulder, trampling a row of seedling maples. Steering with both hands, he guided it into the lane.

Brownfield said, "I hope Greeley's out of bed by now."

"I hear you," St. Germain said. "I could do with some sleep myself."

"Did I say . . .?" The young doctor smiled superiorly. "Let me put it another way. I hope he's done with Roundheels. I can sleep when I get home."

St. Germain didn't know if the joke was on him, but he laughed to play it safe. "You younger guys amaze me. I went steady with every girl I dated since high school. The notion of sharing a woman with my friend . . . I can't guess what to make of that."

"Greeley's not my friend."

St. Germain braked the ambulance, sighted down a long straightaway as though they were entering uncharted territory. He looked at Brownfield unhappily. "We're nearly back to Arnold's Crossing. I don't see the lights from the roadblock."

"Maybe they gave up and went home."

"Not those two," St. Germain said. "They'd stay till they were told they weren't needed anymore."

"Well, maybe they're not. Maybe they found who they were looking for."

"It's what worries me." St. Germain leaned on the accelerator, and the blacktop rolled up under the wheels.

"There's the sheriff's car," Brownfield said. "One of them."

St. Germain brought the ambulance to a skidding stop and jumped into the road. His legs wobbled as he saw Art Gray in a puddle stemming from his shattered skull. Ten feet away, Dick Vann lay crumpled on his side. St. Germain put him on his back, stared into the dull eyes, wondering why his own wanted to fill with tears.

He let Vann down with his cap under his head. Inside the Buick Brownfield was crouched in front examining a man laid out on the seat. St. Germain looked over the doctor's shoulder, and Brownfield turned to him, shaking his head.

"That one's Mel," St. Germain said.

"What . . . ? You know him?"

"The boy they were looking for, that's his . . ." He leaned close, satisfying himself that the diagnosis was correct. "Never mind," he said. "It isn't important."

Brownfield went into the rear and felt for the pulse of a big man sprawled with his knees on the floor. "Head shot," he said. "Know who he is, too?"

"Some bastard who no doubt deserved what he got." As he backed away from the station wagon, St. Germain saw another man slumped motionless against a fender. "There's your third—"

Stark moaned without opening his eyes, and Brownfield slipped quickly from the Buick. "Lieutenant, get my bag out of the ambulance."

When St. Germain came back, Brownfield had placed Stark flat on the pavement and was pinching the wound in his throat. "How is he?"

"He's got both feet in the grave, and all I've got to pull him out with are two fingers," the doctor said. "Advise the E. R. of what we have here. And then bring me some plasma volume extender. The Dextran."

St. Germain's upper body pivoted toward the ambulance, but his feet stayed where they were.

"Didn't you hear?"

St. Germain knelt beside the man on the ground. "Where did he go?"

Stark's lips moved. Blood ran out the corners of his mouth.

"I'm asking you where did he go?"

Brownfield said, "This man will die if you don't—"

"Hear that?" St. Germain bent lower and spoke into the trusty's ear. "Where is he?"

Stark opened his eyes, gazed blankly past St. Germain.

"Conklin. Where do I find him?"

"Don't know . . ."

St. Germain spread his palm in front of Stark's face, then placed it over Brownfield's hand and yanked it away from the wound. The blood spurted down the trusty's shoulder and then his side and he tried to stanch the flow himself. Seeing color between his fingers, he exhaled deeply, making a gurgling sound in his nose. Brownfield reached out to him. St. Germain blocked the doctor with his back.

"I figure you've got thirty seconds' worth of blood you can spare," St. Germain said. "If you don't tell me what I want to know, we won't have to waste much time watching you dry up."

Stark shook his head, shut his eyes again.

"Your choice."

Brownfield started back to the ambulance. "I'm not going to stand for this."

St. Germain chased after him and threw him easily to the pavement. "You even think of touching that radio, son, I swear I'll knock you silly." He took quick steps back to the wounded man. "Where?"

Stark spit some more blood. "Conklin says he knows a way . . ."

"A what?"

"A road . . . some kind of shortcut he was always talking about. Said it was a back door to Canada nobody but him knew."

St. Germain clamped the wound the way he had been instructed during his brief training as a paramedic and held his hand there until Brownfield returned with an IV bag. Then he stripped the gun belt from Dick Vann's body and cinched it around his waist.

"What do you think you're doing?" Brownfield said.

St. Germain ran to the ambulance and squeezed his legs under the wheel. Dome lights flashing, the big Ford pulled around the doctor and his patient, the answer lost in a scream of burning rubber.

14

St. Germain hugged the center stripe, shortening the road. He ran the light onto 108 past a sign that warned the route was closed through Smugglers Notch. As if anyone would be crazy enough to try the pass in April. Anyone, he was thinking, in a fat-ass Ford ambulance that was even money to come back on the hook from a run around the block. A hot car might make it, say a turbocharged sheriff's cruiser in cherry shape. But only if it was equipped with the lugged tires that should have been replaced long before Easter.

A black Cadillac with Connecticut tags crawled away from the Yodler Motel, and St. Germain came up on it sounding his siren. Without waiting for results, he pulled blindly into the oncoming lane, forcing a gray pickup to choose between a head-on and the trees. The driver challenged him to a game of chicken, gunning his motor, drawing a bead on the ambulance— and was the first to flinch. He swerved around St. Germain's right, shooting him the finger in the consolation round, then ran off the pavement, bringing down thirty feet of chain link fence around the Yodler's pool.

Mount Mansfield rose out of the fog, the Front Four dog-legged scars on hardwood stands. Mild updrafts lured clouds to the summit where they hovered over the television mast like moored dirigibles. Sputtering in the cold mountain air, the ambulance struggled to maintain fifty. St. Germain downshifted, searching for easy traction. The crash rail at the edge of the cliff had been pounded into a twisted ribbon of steel. On his right was Bingham Falls and the state ski dormitory and a sign announcing the state forest. Another cautioned: STEEP CURVES AHEAD.

The blacktop paralleled a stream that plummeted from the Notch under a broken cap of ice. He followed it to the Spruce Peak lot, where a row of concrete caissons were set like dragon's teeth across the highway. On the other side of the barrier the pavement continued under a foot and a half of snow. He swung the ambulance close to the water and then angled back onto the road, his lights trained on studded treads climbing the pass.

The big Ford balked, found its footing in the turbocharger's perfect track, and plodded into the gap. The road steepened, the temperature dropping with each added foot of elevation. The rear wheels slid out of the ruts and ground uselessly. St. Germain downshifted again and forced the ambulance up the mountain. If the snow got any deeper he would have to chase the cruiser on foot.

He tried to remember the last time he had been here, decided it was the summer he'd met Annie, when they had driven up in his old Mustang convertible to hike the Long Trail to Elephant's Head on the eastern face of the Notch. The rock formations all had names—The Singing Bird, The Hunter and His Dog, Old Smugglers Face—and Annie had promised that he would recognize each one as soon as he saw it. But no matter how hard he pressed his imagination, every rock looked the same to him, and so they had spent the better part of the afternoon, the very best part, screwing in a field of red trillium and trout lillies above Sterling Pond.

He had told her that he knew all about the Notch, falling for his own story because he had been there twice before as a boy.

But it was from Annie that he learned the pass was named by Green Mountaineers bringing contraband to Montreal before the War Of 1812, and how it had served as a stop for fugitive slaves on the Underground Railroad. In turn, he had boasted of his rumrunner grandfather and how St. Germains had used the gap to bring in bootleg from Canada after the road was paved in '22, making up all of it as he went along.

His ears popped. A boulder flecked with mica jutted out of the rocky wall, pinching the route to a single north-south lane. St. Germain moved his holster closer to his hand and eased the ambulance through the blind corridor. The tread marks continued around a shallow turnout where a tank of radiator water lay buried in the snow. He saw tan paint on a glacial erratic and winced as if it had been scraped from his skin. Then the pass crested without warning and he stepped too heavily on the brake, the ambulance lurching toward a frozen brook so that he had to steer hard into the skid to keep from losing the road.

He was over the hump, looking down at the boarded-up information booth above Big Spring. In summer the small parking area would be overrun with sightseers and rock climbers. But on a frigid spring night he saw only a sign warning motorists to proceed in low gear and a tan police cruiser with steam billowing from under the hood in front of a couple of high-tech outhouses.

He cut his lights, but flicked them on again in admission that he had taken no one but himself by surprise. He coasted past the information booth and parked well away from the cruiser, stepped into crusted snow with his gun out, his finger through the trigger guard. He moved stiff-kneed down the slope, weight back, fighting his momentum in treacherous footing. The turbocharger appeared to be empty. As he circled around the car, an orange sliver of moon dropped its light over the Notch, and he saw footprints ending in a trampled patch at the outhouses. The thin wood doors were unlocked, secured by a simple latch.

He retreated across the brook and picked his way toward them through the woods.

He heard rustling behind him. The gun came up of its own volition at a raven taking flight from a pine snag. St. Germain watched the bird disappear toward its aerie on Old Smugglers Face. For all he knew, Conklin was lurking deep in the trees, had lured him there for an easy target. He studied the snow again; all tracks led to the outhouses. Because his mind already was made up, he told himself the boy had to be behind one of the doors, waiting for him, only pretending to be hiding.

He approached from the left. The .38 felt sure in his hand with the same snug grip and delicate balance as his old Chief's Special. In the weak light he couldn't say that in fact it wasn't the same weapon. All guns, like all rocks, seemed alike to him, which probably explained why he never had been able to work up much enthusiasm about either subject.

He hesitated. Once again he was playing on Conklin's home court, letting him dictate the rules. He stood off to the side, deciding which door to pull. But the choice was not his to make. To step across to the right was to expose himself to possible fire from the door on the left. Nor could he circle behind without giving Conklin a chance to slip out in ambush at the corner. With a shrug of resignation he extended the barrel and fit the gunsight under the latch and slowly raised it. The faint scraping sound seemed to echo off the cliffs. He leaped away from cover and tore open the door and squeezed off a shot into the blackness, heard wood splinter as the bullet passed through the rear wall. Hands reached for him around the door and he turned the gun on them, forcing it aside when he saw twine around the wrists, a diamond chip on an enameled finger.

A blond girl with a handkerchief across her face stumbled against him. Blood ran freely from her upper arm, where his bullet had creased the flesh.

"My God," he said, "who are—"

Another shot, like an explosion, shook the walls, and he heard more wood fragment. He wanted to check the .38, to see how it could have gone off without his touching the trigger, but his thigh was on fire, and then he was on his back in the snow with his feet against the toilet, the upper half of his body jarred by the unexpected cold, thinking, Annie'll kill me for sure when she finds out.

The girl made a screeching sound behind her gag. In the exaggerated silence that followed, he was aware of muffled footfalls. He scrambled onto his belly to see Conklin step from the other outhouse with a long gun across his chest, grinning. "The lady or the tiger?" Conklin said, and aimed down at him. St. Germain squeezed off three quick shots as the long gun went off into the snow. Someone cried out in pain and he assumed it was himself until the boy began to hobble toward the brook. St. Germain rose unsteadily. His leg gave way and he fell back, firing once more in the direction Conklin had fled.

He saw blood on his pants and pressed his hand to the wound. The pain was not as bad as he had thought, the damage done by shotgun pellets and not many of them, the brunt of the charge absorbed by the wood so that the shock was the most awful thing about it. He was picking shreds of fabric out of his leg when the girl, chafing at her bonds, lurched toward him.

"You okay?" he asked, and tugged the handkerchief below her chin, undid the knots.

A child's face empty of color signaled assent. Squatting beside him, she used the gag to sop up some of his blood. "My name is Brenda Jarvis. He took me from a store in Bennington," she recited. "I was working—"

"You're the clerk there?"

"Uh-huh."

"I heard about you. Half the cops in the state are out looking for you, if it's any comfort." He gave her his handkerchief, and she dabbed at her arm, her teeth clicking as the cloth touched raw flesh.

"What's going to happen now?" she asked. "Will the other policemen get him?"

"What policemen?"

She looked at the uniform for the first time, at the snakes on the breast pocket. ". . . But you're carrying a gun."

"I'm an ambulance driver."

"Oh, Jesus," she said, and began to sniffle.

St. Germain pushed himself to his feet. With a hand on her shoulder he moved away from the outhouse, then walked into the snow on his own. "Come with me." He opened the ambulance, climbed in after her, tilted a light over a stainless steel tray crammed with small bottles and racks of ampules.

"It was horrible," she said without being asked. "He robbed the store and shot one of the other men, the one who wasn't mean to me, and then this nice old couple drove up and he shot them, too, and took their station wagon. The deputies got his friends and his brother, so he killed them . . . I'm glad about his friends." She was blushing, the redness surging to her drained cheeks. "They were going to . . . to hurt me."

St. Germain tore the wrapper from a gauze pad and bandaged her arm. He removed a handful of shells from the gun belt and placed them in the .38.

"He did that, too," Brenda said.

"What?"

"When we went in the police car. He found a bunch of red cardboard things, and he put two in the shotgun and the rest in his pockets."

St. Germain loosened his gun belt and tugged his pants below his hips. The cords in his neck bulged as he spilled a dark vial into the wound. The girl helped tape his thigh, blushing each time her fingers came in contact with his skin. When she was done, he stamped his foot as if the heel had come loose from his shoe. "It'll do," he said, and went into the front of the ambulance.

The radio crackled with faint bursts of chatter, the signal

from Stowe blocked by the high peaks. He made out a few words of French, then a blast of static, then a clear call for volunteers to fight a barn fire in Au Sable Forks in the Adirondacks. But he would be glad for whatever help he could raise. He turned up the volume and began scanning the band, and when the girl slid between the seats to watch him, he gave her the microphone.

"We have to keep trying till we reach somebody," he told her. "Just call hello, hello. If anyone answers, tell them where we are and what we're up against. Have them send troopers to Smugglers Notch."

The girl depressed a black button on the mouthpiece. "Like this?"

"Uh-huh." St. Germain hurried into the back and unlocked the door with Brenda right behind.

"What are you doing?" In alarm her voice was small and querulous, fitting the childish face.

"I'm going to see if I can drive the ambulance off the Notch. But before we get started, I have to check around, chase him away if he's still out there with the shotgun. Besides, I want . . ."

"Yes?"

"I . . . it has to be done," he said. "I have to."

"Can't we wait till they come get us? I'm scared."

"Till you talk to them, no one knows we're here, Brenda." The girl brushed her sleeve under her nose, and then he took her hands and tugged them around his hips so she was looking straight at him. "This is important," he said. "I want you to lock yourself in. If anything happens, if there's gunfire or you don't hear my voice, don't open the door. Got it?"

"Yes. But what if he shoots you? What do I do then?"

He dropped her hands. Ask my wife, he wanted to say; she has plans for that kind of thing.

Standing on the bumper, he looked around the Notch. Faded

snowshoe tracks on the eastern face showed the way to the Long Trail. He put a foot in the snow, expecting to hear the shotgun before he could bring down the other, then began inching alongside the ambulance. When he came even with the window he watched the girl stare helplessly at the radio, then reach over to lock the door. Seeing him, she grabbed for the handle instead. As the dome light came on, a yellow flash lit up the scrub across the brook and lead pellets hailed against the driver's side. St. Germain fell back and crawled between the wheels, the girl's agitated footsteps reverberating overhead. "Get down, Brenda," he shouted at her. "And shut the damn—" Another shot, closer, kicked snow in his face; the air began to hiss out of the tire closest to him. The undercarriage brushed his spine, and he scurried out and crouched behind the body of the Ford as the light finally went off inside. Footprints he hadn't noticed before angled back into the cliffs. In the darkness there appeared to be blood in them.

He backed away, keeping the ambulance between himself and the boy. Where a solitary oak offered cover, he ran to the edge of the stream. The banks were at least five feet apart, too far to jump on his injured thigh. He put his foot down tentatively, planted it on the ice, and then came around with the bad leg, sprawling as it buckled under his full weight. He clambered off on his hands and knees and continued into a jumble of boulders the size of Volkswagens. An unexpended shotgun shell in a blob of red restored his confidence, and he allowed himself a moment to knead the throbbing in his leg.

The wind nudged bits of cloud over Old Smugglers Face, trapping them between stunted pines. St. Germain tugged his collar around his throat, buttoned it. He tried to picture what Conklin was wearing, but he had been too busy shooting to have noticed. Still rubbing his wound, he limped out of the boulders. A carpet of loose rock opened beneath him, and icy water deadened his leg to the knee. As he scrambled to the cliff, every shadow was a cave where the boy might be hiding. His injured leg was burning again, the other numb, with a brick for a foot. How, he wanted to know, was Conklin maintaining the pace, leaking blood all over the Notch? He skirted a pine stand too dense to see into. On the far side the boy's trail continued unbending, the sinuous track of a fisher weaving it into a crude figure four.

Away from the trees he was a bull's-eye in brown. He moved quickly, but with caution, not getting ahead of himself. A fallen maple blocked his way, and he had to use both hands to bring his leg over the trunk. The moon highlighted mountain ash growing straight up out of the cliffs. He sent a probing shot skyward, and as he waited for return fire he thought of the chase on Lake Champlain, the situation the same now except the roles were reversed. Or were they? He calculated the likelihood that Conklin was playing him on slack line, measured the odds in cold sweat that stuck his shirt to his back. Clutching his thigh, he dashed toward sharp boulders heaped like steppingstones against the dripping cliff, sixteen in all that ended in a fall of broken rock, the trail evaporating as though the boy had burrowed into the talus and pulled the hole in after him. But then he saw the blood again, more—much more—than before, and any doubt that he'd been suckered was dispelled as the long gun went off from above. Two guessing bullets answered for him as a second blast chiseled quartz chips into his cheek, and he turned to kiss the face of the cliff.

But Conklin was perched where no bullet would find him till hell froze over, or till they both did. St. Germain looked too long at a flash of white on a stone shelf, and a boulder the shape of a football nearly smashed into his teeth. Another large rock rumbled down, taunting laughter after it. "Still with me?" the boy called out.

The overhang provided cover while he reloaded. He brought up the .38, aimed it with his ear. The bullet soared along the cliff wall, rousting the ravens in the crags.

"That's what I thought," Conklin said.

As St. Germain poked his head from under the shelf, the shotgun discharged and the pain in his leg reasserted itself in his shoulder, so crisp and hard-edged in the frigid air that he would have sworn he counted three pellets against the bone. Spasms of nausea swept over his body, and to keep from losing the revolver he had to squeeze it with both hands, wrap it in his chest.

"Careless of you, Larr." The voice was husky, distant, as if it had traveled far just to reach the boy's lips. "Like last time." Worse than last time, St. Germain was thinking, stupider and without the excuse of having been taken by surprise. He put his hand to his shoulder and then plunged it in snow, washed away the blood before he could look at it. Ten million times he had replayed the night at Malletts Bay, rearranging events, casting them till they came out right—his reward never the absolution he craved, but a triumph in his mind that repetition had made more real than his disgrace on the ice. And now, improbably given a second crack at the boy, he'd blown it, Conklin's toy again. He wanted to cut down the shelf, rattle the cliff till Conklin dropped into his lap, and crush him. Forced to consider his actual prospects, he concluded that they were nil unless Brenda had the good sense to try for help.

But he knew it was pointless to expect anything of her, that she would remain in the ambulance, still Conklin's prisoner— as he still was—until one of them came for her. The wind hurtled through the Notch again, pushing cold air over the cliff, and he stamped his feet on his tiny platform and then swept the walls for a handhold, anything better than staying here to freeze.

His dead toes found a V-shaped cranny in the cliff, the pain dispersing through his system as he inched above the platform. He scraped the other foot against the wall, but the rock was smooth and impregnable, and he would have fallen if his fingers hadn't caught in a tangle of broken roots. Using only his arms, he raised himself the length of his body. He was moving straight up in a way he didn't believe was possible, so that he would have said a fly on a windowpane had nothing on him.

An overhang with a mossy underside blocked most of the moonlight, the darkness on his shoulders like a comforting blanket. He guessed he had twenty feet still to go, but most of it was easy, with toeholds he could spot even now. Then a jolt of pain paralyzed his legs, suspending him in mid-stride, and his breath came in wheezing bursts. When he reached for the trunk of a hemlock sapling, his fingers curled around something slippery, and he pulled back to see them colored with the boy's blood. He grabbed the tree again. In his hurry to get moving he pried loose several stones, an avalanche sounding in his head as they rattled down the cliff.

He craned above the overhang. He was clinging to a rim of wet rock that extended two feet out from a ridge of wind-whipped snow behind which he couldn't see. As he brought his gun hand up, a foot swung over the snowy wall and stamped on the barrel of the .38. The twin muzzles of a shotgun came briefly into focus, then slammed between his eyes. He felt wetness running down his thigh, a moment of self-loathing until he realized his wound had opened again.

"Don't go anywhere, Larr. Be right with you."

The voice seemed strained, its jauntiness artificial. And when the boy stepped over the barricade, looking more bleached than a year in prison would explain, St. Germain saw that he was wearing only a thin T-shirt splotched with blood.

Conklin followed his gaze, tugged the sticky cloth from his side. "Lucky shot," he said. "Move your hand away. Leave the gun where it is."

But St. Germain had taken that advice before, and he tightened his grip. Conklin stood heavily on his knuckles and began to grind them into the rock. "I can keep this up all night if you want. Your choice."

Except he had no choice. His hand opened on its own and

Conklin kicked away the gun, then stepped back to give him room to climb up. The shelf was larger than he had expected, fifteen feet wide and almost as deep, much of it under a sheet of meltwater that stirred with the wind.

Conklin went behind the wall as proudly as a child entering a snow fort. Away from the water he squatted on a boulder where the snow appeared to have been piled higher and motioned St. Germain to sit facing him. St. Germain was trying to understand why the boy had wasted energy on the flimsy rampart when the wind blew harder and his teeth began to chatter and he huddled down, trying to stop his shivering.

"Think you're smart, don't you?" Conklin sat back with the long gun across his chest, looking satisfied. "Always did, too. It's your problem, Larr. One of them. Look behind if you don't believe me. Just look."

St. Germain glanced where the boy was pointing and caught an unimpeded view of the rocky ground all the way to the trees.

"I could've taken you out any time I wanted," Conklin boasted. "Know why I didn't?"

But that was ridiculous, St. Germain began to say; he'd been out of range of the shotgun till he was almost at the cliff.

"I wanted the company. It's lonely up here and, you know, I've always thought you were a very entertaining guy and . . ." His eyes shut suddenly and his head tilted back, and as St. Germain started to push himself up, he sneezed. "Excuse me," he said, and tightened his hold on the shotgun. "You look colder than me. Smart guy like yourself, what are you doing up in the Notch dressed for the Fourth of July?"

St. Germain scrunched closer to the wall, watched the blood spread across his thigh.

"Am I scaring you?" Conklin asked abruptly. He pulled the gun away as if aware for the first time that it was pointed at St. Germain. "It's nothing to be proud of, giving an old scairdy cat like you another fright." The wind tousled the spiky hair, and he slunk down with his feet straight out. "Tell me something, Larr, you a religious man?"

"I believe there's a time when everyone is called to account for what they've done on earth . . ." The words slipped out. "If that's what you're asking."

"That's not real profound, Larr. I hope you're not some kind of agnostic."

St. Germain felt vaguely foolish, as if by opening his mouth he had eliminated himself from a game of Simon Says.

"This is one subject that really interests me. You're saying you believe in heaven and hell and all that?"

St. Germain resumed the expressionless gaze he found harder to maintain than any display of emotion.

". . . I was hoping you would," Conklin said happily, " 'cause I need someone, someone who feels like you, to do me a favor." He bent forward, cradling the long gun. "Mel got killed tonight, and I didn't get a chance to let him know how much I'm going to miss him and how sorry I am I was always dumping on him in front of people. I want you to tell him for me, when you see him. Will you do that?"

"Anyone ever tell you you're out of your mind, Paul?"

"All the time. But you got to remember I have a paper from the State Hospital saying I'm not. You have one of those? You have a nice Remington shotgun like mine? No? Then you tell me which one of us is the nut case." He laughed. "And that's Mr. Conklin, Larr, if you recall."

He sat back. "There's another favor you can do right now. I want your shirt, and I don't want to have to put another hole in it first. So how about handing it over, and we'll both avoid a lot of pain and suffering."

The wind relented, and St. Germain raised his head over the top of the wall and glanced down at the boulders at the base of the cliff.

"Looking into flying lessons, Larr? Just to keep your lousy shirt?"

St. Germain was waiting for panic to sweep over him but felt nothing worse than a mild case of butterflies. He stood up slowly and began to undo the buttons, thinking how easy it would be to rush the boy and let his momentum carry them over the shelf before the pump gun stopped him, his only other choice to surrender the shirt and get his head blown off, two paths converging on the same sorry end. Okay, then, he would take Conklin with him, have the satisfaction of that. But even his one small victory was marred by the realization that after dominating his life Conklin now was setting the ground rules for his suicide. Only how could it be suicide when the best part of him already was dead, destroyed that night on the ice?

There was nothing left to think about. He stripped off the shirt and held it at arm's length, and when Conklin said, "Give," he tossed it and then lunged for the boy. His leg collapsed and he rolled under the gun as the muzzle flamed, came up on his toes and wrenched the weapon away, the barrel warm in his hands as he swung it in a low arc with all his weight behind it, like a batter golfing at a ball down and inside and connected with the boy's knees, and followed through. The cherry stock shattered, and Conklin dropped as though his legs had been sawed off and splashed down in the puddle.

St. Germain's ears were hissing. He sat on Conklin's boulder and rubbed his shoulder and thigh while the boy thrashed around as if the cold water were consuming him.

"God, it's freezing," Conklin said. "My knees . . ."

St. Germain picked up the shotgun and extended the barrel. As Conklin reached for it, he slid his hand to the trigger and the boy let go and fell back in the puddle.

"Problem?" St. Germain asked.

"I slipped."

"Let's try again."

St. Germain kicked the weapon off the ledge, then took the boy's wrist and dragged him into the snow. As Conklin lay on his back beside the wall, St. Germain cupped a hand over one knee and then the other, felt them through the sodden cloth.

"Bad news, Paul. They're busted."

A fit of terror contorted the boy's mouth. "I'll be able to play basketball again, won't I?"

St. Germain poked his finger through a scorched hole under the collar, then pulled the shirt on and fastened the buttons, rolled a wet sleeve above the elbow.

"I didn't think you could," Conklin said.

"What's that?"

"I never figured you'd take my gun away and . . . and do this to me."

"Neither did I." St. Germain sat on the edge of the shelf, dangling his legs.

"Where you going?" Conklin asked. "You going for help now?"

St. Germain found footing in the rock and stepped off. "I don't need help now."

"Hey," Conklin said, "you can't leave me here. I'm soaked, I wouldn't last an hour." His body was shaking uncontrollably as he tried to raise himself. "You're a cop, you'll get in trouble."

"Haven't been a cop for a year."

"An ambulance driver, right? Yeah, you had to take the oath, the Hippocrites oath, so you can't—"

The Caducean patch tore easily off his chest and he tossed it to the boy. "I'm a management trainee," he said, "a paper pusher. Makes my wife happy to know I'm keeping out of harm's way."

". . . Can't just let me freeze to death."

"It's out of my hands."

"Huh? Then who's it—?"

St. Germain tilted his head back and stared solemnly toward the stars.

"That's not funny," Conklin said.

"You bump into Mel, you can tell him something for *me*."

"What—?"

"He had a real jerk for a brother."

"What if I don't . . . if I go to . . . What if he's not there?"

St. Germain shrugged. He put his other foot down and then stopped and fished inside his pockets, came out with a quarter and flipped it after the patch.

"What's this for?" Conklin asked him.

"Maybe you can call."

He watched the boy struggle some more, then collapse and scratch spastically at the snow. He lowered himself to the boulders and leaned against the cliff, listening to him howl. With a pine bough for a walking stick he made his way over the loose rock. Someone was coming toward him from the trees. In the moonlight he thought he saw a sheriff's officer or trooper and was furious with himself for not finishing off Conklin while he had the chance. But then Brenda ran up to him, and he said, "What are you doing here?" and put his arm around her, letting her take some of the weight off his leg.

"I was afraid you were in trouble and I could help," she said shyly.

"That was a very brave thing for you to do."

The girl cringed, looking past him toward the cliff. "Did you hear that? It sounds like someone screaming."

"It's an animal," he said.

"He's dead, isn't he? I heard shooting."

St. Germain nodded and Brenda felt moisture against her neck and saw that he was bleeding. "He hurt you again," she said. "I thought . . . I thought he'd killed you."

"He did." The stick fell from St. Germain's hand and he walked with her into the trees. "But I'm over it now."